PRAISE FOR MIRANDA WARNING:

"Tess Spencer will make you fall in love with her, then push you away, then charm you back into love again. She's got a past she'd like to forget, a future she's still learning to embrace, and a few skeletons—er, ghosts—in her closet, but when those she loves are in jeopardy, watch out! This West Virginian, Glock-wielding mountain mama goes all Mama Bear! Deliciously creepy mystery, well-rounded cast, delightful small town setting. Can't wait for Book Two!" ~ **Becky Doughty**, author of *Waters Fall*

"The perfect blend of spine-chilling suspense and cozy mountain mystery, *Miranda Warning* is that rare novel that has it all: a unique setting, rich characters, and a plot so riveting you can't look away. Best of all, it has Tess Spencer, a tough young heroine with a tender heart for those she loves and sense enough to pack a Glock when she needs to." ~**Karin Kaufman**, author of *The Witch Tree*, a 2011 Grace Award finalist

Miranda Warning

A murder in the Mountains Novel

Heather Day Gilbert

Hope you enjoy the start of this mountain mystery series!

~ Heather Day Gilbert

MIRANDA WARNING
BY HEATHER DAY GILBERT

Copyright 2014 Heather Day Gilbert

ISBN-13: 978-1499154870
ISBN-10: 1499154879

Cover Design by Jon Day

Published by Heather Day Gilbert

Author Information: http://www.heatherdaygilbert.com

*Dedicated to the grndmas whose prayers hold up the
mountains on their backs—
I hope to join your ranks someday.*

*And to my sister-in-law, Kathleen Taylor, for reading this book
and encouraging me to publish it.*

*To my mom and mother-in-law, Betty and Jane, for being there
for me, just like Nikki Jo is for Tess.*

*And to my husband David, for being honest on early drafts of
this story and pushing me to dig deeper into Rose's personality.*

*And to my children, my parents, my siblings, my friends, and
my readers. I hope you enjoy this story, because it would never
exist without your support.*

1

I chose the day I would die.

My husband's deep brown eyes glowed as he handed me the cocoa. "Maybe you'll sleep better tonight, Rosey."

I was tired of the charade between us. I never wanted to smile at his dinner parties again. Never wanted to beg him for the children he wouldn't give me. I'd never again clean up his clothes, covered in moonshine vomit.

I gulped the foaming, lukewarm liquid, a smile on my face. And that was the last time Paul Campbell would ever see me smile.

"Checkmate, girlie! Put that in your pipe and smoke it!"

The steely-haired matriarch sitting across from me clicks her heavy rings together, eyes sparkling over her glasses.

Miranda Michaels has a heftier dose of spunk than your average assisted living home resident.

"Are you sure you didn't cheat? Seems like that rook was over one..."

She smiles broadly, rolling her wheelchair back from the marble-topped table. "Listen, young'un, not to be mean, but you haven't played for a while. Maybe you just need to practice some?"

I can't resist it when she kicks in the Southern charm.

"I know you didn't cheat. I just can't concentrate today—sorry." I reposition the ivory pieces on the board.

Miranda rolls around to my side. "Can we talk in my room? I've had something on my mind, too."

The comforting smell of her favorite Black Cashmere lotion surrounds me. She doesn't douse herself in Youth-Dew perfume, like most of the older ladies here.

I pat my hair, trying to smooth down a particularly willful cow-lick. She picks up on my insecurity before I say a word.

"That bob is quite becoming on you, what with your sleek dark hair. Reminds me of a flapper."

"Thanks, but I think she cut it a little lopsided." I roll her chair toward the long hallway. The usual suspects populate the Recreation room. Blue-haired women gossip as the assistants give them eye drops. Grizzled men watch TV, snatching peeks at the prettier assistants.

Miranda cranes her neck at me. "Tess Spencer, when are you going to learn to take a compliment?"

Even though Miranda has had a heart attack and a stroke, her keen insight still amazes me. At home, I secretly call her the *Grande Dame* to Thomas. For a sixty-nine year old near-cripple, she's *tres formidable.*

In her suite, which is more like a small apartment, I roll her over to her blue satin couch and help her sit. I set the kettle brewing on her small stove for her afternoon cup of Earl Grey—a ritual she's maintained since I met her four years ago.

"Do you believe in ghosts?" Miranda leans forward so precariously, I'm afraid her skinny legs will buckle and she'll slide right off the couch.

"Hm. I've heard plenty of ghost stories, what with all the hundred-year-old houses around Buckneck. But I haven't really decided. Why?" I glance around for some sort of food to go with her tea. Nothing but a package of peanut butter crackers that's been open for about three weeks.

She grasps one of the overstuffed peach pillows close, sinking back into the couch. She takes a deep breath.

"I think one is trying to contact me."

Most people might coddle an older person and tell them they're imagining things. Quite possibly, Miranda's own daughter would do that, if she ever came to visit.

But I'm not her daughter—I'm her best friend. And I know Miranda's the last person on earth given to flights of fancy. I pour the tea into her gold-trimmed Lenox teacups and sit in the rocking chair opposite her. "What's going on?"

She fingers the lacy white sweater draped over her shoulders. "I got a letter the other day. The letter itself was odd, but I recognized the handwriting."

She pulls the letter out of a drawer in her French provincial coffee table. I take it, reading quickly. It's handwritten on plain copy paper.

Dear Miranda,

I know you have been seeing Mr. Paul Campbell. For your own sake, I hope you stop doing so.

I'm watching you.

"You're right. It is weird. Is it a threat or a warning? And more importantly, you didn't tell me you were dating someone!" I fold it up into the envelope, noticing its postmark from Sedona, Arizona.

As I hand it back, Miranda's fingers tremble. "Yes, Paul Campbell has come to call on me a few times. I didn't think anyone knew yet."

Something tells me the older women at The Haven assisted living facility have indeed noticed a man coming to call on the Grande Dame.

"But what about the handwriting? You said you recognized it?"

She nods. "That's where it really gets strange. It's my old friend Rose's writing."

"Does Rose live in Arizona?"

Miranda's milky-pale skin blanches even further. "No. Rose Campbell's ashes sit in an urn on Paul's mantelpiece. She's been dead for forty years now."

Understanding hits me. "So you're dating Rose's husband. And you got a note that looks like it's from his dead wife."

She nods, lips tight. A fresh cup of tea would do us both some good, so I head for the kitchenette. I pour liberal cream and sugar in both cups before returning.

Miranda takes the cup, which clatters on its matching dish. Time to change the subject.

"Well, I have some news." My announcement sounds forced, even to my ears.

"Ooh, do tell." Her dark blue eyes widen and one expertly-penciled eyebrow shoots up.

"We're expecting." After a mere two years of marriage. Before I could even land a job. While Thomas has no health insurance. Whoopdie-do.

Miranda's eyes fill. "God bless you...you weren't ready, were you?"

As usual, the Grande Dame cuts straight to the heart of the matter. I take a deep breath. "No, I wasn't. But we'll get through."

"You're right. God knows just when those babies need to come, whether we've planned them or not. He'll provide, just you wait and see."

Miranda has a biblical application for everything. And it's more comforting when she says it, no matter how self-evident it may seem.

She looks out her large bay window at the mountains, covered with a soft red and gold blanket of leaves. The rich colors shimmer and shake loose, making way for the monochromatic lines of winter. She takes a moment to speak. "You know, my friend Rose always wanted a baby."

I grip my still-flat stomach. Why does God drop babies on those who aren't ready for them and withhold them from those who want them most?

Miranda interrupts my thoughts. "I'd love to have you over for dinner Thursday night. Paul will be here, and we can talk about the letter. I haven't showed it to him yet."

"Sure." After all, Thomas works late at his low-paying law

office every night. I'll use my free time to figure out why some ghost is bugging my sweet elderly friend.

2

At first, Paul's close attention didn't bother me. When we were newly married, I thought it was sweet how he hated for other men to look at me. And they always looked. "Beauty is your curse," my mother always said. "Find a strong man who can protect you."

Protecting was all Paul did. I'd be black and blue from his harsh grip as he steered me back to our car, every time we went to town. Then it happened every time we went to church. It got to where he didn't let me go out. We'd have dinner parties at home, to entertain his boss and friends.

One night, Paul's friend Russell brought his wife, Miranda. She walked into my dining room, cracked a joke with a wide-open smile, and wrapped me in a hug like we'd known each other forever. I admired her from that day on—she was someone who didn't measure every word before she spoke it. When Paul would make his blanket statements, she'd challenge him and shoot me conspiratorial looks.

I loved my auburn-haired friend. We planted flowerbeds together and sewed quilts for other women's babies. We shared gossip and recipes. But there were two things I never mentioned to Miranda: Paul's possessiveness meant my slavery, and now his attentions were shifting to her.

One thing about my mother-in-law: she's the best cook I've ever known. Tonight, she's dropped off a container of her famous sausage lentil stew, along with six cornbread muffins. Ever since Nikki Jo heard we're having a baby, she's committed herself to fattening me up. And since Thomas and I live in the cottage right behind her big house, that means I've been getting lots of free meals lately.

About the time I've snuggled in on the couch with my steaming bowl to watch a rerun of *MacGyver*, Nikki Jo calls. Her familiar chirpy voice is always a little too loud.

"How are you, honey? Did you see the soup? I left it right on the counter."

"Yes, Mom, I sure did. Thanks so much—it's delicious." I pull my favorite green afghan around my shoulders. Even though the days are chillier, I'm determined to save money by keeping our heat turned down.

"Now, I know Thomas won't be home till late. But you tell him not to forget his school reunion is tomorrow night at seven."

"Will do." The Buckneck High School is so small that all their graduates are invited to their yearly reunion. Thomas will doubtless take me along as what he calls "arm candy."

"Now, you just get some rest and don't worry about looking for a job." Uh-oh. Here it comes: the "I-was-a-stay-at-home-mom" speech. "You know that Thomas and his two brothers grew up fine with nothing but their daddy's income from the railroad and the National Guard."

"True, but it was also thanks to their momma's good cooking." I smile in spite of myself. I haven't figured out how Nikki Jo kept it all together, with Roger traveling most of the time.

In the background, Dad shouts, "How about some more of that stew, Nikki Jo?"

She sighs into the phone. "How's Miranda doing over at The Haven? I worry about her—stuck in that wheelchair."

Nikki Jo lived near Miranda when she was a small girl, and the Grande Dame was somewhat of a legend in small-town Buckneck. She was the classy woman in the huge green house, who gave out *real chocolate bars* for Halloween.

"She's doing well. Actually...she's dating Paul Campbell. Do you know him?" Putting out some feelers can't hurt.

"*Dating* Paul Campbell? Good lands! Now doesn't that just take the cake?" She takes a deep breath. "Paul was an early widower. His wife, Rose, was well-nigh the prettiest girl ever born in these parts. Doc Cole—that's her doctor—said she took a heart pill overdose. Suicide."

Dad's voice drifts into the silence. "Nikki *Jo?* What you doing, honey?"

She ignores him and continues. "Would you believe Rose dropped dead right there in her favorite chair? I can't figure out how Paul's lived in that same house all these years."

Nikki Jo gets quiet, and I know she's processing the implications of Miranda dating Widower Campbell.

"I'd better eat some of this stew now, Mom. Thanks for calling."

"Sure, honey. You have a great night."

It's still a little strange for me to call Thomas' parents *Mom* and *Dad*, but *Nikki Jo* and *Roger* seem too fancy-schmantsy. Besides, they're the closest thing to real parents that I've got.

Hm. A heart pill overdose. Like Nitroglycerin? Miranda has to pop those little pills occasionally, since her heart attack.

I ponder this as I watch MacGyver disarm some lasers with a piece of glass. Man, that mullet still works on him somehow. He has warm brown eyes, just like Thomas.

The old brass knob moves on our front door, and Thomas walks in. We don't even have a lock. Thomas' parents live so far out in the woods, I'd be surprised if the UPS man ever finds us.

"Hey babe, you're home early." I jump up to greet him, but sober down my smile when I notice his face. "Rough day?"

"You said it, hotcakes. What's that smell? Is it stew?"

Food wins out over chitchat every time for my boy-man. "I'll get you a bowl," I say.

Rumples crease the back of his blue striped shirt. His hair looks like he's run his hand over it, back and forth, all day. He kicks his shoes off in the middle of the jute rug and heads up the rickety steps to our attic bedroom—one of the four rooms in this farmhouse-style cottage.

"What's up?" I shout up the steps to him.

"Job stinks. That's all."

It irks me when my brilliant husband gets no street-cred at

work. "You need to go rogue! Start your own business! After all, you did go to UVA!"

"Tess, no one around here cares where I went to school. They just want a lawyer to handle all the grunt work. I'm too young to start my own place."

"Whatever, babe," I mutter, scrounging under the piled dishes in the sink for my ladle.

"I heard that." Thomas sneaks up behind me, grabbing me around the waist.

I turn, taking in the spiky blond hair, the faded red tee, and the boot-cut jeans. Too much. I kiss him, full on the lips.

He grins. "Woman, can't you see I'm famished?" He grabs the ladle, deftly washes it and helps himself to a bowlful of stew.

We both settle into the couch before I drop my news on him. "Thomas, the Grande Dame has a stalker."

"What?" He eats his stew like some high-class laird, placing the entire spoon in his mouth. Not a drop of it hits his shirt.

I explain about the note and tell him Rose's story. Thomas assumes his lawyerly, pensive look until I'm finished, then starts his questioning.

"Let me get this straight. Rose took an overdose? In her twenties? What would make a woman do that?"

I've been wondering the same thing. "Maybe because she couldn't have kids? Miranda said she wanted them so badly."

Thomas peels his muffin from the wrapper, meticulously dropping each tiny yellow crumb into his napkin.

"Thomas, you make me feel like a peasant when I watch you eat. I have to stain spray my clothes every day from spilling stuff on them!"

"You're just pregnant, little missy." He lightly pats my stomach. "It's common knowledge that pregnant women can be klutzy."

"Thanks a lot. I—"

The door flies open and Thomas' youngest brother runs in, skidding to a stop on our rubber doormat. The twelve-year-old reminds me of a self-contained tornado.

"Petey, what on earth? Have you no manners, boy?" Thomas stands to greet him, not a crumb escaping the napkin gripped in his hand.

Petey's red curls have grown over his ears, so he looks like a cross between a street urchin and a skater dude.

"Sorry, bro. Hey, Tess. You look nice."

Thomas shoots me a sideways grin. Petey has a little crush on me, and everyone in the family knows it.

"Thanks, Petey. What's your hurry?" I fold the afghan over the back of the couch.

"Just wanted to tell you I followed Thor out into the woods. He was hot on the scent of something, barking his head off. Turns out, someone took off—they were right near your house!"

Thomas' family must've been feeling ironic when they named their miniature Doberman *Thor*. I keep telling Thomas they should get a full-sized Doberman, and name it *Thor Senõr*.

Thomas runs upstairs, no doubt retrieving his twelve-gauge—typical protocol in our deep-woods locale. Petey and I head outside.

"Right over there, behind that bush." Petey points, and we close the distance quickly, a yelping Thor on our heels.

The leaves are smashed in a circular pattern, but nothing

else looks strange. Thor noses into the flattened leaves, destroying any kind of evidence. Why am I thinking I need evidence, anyway? This whole thing with Miranda is freaking me out.

Thomas bolts out the door, shotgun aimed toward the sky. "Get back, you two!"

He's nothing if not heroic. And quite angry with Petey and me, to boot.

"What are you *doing*? What if someone were out here with a gun? You could've both been killed!"

Petey and I edge back toward the house. Thor pulls his nose from the debris, takes one haughty sniff, then pees all over the leaf evidence. Charming dog.

Thomas looks around the perimeter, lowering the gun slightly. He glares at Thor. "Maybe we need a bigger dog."

"Or a lock on the door," I suggest.

"This isn't funny, Tess. We're out in the middle of nowhere with no protection."

Petey gets serious, too. "Don't worry, bro. I'm around after school. I'll watch out for Tess. And Dad's around too. You know he's got a whole arsenal up at the big house."

I chime in. "I'd prefer a throwing star, so I could practice my rare ninja skills."

Petey laughs, and even Thomas cracks a grin.

"We'll figure out what's going on." When Thomas says this, it sounds like a declaration of war. He won't stop until he finds the person who's been watching us. He trudges off into the woods, gun at the ready.

A nice sentiment, but what if I run into that person first?

3

One man who came to our dinner parties always tried to catch my eye. Every time Paul was out of the room, he'd scoot his chair closer, asking questions about my flowerbeds. Once, he grabbed my hand, turning it over so it exposed the bruise on my wrist.

"Rose, do I need to get you out of here? I'll do it in a heartbeat." From his concerned look, I could tell this idea had simmered for a while.

There was no time to answer as Paul pushed open the dining room door, cigar in hand. "Ready for some poker, boys?"

It was my cue to make myself scarce. I piled up the dishes in my first of several trips to the kitchen, but almost stopped when my would-be protector spoke up.

"I've got no money for betting tonight, Paul. You boys go on without me. I'm heading into the parlor to sit by your fire, till you shoo me out in that snow."

I knew he'd be waiting to talk with me. It didn't matter that the whole town knew him. It didn't matter that I was already married. I fell in love for the first and last time that night.

As I sit next to the disturbingly inebriated town dentist at the Buckneck school reunion, two thoughts keep running through my head. First, a drunk dentist must be some kind of oxymoron or a contradiction in terms...Thomas would know the right word. Second, my flip-out knife is burning a hole in my pants pocket, and if this dorky dentist hits on me *one* more time, I'll pull it on him.

Thomas, deep in conversation with one of his elderly teachers, has yet to notice that his bride is garnering all the wrong kind of attention. It's time for the eye candy to take a little trip to the water fountain.

"You going somewhere, gorgeous?" As I stand, the dentist puts his hand up to stop me. Thomas looks over at the word *gorgeous*. Maybe he's wondering who fits that description around here.

I motion to the door. Thomas nods before resuming his conversation with the white-haired woman. Dropping my hand into my pocket, I finger my knife's familiar grooves. After the watcher in the woods incident, I've practiced pulling my knife every day.

In the wide hallway, predictably lined with trophy cases, bulletin boards, and beat-up lockers, I nearly run into a silver-haired man who's hurrying into the cafeteria. He's dressed immaculately—far dressier than most of the men inside—with a fitted, camel-colored suit jacket and striped tie that makes him look like a J.Crew model. Who on earth?

"Oh, sorry." He gives me a distracted look, then focuses more closely. He holds out his hand. "Bartholomew Cole. Sorry, just got off hospital duty."

He must be a doctor. Only a doctor or a lawyer could afford that getup. Wait—Thomas *is* a lawyer and we have a half-lifetime of debt. I shake off my judgmental thoughts as something niggles at my memory.

"Tess Spencer. Don't worry, I was in a hurry to get out of—to get some fresh air."

He gives me a sympathetic smile. "I know these reunions can be a trial. I do like seeing old classmates, though. No promise of the morrow and all that." He studies my face. "Sorry, morbid thought. That was the doctor in me talking."

Doctor Bartholomew Cole. As in *Doc Cole*, Rose's doctor? Curiosity overtakes me. "So, did you grow up here?"

"No, no. We moved here the year I graduated from high school—1965." He glances toward the cafeteria.

No time to waste, so I plunge in. "By any chance, did you know a woman named Rose Campbell?"

I've never seen someone's jaw drop, but the Doctor's does. His eyes widen and he slides both hands into his jacket pockets.

"Yes—how do you know Rose?" He leans toward me. He must be six foot three, making me feel like a tiny speck at five foot six.

"My friend Miranda—"

"Miranda...Miranda *Michaels*? Oh—sorry to interrupt." He takes a small step back. "I saw Miranda today on my rounds.

She's always been a dear friend."

I don't try to get a word in edgewise. The Good Doctor seems determined to fill me in on things.

He looks at the ceiling, as if peeling off the mint green plaster layers and seeing deep into the past.

"Yes, Rose. She graduated the year before I did. Beautiful woman; the whole town said so. Married Paul Campbell—bit of a blighter, as my British grandma would say. Paul was always having poker parties, but he called them 'dinner parties' so the church-people wouldn't gossip."

"So you knew Rose well?" I can't put my finger on it, but there's something about the way he says *Rose.*

He looks directly at me. His eyes are what can only be described as battleship gray. Enchanting, really. Maybe Rose was enchanted by the Good Doctor?

"Her husband was quite overprotective. No one really got to know Rose well—in fact, she never left her house and her flowerbeds. As far as I recall, Miranda and I were the only ones she talked to. I was Rose's doctor."

With that, the conversation snaps shut like my laptop computer. The Good Doctor stretches his arm, checking his pewter-color watch.

"I've got to run." He nods and heads toward the heavy smell of overcooked chicken and instant mashed potatoes.

I'm left examining my black dress pants and my scuffed slingbacks from Payless. Next to the Doctor, I feel shabby. He seems high-class. Like Thomas, only older and more settled. Why do I always have to feel so—

"Tess!" Thomas jogs out of the cafeteria. "You hardly touched your food! Are you feeling sick?" I barely have time to

17

shake my head. "They already gave out the Outstanding Teacher Award. Mr. Irwin got it, the old coot. I always got in trouble in his lab class...Tess?"

The idea of returning to the cafeteria for more tasteless chicken with a side of leering and innuendo revolts me.

"Can we just hit Wendy's and go home?" I pull my leather blazer tighter, a hand-me-down from Nikki Jo. I feel exposed and raw.

Thomas' eyes soften. He slips his arm around me. "Sure, babe. Let's get outta here."

4

The jealousy ate away at me, though I tried to stop it. Every time we talked, Miranda had to bring her husband into the conversation somehow. Their marriage was perfect—Russell was perfect.

But I found a way to escape. I carved my own alternate reality outside the influence of my husband. When Paul had to work overtime, I'd call my true love and we'd meet beneath my wisteria arbor, regardless of rain or snow. Paul never set foot in my gardens, claiming to be allergic. In reality, he didn't want to do any work around the house.

One bright winter day, Miranda's pale skin glowed beneath her crimson lipstick. She could hardly contain herself as we ate her chocolate-chip pumpkin muffins. I knew before she told me: she was expecting.

I was not. I never would be. Twenty-six years old and my husband deliberately treated me like a nun.

I knew why. But I had my own plans.

How the Grande Dame managed to get this gargantuan, antique white dining table into her sitting room, I'll never know. She sits at one end, wearing her diamond-blinged glasses and red satin dress. I anchor the opposite side, hopelessly underdressed for this apparently "cocktail-wear" meal.

Paul sits between us, his skinny frame angled toward Miranda. From the moment he shook my hand, I've been taking mental impressions like a sketch artist.

Soggy-biscuit handshake. Too much Old Spice, possibly to mask another smell...alcohol? Body odor?

I try to cut him a break on his appearance. He is a widower, after all—no one to cook and clean for him. But then again, if that's what he's searching for, why's he dating Miranda? She can't get in and out of the shower by herself, much less do someone's laundry.

Once Paul starts talking, I begin to see some of his charm. He asks lots of questions about Thomas' job, my parents-in-law, and my pregnancy—all the while watching me with sharp brown eyes. It should be encouraging to get such undivided attention, but it unnerves me.

A catering woman in a crisp white oxford shirt and black pants brings out our first course: rosemary corn soup. When I'd asked, Miranda had refused to let me bring anything, even dessert. "You just come and enjoy, Tess. I should be able to afford a meal for three people."

Where had Miranda's husband worked, anyway? I make a

mental note to ask Nikki Jo. He must've left her some money, since The Haven is practically a resort facility for the elderly. It's not every day you see assisted living homes with Keurig coffee makers for the residents, much less a lap pool and gym in the basement.

"...I never thought I could learn to live again," Paul says. I tune back in to the conversation.

Miranda reaches out and pats his bony hand, her sapphire ring catching the light from the chandelier and reflecting it on the walls. "It was so unexpected, for all of us. She was in the prime of life."

"Yes, a rose with no thorns." Paul looks at me sadly, waiting for his obviously well-recited phrase to have its effect. Now it's my turn to look into his eyes. He starts to tear up. I'm not buying it. He turns back to the Grande Dame.

"You knew her so well, Miranda. Sometimes I thought you knew her better than I did. And then, when Royston read the will—"

Miranda interrupts, which is completely out of character. "Don't let's talk about that now."

Paul glances at me and nods slightly. Our second course is brought out: some sort of crab cakes on a pile of salsa. I'm sure there's a French name for these.

"Mr. Campbell, if you don't mind my asking, how did Rose die?" I need to hear him explain what happened.

The answer comes quickly. His piercing gaze reminds me of those hawks I see staring at small birds from the fence-posts.

"Please, call me Paul...and my Rose gave up on her own life and took an overdose. I've never known why, Tess."

There's something wrong with his tone as he says my name.

Intimate? Chiding? I store it up for replay later.

Thomas thinks I have a photographic memory, but it really works more like a video camera. I can review scenes—entire conversations, really—in my head. I try to tell him it's *not* a blessing to stroll down my memory lane of bumbling boyfriends and high-school angst. Still, every time he asks me *What was Mrs. Martin wearing at that church meal?* or *What was that crazy phrase my dad used again?,* I obligingly pull up the info on my brain's hard drive. Thomas actually prays that our child-to-be will have this videographic ability, as well as my nose and his math smarts.

Conversation lulls as we dig into our thick pork chops, followed by a light raspberry chocolate mousse served in champagne flutes. Paul eats like a man who's been living on Cheetos and Pop-Tarts.

I offer to help clean up, but the server loads all the dishes into a covered cart, then whisks it out of the suite. I wish Thomas could've come along tonight. It's been ages since we've had a real date. Obligatory church pot-lucks and Republican dinners don't really count.

Paul pushes his chair in and saunters over to the couch before I register how offensive that is. Not only did he forget to excuse himself, he didn't even offer to wheel his hostess over to join him. Possessed by a strange fury, I jump up. Shoving my chair back, I walk to the opposite end of the long table and grab Miranda's wheelchair handles. I feel like popping a wheelie and running over lazy-hiney Paul.

He doesn't seem to notice my self-righteous production, but Miranda does. "I'll get my chair, dear." Her eyes darken as she puts her hands on the wheels. "You know I can handle it."

"Sorry, Miranda." I trail behind her across the room, then help shift her onto the couch. She reaches for the drawer, and I fight an impulse to tell Paul "Goodnight, time to go." Why should Miranda share the letter with him? Why's she dating him anyway? And why can't I stand this guy?

"Do you need help, Miranda?" He leans over and pushes the drawer in for her. Truly valiant.

Miranda charges right in with characteristic openness. "Paul, I got this strange letter. I want you to take a look."

Taking the envelope, he pulls out the letter and slowly reads it. "Hm. Who would have something against me?"

Not a word of concern about Miranda. He doesn't even mention the handwriting. Either Miranda is imagining things—highly unlikely—or Paul paid no attention to how his wife wrote. Who doesn't recognize his wife's handwriting, no matter how long she's been dead? I feel like I have lockjaw, my teeth are clenched so hard.

Miranda gives me a look. I try to read her thoughts. Does she want me to say something? Might as well.

"Paul, do you recognize anything familiar about that letter?"

He looks at the stamp, examining the postmark. "No, should I? This person is from Arizona?" His fingers are long and thin, like his legs. Grandaddy longlegs.

I glance at Miranda, who's picking at her pillow tassels. Her steel-gray and white hair still looks perfect—she probably had it set on hot rollers this afternoon. All for this ill-mannered ingrate.

I force a polite smile. "Just asking—trying to figure out who sent this to Miranda."

He hands the letter back, then yawns and looks at his watch.

"Ten o'clock already? I'd better skedaddle on home now, ladies." He stands, extending those long legs and stretching his hand toward me. "So nice to meet you, Tess. You're every bit as lovely as Miranda made you out to be."

"Thanks. I had to meet the man who's been spending so much time with my friend."

Paul reaches down and gives Miranda a half-hug. "Delicious meal, my dear," he whispers, loud enough for me to hear.

The moment Paul pulls the thin door closed, Miranda launches into me.

"*What* was all that hullabaloo with my wheelchair? What got into you, Tess?"

"I don't like the way he treats you. And Miranda, he didn't recognize Rose's writing!"

"Treats me? He treats me just fine." She sighs and gives me a slight nod. "But I did notice about the handwriting."

I try a different tack. "Just wondering…what was your husband like? You hardly ever talk about him."

"Russell? Good lands." Her eyelids give her tiredness away, despite her careful application of concealer and eye makeup. "Well, Russell always called me his spicy fireball. He was so quiet…but when he talked, you'd better believe he had something important to say."

"Did he get along with Paul?" Suddenly I need to know this.

Miranda peers out the window, as if she can see into the black night. "I'm getting tired, honey. How about we talk more next week?"

This feels like a polite Southern brush-off. I kiss the Grande Dame's head, then help her into her wheelchair. She'll push her call button soon, and an assistant will come and help her get ready for bed. We can revisit this topic later.

In the crisp fall air of the parking lot, silent except for the crunch of leaves beneath my boots, it hits me. Miranda Michaels is the closest thing I've ever had to a grandma, on top of being my best friend. I'll be hanged before some jackanapes takes advantage of her. Paul Campbell had better watch his back.

5

Some winter nights when Paul worked late, I saw things in the woods. With the leafy green cover of summer gone, inexplicable movements often caught my eye when I went to load up the outdoor woodstove. A white light would move steadily through the trees and then stop. Underbrush shifted and branches rattled.

I wasn't scared. I carried Paul's pistol with me every time I went outside. It would have been foolish not to. Our nearest neighbor lived a forest and a field away.

Once, I asked Paul for a dog for protection. His response was, "No mangy mutts, needing shots and flea medicines. You're just imagining things, Rose."

True, my imagination dominated a great deal of my life. I had nothing else to do with my mind, or my time. Nothing but wait on Paul. He didn't want anything else vying for my attention.

Regardless, I never felt threatened by the presence in the woods. I knew it wasn't my true love, because he was working many of those nights. I finally decided it must be a guardian angel.

A guardian angel who'd heard my prayers for freedom, perhaps?

I couldn't describe the smells of Buckneck, West Virginia, even if I tried. It has something to do with the leaves composting in the woods, the cold trickle of little creeks and waterfalls, the ferns greening up everything. But somewhere deep below, I can smell the rock and the coal this state is built on.

My dad walked out on us for the coal.

The chain from our old porch swing grates against its hooks every time I push it backward. It sheds dark green paint chips all over my jeans and the wood plank floor.

I take a swig of my already-cold coffee. We have a French press, because Thomas didn't want to spring for a Keurig. His perpetual mantra is, "Can't afford the K-cups on my salary." Ain't that the truth.

Thomas' friends from UVA can't understand why we didn't head to D.C. after law school—the quickest way to take a huge bite out of his debt. Instead, we both agreed to return to a town in West Virginia so rural it rarely shows up on maps. We don't even try to explain our choice to them, because we can barely explain it to ourselves.

Growing up, I pictured West Virginia as a giant spider's

web, spun tightly around ramshackle houses and trailer parks like the one I lived in. I couldn't wait to get out of our valley to a flat place where skies kissed oceans—a place where everything wasn't hemmed in with trees.

Then college in South Carolina gave me my fill of flat land, red dirt, and heavy traffic. I came home to our valley, only to find mom had taken refuge in pain pills. Even worse, she'd started selling them at a mark-up to teens in the trailer park.

I had no choice. I moved out, but not before I called the cops. I wish I could erase my brain video of Mom, mascara streaking her tears as she shouted, "Tess! *Tess?*" That was just her first time in county jail. Now she's graduated to prison.

Nikki Jo crunches up our stony path in her tan cowboy boots, a welcome diversion from my memories. Her precisely highlighted blonde hair brightens and darkens with each sunray.

I get up, but Nikki Jo throws her hand up to stop me. "No, you sit down and enjoy your coffee, honey. I just wanted to bring you a cheesecake. I made five for church, so I just fixed an extra one. You like chocolate chip, right?"

"Ah, you know me too well, Mom. I'm going to gain twenty pounds before I'm into my second trimester."

Nikki Jo takes the cheesecake into the house before returning to the porch. She plops down in our green plastic Adirondack chair and sighs.

"What's up?" I ask.

"Those boys are about to drive me crazy!" She's talking about Petey and Dad. Thomas' other brother, Andrew, is in college.

She looks at me, her brown eyes a shade darker than

Thomas'. "Maybe you'll finally bring a girl into the Spencer family." Her smile deepens her dimples. "Of course, we'll be happy with whatever the Good Lord gives us."

I like the way she says *us*. One thing about the Spencers—when you marry in, you might as well be a blood relation. They'll watch over you and fuss over you and scold you like one of their own. God knew they were everything I'd missed growing up.

"Mom, I was wondering about Miranda's husband. What did he do?"

"Russell? Lawsie. Well, he got out of high school early and took over his daddy's bank. Always had a head for numbers, like our Thomas. He made a fortune, since it was the only bank around for miles. He built the biggest house in town. Miranda never had to scrape by, that's for sure."

I smile, but the irony is wasted on Nikki Jo, who's too humble to realize she now owns the biggest house in Buckneck.

"And what did Paul Campbell do?"

"Paul was a coal truck driver. He had all kinds of strange hours."

I shift forward, rubbing my lower back. Why haven't I put cushions on this swing yet? "I didn't think truck drivers got paid much. Weren't Paul and Rose wealthy, too?"

"Sure they were. But all their money came straight through Rose, not Paul."

Petey runs helter-skelter up the path, shooting gravel every which way. "Tess! The floral truck's up at the house! Someone sent you flowers, but you have to sign for them."

Nikki Jo hides a smile. "I think you could've signed for

29

those, Petey."

"No, Ma, he *specifically* said Tess has to sign. I told him he'd just have to wait." Petey's chin juts out, and he stands with his hands on his hips. "Those flowers came all the way from Point Pleasant!" The riverfront town is a good forty-minute drive from here.

I stand, brushing off the paint chips. "Guess we'll go see what it is, then." I say *we,* because doubtless Nikki Jo and Petey will stick with me like white on rice until we get to the big house.

Yellowed hostas wither beneath the scraggly rhododendrons lining our footpath. Nikki Jo's landscaping around the big house looks twenty times better than ours. The woman is a regular whiz with flowers, food, and anything remotely housewifely. Thomas says I have a brown thumb, since I've killed every bush and bulb we've transplanted from his mother's gardens.

Who on earth would've sent flowers? Thomas knows better than to do that, given our budget. It's like burning money—why buy something that'll die in a week, instead of saving for the baby furniture we need? My Scotch-Irish roots run deep, and I've already told Thomas we're not asking his parents for money to gear up for our accidental baby.

As we cross Nikki Jo's wraparound porch, Petey runs ahead of us. He jumps over the low-lying azalea bushes and shouts at the flower guy. "Hey!"

The tall blond man turns so I can see his face, giving me an even bigger surprise than the potted yellow plant he's holding.

Axel Becker.

The German who stalked me in college. In *South Carolina.*

What's he doing in Point Pleasant, West Virginia?

6

Crisp red-orange leaves swirled and fell, dusting my porch like confectioner's sugar on a Bundt cake. Each one seemed to whisper "Your days are numbered."

But the writing on the wall should've been for Paul. How I longed to shout in his face, "Mene, Mene, Tekel, Upharsin— You've been weighed in the balances and found wanting. You've treated me like a hired hand, not a wife. You've withheld good from me at every turn."

Judgment doesn't always fall on the unjust in this life. Sometimes you have to make your own way out.

I'd wait till winter. In the meantime, I watched Miranda, to see if she reciprocated any of Paul's smiles. If she clasped his hand a bit longer when he greeted her. If she joked with him more than her husband at our table.

She never did. In very fact, from the time she was pregnant, she seemed to shun him. But she was hiding something from me. She didn't visit as often, and when she did, her bright eyes rarely met mine.

What did she know?

Fall birds around here have their own burbling song, completely different from the robins of spring. Miranda and I sit at the white metal bistro table, soaking in the warmth of this unusually bright November day.

She pats her hair, a nervous gesture that speaks more than words. Suspicions creep into my mind and push all niceties aside.

Seeing Axel Becker in town makes me feel like I'm being followed. Sure, he *seemed* surprised to see me. Nevertheless, I scrawled something illegible on his delivery slip, grabbed the yellow plant, and high-tailed it back to my house before Nikki Jo and Petey could ask "What's going on?"

Better figure out who Miranda's stalker is, in case I attract one of my own. The yellow plant didn't come with a card, but it's unnerving, nonetheless. I lean forward on my elbows. "Did you get another note?"

Miranda sucks in her breath. "No, my dear, I did not." She focuses on a bare oak tree, where a crow caws forlornly.

"How's Paul doing?" I can't protect the Grande Dame if she doesn't open up a little. It's not like her to be so cagey.

"Paul? Oh, he's just fine—coming to see me tomorrow night. There's a gospel group coming to the forum."

The forum is a fancy term for *reception hall*. Everything about The Haven is fancied up to make family feel better about shedding their elderly cargo.

Sunlight glistens in the air. A caregiver with a dark navy shirt stands on a ladder nearby, using a rake to knock leaves from the gutter. Is it my imagination, or is he tilting his head our way?

"How's the baby doing?" Miranda adjusts the gauzy taupe scarf around her neck, as if to ward off some invisible breeze.

"I'm still in the first trimester, so I don't really know. I've only been nauseous a couple of times. It's too bad I'm *not* getting sick, with all the comfort food Nikki Jo keeps sending over."

Miranda adjusts her darkened glasses so I can't see her eyes. "Nikki Jo. I swan if that girl isn't the best thing that happened to Roger Spencer. He always had the big-head growing up, being the football star and his momma's only boy. Then here comes Nikki Jo, a skinny blonde girl with a big attitude, ready to give him a what-for."

The cadences of Miranda's West Virginia dialect soothe my suspicions. I fall into her words, like a plump earthworm slipping back into the dirt.

"Anyway. How's Thomas' job going? Royston have him working long hours?" Miranda's glasses slip down her nose, revealing her concerned eyes. "You know, those nights when Russell worked late, I wound up baking through the entire *Better Homes and Gardens* dessert section. Never learned a blessed thing from it, either. My cakes always went flat— cookies too." She chuckles. "Hope you've got something better to do with your time?"

Now would be a perfect time to mention the watcher in my woods or to discuss how Axel Becker moved to this part of

West Virginia. But I'm going to return to the issue at hand.

"I've just been thinking about Rose. So...Paul worked long hours with his coal hauling job?"

Miranda straightens, back stiff. "Who told you that?"

"What, that Paul worked late? Nikki Jo. I was asking her things—trying to get a good picture of Rose in my head."

The caretaker gets off the ladder and moves it closer to us—and farther away from the actual gutters.

Miranda sighs. "You want a picture of Rose? I've got a whole album of them. Only thing I could do to keep my friend close—take Polaroids of her and put them up on my fridge. She never visited me at my house. Instead, Russell and I would go over to their house for dinner parties."

She leans in toward me, our elbows touching on the table. "Rose never told me why she didn't like leaving her house. I figured she was shy. Her mother said something to that effect once. Anyway, if Rose wasn't out in her flowerbeds, she was reading books about flowers. She'd have me bring books from the library."

"Are the flowerbeds still there? Paul still lives in their house, right?"

"Oh, law; I don't know about those flowerbeds, but Paul does live in the same house. I haven't talked to him about it. Honestly, there are so many memories wrapped up with that place."

Indeed. Which makes me wonder how Paul's been living there cozily since Rose's death. Paul, the widower of a beautiful, agoraphobic wife, whose handwriting he doesn't even recognize...

"What's going on in that pretty little head of yours?"

Miranda smiles, her ruby lipstick hardly faded. The Grande Dame has a habit of telling me how pretty I am, which fills me with hope—a hope I'll age half as well as she did.

I've seen pictures of Miranda when she was Rose's age, and she was lovely in her vivid contrasts—dark red-brown hair, luminous eyes, and Snow-White fair skin. But her beauty's only grown more pronounced with age.

And now Paul's falling for her. I wonder...two young couples always getting together for dinner. Two beautiful wives.

"Did you and Paul always get along?" That question didn't come out right. Why am I always thinking the worst?

The deep blue eyes looking over the large glasses fill with tears. Blast it, I hit a nerve.

In my peripheral vision, I catch a navy shirt with light chinos moving behind my chair. Time to stop this dude's leaf-cleaning façade.

I jump up, knocking my chair backward into his leg.

"Ow!" The dark-haired man hops on one foot. "Lady, didn't you see me here?"

"Oh, so sorry. Maybe you should get some ice on that?"

Wraparound sunglasses hide his eyes, but I'm sure he's glaring at me. "Shoot, lady." He drops his rake and limps off to the main building.

Miranda coughs—a small, ladylike sound—and grins at me. "I wondered when you were going to do something about him, my little spitfire."

Yes, for an older woman, Miranda still sees plenty.

I yank up the back of my low-rise jeans before sitting. The person who created low-riders must've either been a guy or a girl built like a pencil.

"We were talking about Paul." I wait for her to fill the silence.

The crows have evacuated the oak tree, but the Grande Dame returns her attention to it, lost in thought. Finally, she covers my hand with her own and looks at me intently.

"I've never told anyone this. You know my Russell and I were crazy in love. He may've been quiet, but he worshiped the ground I walked on. Sometimes I think he would've given me anything I asked for—so I tried not to ask for much. Still, he could be...distant. He'd retreat into his study with his numbers. I needed flesh and blood, someone to talk to. I thought I'd found that friend in Rose. But she wasn't always open about things, like her marriage. And once I got pregnant, she seemed to pull back from me—didn't ask for library books, and we weren't invited over as often for meals."

Miranda takes a deep breath. "But when we did go over, Paul always wanted to talk with me. See, we had so much in common, like Edith Wharton books and *The Twilight Zone*."

My lips inadvertently quirk upward, so I focus on the fine metal weave of the table.

"Once, I was doing dishes in their kitchen, while Rose was cleaning off the table. Paul said something that made me laugh so hard I started crying. Then he put his arm around my shoulders; I guess to calm me down." Miranda's eyes tear up again, but not with happiness. "Russell came in at that moment. He wondered what I was laughing about."

Oh, no. A love triangle, with my beloved Grande Dame smack in the middle of it.

She squeezes my hand. "No, no, it wasn't like that. I know

what you're thinking. That one time was it. We avoided each other like the plague after that night."

An image flashes into my mind—a video, really. My mom, denying she'd sold her pills to anyone. Even after she'd been doing it for months.

Thomas always tells me I'd be a great prosecutor, because I don't take anything at face value and I don't believe people until I've hunted down the facts.

Only now, my mind has tried and convicted my best friend in the whole world—the Grande Dame of The Haven.

7

The best therapist I ever found for my marriage was a pair of sharp pruning shears.

In my shrub garden, I attacked the greenbrier vines that wanted to twine their way up my rhododendrons. Even with my gloves on, the long thorns would jab my fingers, drawing blood and making them throb for days. Still, I wouldn't stop until I chopped every vine and pulled it down.

My flowerbeds demanded even more attention, especially my roses. I read every book I could get my hands on, even concocted an elaborate watering system for them. Some years they got black spot, some years they got Japanese beetles. But they never failed to produce. I felt like God was smiling on me, honoring my name and giving me some small happiness in life.

What Paul didn't know was that I had a regular arsenal of poisons thriving in my flowerbeds. Foxglove, belladonna, hellebores....even the hydrangea in my shrub garden and the potatoes in my vegetable beds could be utilized, if necessary.

Day and night, I plotted my revenge on my husband. He could not withhold children and civility from me and expect to get away with it.

Most people saw me as a timid rabbit, scared to come out from my burrow and socialize. But I knew who I was—a mountain lion, silently watching my prey before I jumped on it and tore it to pieces.

The turnoff to the Spencer driveway looks like someone threw a bucketful of gravel across the shoulder of a one-lane road. You feel like your car's going to fly off the face of the cliff when you pull in. *Blind drive* would be a handy sign to post, but no one bothers.

Still, the florist—rather, Axel Becker—made that turn. Weird.

I remember the nudges and comments my roommates gave me, every time the blond giant stared at me across the college commons. "He's *fixated*, Tess. Why doesn't he just give you a call?"

He never did, even though he'd often show up in the same classes I took. I had the freakish feeling he'd employed spies to deliver my semester schedules to him. In Modern Philosophy, or British Literature, or any other random Liberal Arts class, he'd watch the back of my head, or the side of my head, or even turn around to full-on stare at me.

For a while, I made the mistake of trying to read his mind. I'd interpret the drawn blond eyebrows as misplaced anger, or the pale blue eyes as devoid of pain. I tried different tactics: staring at him, ignoring him completely, smiling. The one thing I couldn't control was the blush that crept up my cheeks every time he stared back. Really hard to look cool and haughty when your face goes scarlet.

Then, as we were leaving Pottery class one day, he caught up with me. I gripped my seafoam-green, asymmetrical vase closer, as if he'd try to snatch it from me.

"Tess Spencer?" His voice sounded almost formal, then I realized he had a German accent. "Axel Becker."

He stretched his long arm out, I assumed to shake my hand. Instead, he stepped in front of me, his arm barring my way.

And then, right there in the middle of the green, he kissed me.

I should have screamed and run like a maniac. Instead I stood, transfixed by this German stalker of few words, who also happened to be an incredible kisser.

That was the last I saw of Axel Becker. He disappeared from campus. I wondered if a friend had turned him in for being a predator, or if he was so disillusioned with my limited kissing abilities, he gave up on American women altogether.

One hand on the steering wheel, I absently let my red SUV coast down the hill, heading past the big house. A whir of black fur darts toward my tires—Thor! I slam the brakes. Gravel sprays against the white siding on my in-laws' house.

"You teeny crazed mutt, you're going to get yourself squashed like a grape—" Petey sticks his head through my open window, interrupting my mutterings.

"Hey, Tess. Mom left some pumpkin bread on your porch, up in that metal box thingy." He leans closer and whispers,

"I've been watching out my window with the binoculars. No action in the woods lately. But I've figured out a way to catch him—booby traps!"

"Petey, this isn't *Hardy Boys*, or *Choose Your Own Adventure*. This could be something dangerous." Petey's been reading through all Thomas' old books at breakneck speed.

He scrunches up his freckle-splattered button nose. "'Course I know that. But if I set the traps ahead of time, I can't get hurt, right?"

His imploring brown eyes make it impossible to refuse. "Okay, Petey. But don't do anything expensive—no buying traps. And no…spikes or explosives. And let me know where you put them, okay?"

"Yes, ma'am. Agent Petey Spencer, reporting for duty." He mock salutes, then picks up Thor. The dog was so close to my tire, I have no doubt he was relieving himself on it.

I can practically taste a golden slice of Nikki Jo's eggnog pumpkin bread, slathered in butter. All thoughts of Axel are obliterated as I walk up to my door. Sure enough, the pumpkin bread is neatly wrapped in a cellophane bag decorated with fall leaves. Nikki Jo likes to class things up, unlike my own mom, who frequently served ketchup sandwiches on white bread for supper.

The phone's jangling as I open the door. Is it just me, or is my stomach getting in the way a little? Sure, my jeans still fit. But there seems to be a bit more of *me* these days. I need to lay off the goodies. Then again, Thomas is always telling me that I should eat whatever I crave, for the baby. No doubt, his font of childbearing wisdom springs directly from his mom.

I grab the phone and shove it between my shoulder and face,

nearly dropping my precious bread. I yelp. "Yes?"

"Tess, what's up?"

"Sorry, babe; just trying to keep hold of your mom's bread. Hey, when you coming home tonight? Should I wait up to eat?"

"No, go ahead. Royston needs to close a big deal tomorrow, so I have to get the paperwork ready to go for him."

Please. *As if* Royston can't do that himself.

"What are you going to eat? You don't have anything left in the fridge there."

Thomas sighs—more a huff than a full-body groan. Even his sighs sound high-class.

"I'll grab something from the Stop-N-Go."

Bad idea. Last time I got a sub from there, the roast beef was green. "I'll bring you something, since I need to go to the library tonight." He might as well enjoy some pumpkin bread before I get going on it, and I want to do some research on Rose.

His voice brightens. "Sure, come on by. I'll leave it unlocked. And wear something *nice.*"

Yeah, right. "Dude, I'll be wearing my regular jeans, a turtleneck, and boots. Standard fare. I said I'm going to the *library.*"

"Okay, gotcha. See you soon, beautiful."

By the time I pack up leftover meatloaf and scour my fridge in hopes of finding edible side dishes, it's nearly dark. This is one of two nights a week our library stays open late, so I'm going to capitalize on that. Our modem connection in this hollow is so patchy and my laptop is so dated, I might as well drive the fifteen minutes to downtown Buckneck for normal internet speeds.

Petey waves at me from our back woods, then kicks at Thor, who's running circles around his legs. My nephew wears thick yellow work gloves and holds a circle of barbed wire. I'm just going to keep on driving. I'll have to figure out where he puts that later.

Meredith and Jenkins, LLP, is located right on the main street in Buckneck—ideally situated between a funeral parlor and a real estate office. It's one of the original brick two-stories in town. People have been known to enter the law office and promptly exit upon seeing its dark paneling, sure they've entered the funeral home by mistake.

Thomas opens the back door for me, grabbing the food bag before he grabs me. "Come on into my *lair*, dearie." He swings me into an embrace, his brown eyes soft.

I kiss him, then extricate myself.

"Thomas! I said I have work to do."

He holds me at arm's length. "Did you land a job I wasn't aware of?"

"No, nothing like that. Just doing some research for the Grande Dame."

Thomas' smile wavers, then he gives me a resigned look. "It's for the best anyway. I'll probably be here half the night."

I kiss him goodbye and get going. I know from experience when the library says it closes at nine, they'll kick you out at a quarter till.

An hour and a half later, I've managed to print a copy of Rose's obituary, along with the scanty news report on her unexpected death. I tap my pen on the piece of library scrap paper, until the older guy next to me clears his throat. Ooh, so sorry to interrupt your important web browsing session, which looks to consist of checking out pictures of teen models. Pervert.

A cough sounds from the loft above. Another hint to quit my tapping? I look up, only to lock eyes with the Good Doctor. It takes me a few minutes to recall his real name: Doctor Cole. Bartholomew Cole.

Again, he looks quite snappy, sporting a gray shawl-collar cardigan, complete with those old-fashioned leather buttons and elbow patches. He's wearing round tortoise-shell glasses that shout Ralph Lauren. A massive tome sits open on his lap— maybe a medical book from the 1800s?

I write *Dr.* on my hand, so I'll remember to ask Miranda about his relationship with Rose. He waves slightly, then stands and disappears. Quiet shoe-steps sound on the marble stairs and it hits me—he's coming to talk.

A chill runs down my back, making my shoulders shake. My old-dude neighbor shoots me an undisguised glare. My spidey-senses are tingling. Maybe I'll get out of here; pretend I was already leaving.

I grab my quilted bag. Striding to the unmanned librarians' desk, I toss the computer check-out card across the counter in the vain hope someone will find it later. When I shove the interior glass door, an arm reaches above me and holds it open.

"Tess Spencer, isn't it?" The Doctor's deep voice surrounds me. He follows me into the hallway before I can get to the outer set of doors.

I turn, smiling my brightest. "Yes, Doctor. How nice to see you again."

"You shouldn't have to open doors—you're expecting, aren't you?" Though his chiseled jaw and white hair combo distracts me, I do have some brain cells left. My hand flies to my stomach.

"How did you know? I didn't think I was showing all that much."

He laughs. "No, I do house calls at The Haven, remember? Miranda talks to me quite frequently about her young protégé. Or should I say *friend*? You're very good for her, Tess. Widows should not be forgotten—that's biblical, you know."

Is that an insult? As if I don't know the Bible? Just because I don't show up at any of the four churches in town...

He steps closer, blocking the cold draft from the outside doors. "I see too many widows and widowers who are completely forgotten by their families. Speaking of widowers, I hear you've met Paul Campbell? What do you make of him?"

A flicker of ice creeps into the Good Doctor's blue-gray gaze. Looks to me like he doesn't care for that *blighter,* as he called Paul. Neither do I, but I don't have anything solid to base my opinions on.

"He's tolerable," I finally answer.

He buttons his sweater and motions to the door. "May I walk you to your car?"

Sure, why not? As usual, I've got my knife on me.

I click open the SUV door and jump in, turning the engine on to get some heat rolling. The Doctor stands at the open door, hesitant. He looks like he wants to tell me something—and every instinct tells me it's important.

"Did you want to talk, Doctor?" I motion toward my passenger seat. The tall, dapper man nods and comes around. Let's hope I'm trusting the right person.

8

Every time the doors were open, we were in church. My mother would braid my hair and help me get into one of my frilly, pressed dresses. She never stopped humming as she did it. "We're going to the Lord's house today, my little Rose."

I must've been about six when it hit me that my father never came to church with us. He owned a steamboat on the Ohio River, and he ran it on Sundays. Funny thing was, absence must've made the heart grow fonder for Mother—when he was gone, she was happy.

Sometimes I wondered if my mother fell for Paul every bit as much as I did. He'd bring her flowers and chocolates. They'd sit on the porch and talk for hours. She soaked up the attention, something Father never gave her. Or me.

So I married Paul, and had more than my share of attention from then on. Attention if I ate too much pie. Attention if my hair was askew. Attention if his pants weren't pressed for company. Repercussions came when those details were amiss.

I planned my way out, even as I subjected myself to the sham of marriage. Justice was thwarted, but not forever.

The clove-like smell of the Good Doctor's sweater draws me closer as he starts talking.

"To be frank, I've noticed your curiosity about Rose. I wonder if this stems from Miranda's recent relationship with Paul?"

All right. You want frank, Doctor? I'll be frank.

"Yes, I'm concerned, and I'll tell you why. Miranda got a note from someone, warning her away from Paul."

"A note? Any idea who it came from?"

"This is where it gets strange. According to Miranda, the handwriting matches Rose's."

The Doctor's face struggles between surprise and denial. Denial wins out.

"I pronounced her, Tess. She overdosed on her Digoxin. I knew that's what it was because I prescribed it to her, yet she had no significant premorbid illness. It was toxicity, pure and simple."

"Doctor, I don't know how to explain it. Maybe someone knows her writing and copied it. Paul didn't even recognize it—or so it seemed. And why would he want to warn Miranda off from dating *himself*? Maybe someone just hates Paul."

My cheeks feel hot as fireballs, so I turn off the car. I don't have any good theories on this. And I find it hard to believe the note came from a ghost.

"There *is* the issue of the will," the Good Doctor says.

My mind re-runs Paul's comment at the dining table. *"You knew her so well, Miranda. Sometimes I thought you knew her better than I did. And then, when Royston read the will—"*

"What issue?"

The Doctor takes off his fogged-up glasses and starts wiping at them with his pocket handkerchief. I don't know if I'm more entranced by the old-fashioned handkerchief or by the compassionate eyes focused on me.

"I thought everyone in town knew. Of course, you're young. Rose left all her money to Miranda, since she was her best friend. Left nothing to Paul but the house. Caused a real stir in Buckneck, believe you me."

So *that's* why Miranda changed the subject at the dinner table. Awkward topic when you're dating your best friend's husband. And are they just dating? I need to talk with her...

The Good Doctor's still watching me. "You're very observant, aren't you, Tess?"

This is starting to feel uncomfortable. It probably wouldn't be uncomfortable if I didn't find Doctor Cole so attractive, much less mentally refer to him as the Good Doctor.

"Have you ever thought about studying counseling? Miranda truly feels you have a gift for reading people. I can see that."

"Thanks, Doctor. I'll think about that." I turn the key, making a point of looking at the clock. "Oh, look at the time! I've got to get home." To my empty house.

He gets the hint. "So sorry to keep you. Keep your eyes open, my dear."

My cheeks flame as he closes the door.

All the way home, those words ring in my head. *A gift for reading people.* More like a curse. I told my mom something was wrong with Dad, a week before he walked out on us. I figured out Mom was doing some kind of pills, just from a phone call. And now I know someone has it in for Miranda. It's not even the note. It's just a feeling that something's still wrong—the same thing that was wrong forty years ago when Rose died. A malignancy, a tumor, slowly growing in someone's heart. A conscience that's seared.

What if Rose's death wasn't an overdose, no matter what the Good Doctor swears to the contrary?

Once I'm home, I change and get onto my stationary bike. I need to process my recent conversation. Why's the Doctor being so friendly? I don't think he's fake. But I'm pretty sure Paul doesn't like me. Maybe because I'm too close to Miranda?

My bike sits toward the back wall of our cottage, in a room the size of a closet. The window is practically flush with a sprawling oak tree. I try to check my reflection in the darkened glass as "Don't Stop Believin'" plays on my mp3 player. Yeah. Wish I knew what I believed.

Back in Sunday school, I believed Jesus loved me, probably because I was painfully aware my own daddy didn't. This love filled me up until college. Then a few guys stomped all over my heart, I figured out my mom was doing drugs, and my roommate died when a drunk driver crossed into her lane in broad daylight.

In the end, no one loved me; least of all God. He didn't give—He took away.

Thomas has taken me to a few church dinners. They always turn out badly, because I hardly know anyone in town. To them, I'm simply "Thomas Spencer's wife."

Nikki Jo's tried harder, inviting me to every imaginable women's Bible study. She must think I'm a mess. Still, she doesn't *treat* me like a mess.

I make a mental checklist of to-dos for the week. Talk to Miranda about the Doctor's income and relationship with Rose. Go to my first prenatal appointment. Figure out if I still believe in God. Because we want this baby to go to church, right? Otherwise the poor child might end up like my absentee dad or my jailbird mom.

I project a grim smile to my wavery window-reflection. Those panes must be a hundred years old. I look pale, and not in a good way. I push down again at my cowlick, which manages to protrude despite my headphones. I'm not going to that beautician again.

Turning back to my bike, I glimpse something moving outside. Something very close to my window.

I jump off, peering into the blackness.

There, by the tree trunk, our house light illuminates a face— a woman's face. It's familiar somehow.

I kill the lights and run upstairs. Taking our subcompact handgun from the drawer, I eject the magazine, feeling in the darkness to make sure there's a bullet in place. Nothing like a loaded Glock in hand to endow me with a healthy dose of bravery.

I move through the dark house, grabbing a flashlight before silently turning our front knob and stepping outside. Flashlight held high, I rush to the back of the house and click it on, straight toward the tree.

Nothing. She's gone.

Who is she?

As I round the house again, Thor yelps his way down the path, Petey running behind.

"Tess! I saw the light! What's going on?"

I'm beginning to think Petey's my real stalker. "Petey, you should be asleep! You have school tomorrow!"

He ignores my words of wisdom. "Why do you have your gun? Was someone out here?"

I nod. "A woman."

"Did you check my traps out back? Maybe she's there!" Petey grabs my flashlight and runs. I follow him, stepping carefully in the dark as Thor darts around. At least his incessant yipping gives his position away.

Petey pulls branches off a deep hole behind the oak tree. "Nothing in here. I'll check my other traps." I wait as he makes his rounds, imagining the kinds of traps a twelve-year old could have come up with. I'd better have him sketch me a trap-map before I venture deeper into the woods.

It doesn't take long for him to get back. "No one around. How'd she miss all my traps?" He shakes his head in disbelief.

She must have been here for a while, figuring out which way to go...watching and waiting outside my window.

Looks like I'm going to have to drag Thomas into this sordid mess.

9

Our second year of marriage, after I'd stopped leaving the house, Paul brought home a new red lace dress for me.

"Get yourself all fancied up, Rosey. We're having a date tonight."

I spent all day wondering if my desperate prayers were finally answered. Maybe Paul had come to his senses, realizing he'd beaten his wife into submission. Maybe he was ready to make amends. After all, he'd never once apologized for hitting me.

I pulled the rollers out of my long hair, awed that it was still strawberry-blonde. I should've had thousands of white hairs, given the things I'd been through. God had a sense of humor. Miranda was already getting white hairs, and she had an idyllic life. Big house, perfect husband, and now, a healthy baby girl named Charlotte.

Mascara and eye-shadow, which I seldom used, brought out a sparkle in my eyes that had died with my girlhood. I started to see what my lover saw, every time he complimented me.

Determined to please Paul—to give him a chance—I put on my highest black heels and waited for him to get home, though it was already five-thirty. He wasn't leaving much time to clean up before our date.

He arrived at eight that night, filthy with coal dust. He took one look at me and smiled. "Let me change, and we'll have our date. Is there any of your leftover pot roast in the fridge?" My empty stomach turned as he spoke.

All along, our date was to be at home. With leftovers.

I went into the kitchen, got my scissors, and came back out as he was shaking one of his black boots over the doormat. He turned, smile still frozen in place. I made a long, deliberate cut from the bottom of my dress to my thighs. Then, summoning all my strength, I ripped the entire dress in half. As it fell to the floor, I stood there, in nothing but my underclothes.

Paul just stared as I said, "You'll never hurt me again, Paul Campbell. The day is far spent, and the time for repentance is past."

Thomas crawls into bed around three in the morning, effectively nixing any time for chitchat. At breakfast, his zombie-eyes seem out of focus as he downs his fourth cup of coffee. He grabs his lunch bag, almost forgetting to give me his usual goodbye kiss.

I wait till his lunchtime to call, hoping he'll agree to go out to eat tonight. We need to talk, and I need to get away from my invisible cottage stalker. To my surprise, Thomas accepts. We set up a meeting time for our favorite Point Pleasant restaurant, Bistro Americain.

I wander around the house, my thoughts disjointed. I should do the stationary bike, but I don't want to go into that room. Curled yellow buds open on my potted plant in the front window. A begonia, Nikki Jo said. Even though Nikki Jo likes flowers, she's not obsessed with them like Rose was.

And why was Rose so obsessed? Maybe she needed a hobby with the agoraphobia. Something tickles the back of my mind…I'm missing something.

I visualize Nikki Jo, touching the deep green leaves on my plant. "Unusual gift, this time of year."

Unusual? Or *deliberate?*

I call my in-laws. Nikki Jo picks up, but I hear the Fox news channel blaring before she speaks.

"What you need, baby girl?" My mother-in-law's endearments make me grin from ear to ear.

"Mom, do you have any old books on flowers? Like, the meaning of flowers and stuff?"

"I might have some in that jam-packed bookcase in the attic. It's going to break down the rafters someday. I keep telling Roger to go through it, but he won't. Anyway, why don't you come over and take a look?"

"Will do. Thanks." I grab several of Nikki Jo's clean dishes to return. I look at my stomach to see if the contents of those dishes have fattened the baby up. Sure enough. At least, I hope it's just the baby.

Nikki Jo's burnt-orange front door perfectly matches the plaid ribbons on her twig wreath. Twin hunter-green urns flank the door, overflowing with profuse purple and yellow flowers. People with this level of decorating skills are born, not made.

Roger opens the door and throws his arms around me. "How's the little momma?"

I pat my stomach. "Getting bigger, I think?"

He laughs. "You ain't showin' yet. C'mon in where it's warm."

The blonde wood floor in the hallway is polished to perfection. Nikki Jo comes down the curving staircase, triumphantly brandishing a book.

"I went up there to poke around. And blamed if this book didn't fall right out in front of me! The very one I was thinking about." She hands the thin green book to me. *The True Meaning of Flowers* runs up the spine. "Is that what you wanted, Tess?"

"Sure was."

Roger kisses my cheek and takes his leave into the TV room—back to his news channel. Nikki Jo and I discuss town issues, like how the beautician is divorcing her husband and how the funeral director's retiring. Nothing gets past Nikki Jo, but she doesn't spread the news in a malicious way. She's just disseminating information. I find myself wishing Miranda had Nikki Jo's sharing abilities. I feel like she hasn't told me anything important yet about Rose. But maybe I haven't dug deep enough.

When we finish talking, I give Nikki Jo a quick hug, ignore Thor dancing around my feet, and head back to the cottage.

Walking along Nikki Jo's brick path, I admire her perfectly manicured holly bushes. If only we had the money to fix up our place more. Still, I'm thankful Thomas' parents let us use their cottage rent-free while we're paying off student loans.

My mom was thrilled I was marrying a lawyer, convinced we'd have a huge house with an extra room so she could move in. Of course, this was contingent on her ability to stay out of prison, which proved impossible. If she ever sees our small cottage, she'll still think I married up, compared to the trailer park.

I grab a fleece jacket, then sit on the porch to read the flower book in the streaming sunlight. The thin pages have a musty smell that's not unpleasant. I run my finger down the words. Baby's Breath. Bachelor's Button…Begonia. Yellow Begonia: *Warning* or *I am fanciful*.

Warning.

Someone is trying to warn *me*, not just Miranda.

I slam the book shut, looking toward the woods. The light glints off something metallic, probably one of Petey's traps. Let's hope little Thor doesn't get messed up in one of them. Usually Nikki Jo keeps him inside till Petey gets home from school.

Back inside, I lay out my black pantsuit and my silky moss-green blouse. I'll wear my favorite high-heeled boots tonight, not to mention makeup. Maybe if I look good, I'll divert Thomas' attention from the heavy stuff I'm saying.

After a hot bath and liberal application of Thomas' favorite perfume, Cool Water, I feel halfway presentable. Thomas will be wearing his office attire—dress pants, a suit jacket, and tie. It's more intimidating when a lawyer dresses up for work, he says. And he needs all the intimidation factor he can muster, as the lowest lawyer on the totem pole. Even though his degree supersedes anyone else's, his age and inexperience knock him down several rungs in the eyes of Buckneck residents.

I run over my mental list of discussion points. It's probably a dumb evening to set up a date—right after he's pulled a half-nighter. But I feel I need Thomas' go-ahead before getting more deeply enmeshed in this mystery surrounding Rose's death.

Right before I walk out the door, my sky-blue cell phone rings—playing the *Doctor Who* theme song. Thomas thinks I'm a total geek for loading that one up. Like Miranda with her *Twilight Zone* fascination, I'm a bit of a sci-fi freak.

The number shows up as The Haven.

"Hello? Miranda?"

"Yes, it's me, honey. Listen, we need to get together. How about tomorrow?"

"I was planning on it. Do you need anything from town? I'm going over tonight."

"Don't you bring anything but yourself. Vesta always gets my supplies when she shops, and I have some coffee cake Paul brought over today."

My jaw clenches involuntarily. "Paul was over?"

She sighs. "Of course he was—he comes over about every day, Tess. Things are getting pretty serious between us."

Pretty serious? What does that mean for a couple of almost-seventy-year olds? I can't ponder this.

We nail down the details, my mind fixated on the *pretty serious* news. What if she's going to tell me she's getting married? How can I feign happiness?

Absently, I change the contents of my purse to my favorite eel-skin clutch, a gift from my Chinese roommate in college. I'll try to look high-class tonight, even if I did grow up in a smaller town than this one.

It's still light out when I get to the bistro. I pull into the parking area, where Thomas stands, lanky limbs propped against his old navy Volvo. Somehow the man and the car belong together. As I get out, he winks and bows.

"Shall we take a jaunt along the waterfront first, m'lady?"

Hand in hand, we stroll down the walkway, which runs along the Ohio River. We slow to scrutinize the scenes on the long mural wall, which depicts the battle between the Shawnee natives and the Virginia Militia. When we reach the concrete outdoor amphitheater, we stop, sitting on a cold built-in bench and silently watching the men work on their docked ferryboats. One of the boats' deep air-horns makes me jump.

"You seem on edge lately." Thomas' eyes are fixed on the metal bridge in the distance. "You worried about your doctor appointment?"

"No, no, nothing like that. Just some stuff going on with Miranda."

"Drama for the Grande Dame?" He laughs.

"Actually, yes. Someone's bringing the drama to her. And to me." The words pop out before I think.

Thomas turns, his brown eyes narrowed. He must've combed his hair, since it's not as spiky tonight. He has just a hint of five o'clock shadow. His crisp white shirt and charcoal-and-orange striped tie exude power somehow. He gently turns my shoulders toward him. "*What* did you say? Who's bringing drama to my wife?"

I chuckle inside, remembering the lusty dentist at the reunion. Last time someone brought the drama to Thomas' wife, he was completely oblivious.

I open my mouth to explain, but a tall blond man on the sidewalk above us draws my eye. In the twilight, I can't see him very well, until he turns around and stares at me.

It's Axel Becker. Date night is off to a roaring good start.

10

Once baby Charlotte was born, Miranda pulled away from me. Some days, I'd go down to the creek and swirl my feet in the icy water, just to feel alive. I'd sit on the rocks in our woods, watching the clouds sift between the bare branches. I wondered if I had any real friends at all.

My lover had disappointed me. He didn't want me to follow through with my plan. He had another plan, he said. A better one. But I'd have to do something for him first—something I refused to do. I began to see him through different eyes. He was merely another self-serving man, like Paul. He'd never had my best interests at heart.

I decided that love was fickle, and nothing but pain. I would continue to make my own happiness, and I would use my lover to do it. I would promise the world and give him nothing in the end. Why should I? Nothing was free in life, not even love. My own father never loved me. My husband probably hated me. My lover only thought he loved me. I didn't even have a God who loved me anymore.

All the Bible verses I learned in Sunday school felt empty. Songs like "Jesus Loves Me, This I Know." I didn't know that. Perhaps I needed to read my Bible; try to understand more. But I couldn't even go to church, couldn't ask the questions burning in my heart.

Still, I needed to talk to someone. Someone not associated with Paul in any way. A name jumped to mind, the name of a classmate and friend I'd had in grade school.

Cliff Hogan. Now he was pastor of the small independent church in town. And Cliff knew how I grew up, in that big house with no father to speak of.

I called him and explained I couldn't leave the house. He agreed to come over during the day, so Paul wouldn't know we were talking. This was very unwise, but he was a young, single pastor and didn't know any better. Neither of us could have foreseen the consequences we'd bring upon ourselves.

As soon as I recognize Axel, I do the first thing that comes to mind—I bury my face in Thomas' shirt.

His crisp Eternity cologne combines with the Niagara starch and the faint masculine smell of sweat. He pats my head, doubtless unsure of what upset me so much. "Tess?" he whispers. "You okay?"

I raise my head inch by inch, careful to keep it turned away from my German stalker. Thomas' stubble is rough as I cup my hand under his chin. "Just worried, that's all. But it's getting dark. Let's talk on our way to the restaurant."

Thomas joins me as I stand, veering to the right—the opposite direction from Axel.

"Um, aren't we going *away* from the bistro?" Thomas stops mid-stride.

I offer him a very alluring smile. "Just gives us more time to talk. We'll circle around."

Works like a charm. As we walk, I tell him all about Miranda's note and the unnerving meal with Paul. When I mention the woman's face in our window and my begonia of doom, Thomas groans and mutters ominously about protecting his woman. I finally bring up my conversation with the Good Doctor and share what he said about Miranda's inheritance from Rose.

Thomas nods thoughtfully. "Yes, I think I've heard Royston mention the Darby account. That's Rose's surname—her father was French—and a big-time steamboat owner, back in the day. There was definitely some money to be had there. Rose was their only child."

His arm covers mine, and I squeeze it tighter to my body. The minute the sun set, the cool breeze off the water picked up. The dark wetness seems to bite into my suit jacket and thin blouse. But the chill isn't just outside.

"Thomas, when I put the pieces together, they don't fit. Rose *was* a recluse. She couldn't have children. But would that be enough to make her do herself in?"

"People do it all the time, for punier reasons than that." Thomas speaks like a world-weary cynic.

"And the letter? Why would it have her handwriting?"

"Who told you it's her handwriting?" Thomas' eyebrows

quirk up, and I laugh at his intense look before I answer.

"Well, Miranda, of course. Her best friend. And Paul didn't even recognize it! Imagine not recognizing *my* handwriting..."

"Maybe by the time I get to be an old geezer, I'll forget too!" Thomas laughs.

We finally step up onto the main town sidewalk, heading left toward the bistro. Thomas might be hungry and tired, but he's getting a little too slap-happy for me. This is a serious investigation.

He grins. "I see that dubious look, missy."

"I'm telling you this stuff so I can get your informed opinion on things, Thomas!" My stomach gives a loud growl for extra emphasis. Seductive, I'm sure.

I try to focus straight ahead, determined not to glance at the creepy Mothman statue in the center of town. Those metal claws and glowing red eyes freak me out. Just because Point Pleasant got famous for some alleged alien sightings doesn't mean I have to embrace the insanity. Thomas knows this, and he valiantly steps between me and the statue as we pass it.

A few steps farther, to my left, a gold curliqued name stenciled on a lit bay window pulls me up short. Fabled Flowers—the shop where Axel works. Potted ferns form a soft border inside, showcasing the display itself, which channels Beatrix Potter. A worn, stuffed family of rabbits seems to hop around a white picket fence. Red and white roses are juxtaposed with green cabbages and bright-orange carrots. Rosemary sprigs are shaped into a hedgehog—Mrs. Tiggy-Winkle!

I give a short whistle. "Can you *believe* this? I've never seen such edgy flowers!"

Thomas stretches his arms. "Edgy, for sure. Look, I'm hungry, and you know this town always seems to shut down early. I can't talk until I get fortification."

I peer beyond the ferns and the fence, trying to see if someone's inside. Wonder if Axel runs the shop or just works—

"AGH!" I jump backward as Axel's face emerges, right behind the glass. He's staring at me, pale eyes fixated.

Thomas grabs my arm. "What the—?"

I start walking, fast as I can. We can beat him, we can beat him, I'm hungry…

An old cowbell clangs into the glass door as Axel swings it open wide. This is a nightmare. Right here with my husband, he's going to accost me. Video images of the stolen kiss race through my mind.

"Tess. You like the begonia?" His German accent seems more pronounced than our last meeting.

Thomas stops following me and turns, pointing loosely at Axel. "Begonia?" His tone is quizzical, light. But I know flaming hot lava simmers underneath it.

I step in quickly.

"Thomas, meet Axel. He delivered that yellow begonia, you know, from someone anonymous…" I step right next to Thomas, ready to catch his arm, should he choose to hit the big German with it.

Thomas turns to me. "You and the florist are on a first-name basis?"

Axel doesn't pick up on Thomas' negative vibe. At all. He strides right up next to me. "We went to college together." He pats my arm and looks at me. Oh, good mercy, no. It's the possessive stalker look.

Thomas' perfect white smile is so incongruous, it's downright terrifying. His long fingers bend, tightening into fists. I wanted him to be protective, but he's about to go loco on a German who bears more than a passing resemblance to Dolph Lundgren in *Rocky IV*.

I hug Thomas tightly, getting up in his face before I turn. "Axel, this is my husband, Thomas Spencer. He's a *lawyer*. We've got to get going, though."

Axel nods, looking from Thomas to me. No doubt he's used up his quota of words for the day. He smiles and lumbers back toward Fabled Flowers. I wait for the cowbell clang before I finally let go of Thomas. My arms are shaking.

Thomas' set jaw and the way he power-walks past me lets me know I'd better zip my mouth and let him cool off. By the time I catch up with him, we're at the bistro. Once the hostess seats us, I decide to break the ice. After all, this *is* a date.

"So…how was your day?"

Thomas slaps the menu on the table. "Well, Tess, it was just great, till some whopping guy I've never met came up and leered at my wife like she's a piece of German chocolate cake."

"Come on. He just knew me in college and happens to be the florist."

"And was he the anonymous donor of aforementioned flowers?"

He's veering toward lawyer-talk. Not good. Where's our waitress, anyway? Maybe breadsticks would help. I wave frantically toward the kitchen. Finally, a woman walks our way.

The waitress says, "Today's special is—" She stops as

Thomas turns his smoldering eyes on her. His anger gives him a masculine edge he's completely oblivious to.

The waitress blushes, then continues. She has lovely fair skin with peachy undertones. Even her hair looks peach—some kind of strawberry blonde. She turns full-on toward me to finish her spiel, and I gasp.

Those wide-set eyes. That hair. The pale skin. *She's* the face I saw in my window. The watcher in my woods.

11

The first time Cliff came to talk with me, snow had blanketed the ground. His old orange Dodge truck rumbled up our drive. I put on my rabbit-fur trimmed coat and white leather gloves to go and meet him.

He jumped out of the truck into thick snow that swallowed his boots. "Rose! Good lands, you haven't aged one bit!" He yanked his feet free and tromped over to hug me. "You look like a snow queen, all dressed in white."

I couldn't believe his comments, much less his enthusiasm over seeing me. I felt like the only person in his world. Cliff had always had that way about him. He drew people close without trying hard at all.

He had changed since grade school. His freckles seemed less pronounced, and his red hair had darkened considerably.

I had hot cider waiting inside, along with cinnamon rolls I'd made for Paul's breakfast. Cliff put more wood in the fireplace and we sat, watching the glowing, crumbling logs.

"I have a feeling you called me for a reason. Might as well begin at the beginning." His directness disarmed me.

I told him everything about our marriage. I left my affair out of it. In my mind, that was already over. But Cliff knew I was hiding something—it was like he had a spotlight trained deep into my soul.

"Be honest, Rose. You seem weighed down, and not just from Paul's bullying. What else is going on?"

Bullying. He saw it and acknowledged it. His clover-green eyes stayed on my face, waiting for an answer. It was too much for me. Truth spilled out, like water overflowing a dam. I couldn't stop until I'd told him everything, even my plan for dealing with Paul.

And our fate was set that day.

Before I think, the words pop out of my mouth. "Excuse me, but do I know you?"

The waitress doesn't have a nametag. Nametags are probably old-school, like Flo from Mel's Diner, or Laverne and Shirley.

She blinks. "No. I don't think I've ever seen you before."

Thomas glares at me over his menu. I know he's starving. "Oh, okay. I'd like the Cheddar Onion Burger. And a side salad with Ranch."

The waitress turns to Thomas, her expression softening. Dude, she is totally scoping out my husband, even though she's probably a good fifteen years older than I am.

The nameless waitress takes Thomas' order, then walks through the swinging kitchen doors, swinging a little herself. Thomas ignores her hips and stares at me.

"What?" I take a sip of water. "I've seen her before, and you want to know where? *In our window.* She's the one who's been spying in our woods!"

Thomas' anger dissipates. "Really? But why?"

"I have no idea."

We drop our voices as the waitress reappears with our breadsticks. I smile. "Thanks—um, what's your name? I didn't catch it."

My impromptu probing technique works.

"Rosemary Hogan." She places a tub of marinara sauce in front of Thomas. "Careful, honey, that's hot." Her eyes rove down his shirt.

I interrupt her gape session. "Could I have some garlic butter?"

She pivots and gives me a longsuffering look. "Sure thing."

As Rosemary walks to another table, Thomas leans forward and takes my hand. "I'll pray," he says. "Dear Father, we thank you for this food and this date. In Jesus' holy name I pray, Amen."

"Short and sweet?"

Thomas stuffs a bite of breadstick in his mouth, red sauce dripping onto his plate. "Hungry."

Let it never be said that cavemen are dead. So much for the high-class, patrician husband I married.

After Rosemary drops off our main dishes, we start throwing ideas around. Maybe it wasn't Rosemary in our woods—after all, it was dark when I saw her. Still, her face looks so familiar.

Miranda's note was from someone who doesn't like Paul. I think back to my conversation with the Good Doctor. My face flushes as I visualize his immaculate appearance and replay his deep voice saying my name. These pregnancy hormones have hijacked my brains. I'm more Neanderthal than Thomas.

"…and so I had to make all those copies. Can you believe it? What's our secretary get paid for, anyway? All she does is make gritty, tar-thick coffee every morning." Somehow Thomas has segued into a gripe session about work.

"Good grief." I try to echo his browbeaten tone.

He chows into his loaded baked potato. "And I swear our old paralegal is either dyslexic or blind. He messed up all the measurements on the deed he handed me."

My eyes flit around the room, but don't land on Rosemary. I want to talk more about the Miranda situation with Thomas, but he's off in lawyer-land.

"They think I'm stupid because I'm in my twenties. Who *cares* that I have a UVA degree? The worst is when Royston butchers the wills I draw up. The man can't even write!"

Thomas pauses as I sip my water. "By the way, I don't think I told you, but you look amazing tonight. Pregnancy gives you quite a glow. And that blouse…so silky." His deep brown eyes are soft and intimate. A little *too* intimate for the restaurant.

"Thanks." I drop my voice to a whisper. "Could you get your hands on Rose's will for me?"

Thomas leans closer, putting his hand on my knee. He's still distracted. "You want a copy of it?"

"No, you loon. Just tell me what it says. You know, any weird contingencies or anything."

"No problem. Consider it done. But tell me again why you're in the middle of this? Why do you care so much about whether Rose committed suicide or got murdered?"

"Because Rose's husband is dating the Grande Dame. And if he was involved in Rose's death...if he was, I'll...have to do something."

Recognition dawns on Thomas' face. "You are *not* going to do anything if you uncover something significant. You are going to call the police."

"I'll definitely call the police." I don't quantify at what *point* this will happen in my investigation.

We finish our food quickly, then decide to go home for more coffee and chitchat. Thomas will never admit it, but he tends to leave hearty tips for waitresses who flirt with him. Rosemary picks up the receipt and smiles.

Save that smile, chickie. I'm going to find out if you were in my woods.

We return to our cars. On the way home, I kick myself for not encouraging Thomas about his job. Still, we both know it's just a jumping-off point. He merely has to stay the course without blowing his top, then he can have enough clients to start his own firm.

The drop-off turn into the driveway seems even more harrowing in the dark, as Thomas' Volvo plunges over the edge before I turn in with the SUV. I hold my breath, imagining the side of the mountain sliding off into oblivion in our absence. Halfway down the hill, blue and red lights swirl into vision. *Police?* At Nikki Jo and Roger's?

Petey runs up to Thomas' car, holding one of those lime-green Halloween glow sticks. Thomas parks and jumps out, and I pull in behind him. I step gingerly onto the paved drive, so I don't squash Thor if he's on the loose.

Thomas grabs Petey by the shoulders—a rough gesture, but a protective one. "What's going on?"

Petey bounces around like a plane caught in turbulence. "Guess what? You'll never guess. One of my traps worked!"

12

The first thing Pastor Cliff advised me to do was to keep a diary. He said I needed an outlet for my thoughts. I rummaged around until I found one of my father's yellow writing pads, only partly used. I started writing on December first.

Paul had been acting strangely for a couple of weeks. He was coming home early from work, asking questions about my days, as if I had something to do or somewhere to go. I didn't even have a car.

He made cryptic remarks that insinuated I was having an affair. But my lover and I hadn't talked for a month, after I'd told him what I planned to do.

Finally, it dawned on me. Paul had figured out the Pastor was coming over. I'd been careful to wash our mugs and plates after each visit. I'd even gone out with a snow shovel and smoothed out the tracks Cliff's truck left on our driveway.

Or maybe Paul had noticed something else...something more personal. He never slept in my room, though.

I told Pastor Cliff, but he wasn't concerned. "God will look after His own," he told me.

Cliff might've been a man of God, but it turns out he was wrong.

"Traps? What traps?" Thomas turns from Petey to me.

"I forgot to mention that Petey set up some booby traps in our woods. Just in case the stalker came back. I'm scared to ask, Petey—what did you catch?"

"Come see!" He runs toward the house. Dad's locked and loaded with some kind of assault rifle slung over his back. Thomas goes to talk with him and a thin police officer. Nikki Jo sweeps her arm my direction, as if magically transporting me to her side faster.

She puts a shaky, French-manicured hand on my wrist. "Oh, honey. You just wouldn't believe it. If it wasn't for Petey, who knows what could've happened."

"Mom, what's going on? What did Petey catch?"

She takes my arm and pulls me toward our cottage. "You'll have to see it to believe it."

Near the sparse trees in front of our house, three police officers stand in a group. They're looking into some kind of pit. Apparently, digging pits is trapper Petey's modus operandi.

A bald guy in a tan shirt gets out of a truck with a metal cage in the back of it—animal control? The cops clear a path, and he steps to the edge of the hole. Nikki Jo points at him and covers her mouth with her hand. Everyone watches as he puts a black tube to his mouth, puffs his cheeks out, and blows.

Something zips out of the tube. No way. That was some kind of—

"Blowdart." Thomas comes up behind me and rubs my back, as if he's seen this a thousand times before.

I yank forward, trying to control my voice as I wheel on him. "Thomas. No one has *told* me what's going *on* in my *yard*." Nikki Jo, Petey, and Thomas gape, unused to my wounded tone.

Petey's face reddens. "Sorry, Tess. It's a bear in the trap. Like, a fully-grown, mamma bear."

"What?" Bears have been lumbering around that close to my porch? The place I go to sit and relax? I'm pregnant, for the love of everything...

Nikki Jo puts her arm around me, dark eyes suddenly lit with understanding. "Let's go back to the big house. I'll fix you one of those fancy expressos you like, with vanilla syrup and cream." Even though I know it's "espresso," it sounds best when Nikki Jo says it her way.

Thomas and Petey jog over to the floodlit trap. A patch of black fur moves. Something in my gut tells me not to look. It's not mere pregnancy queasiness—it's some kind of deep need to protect this baby from lumbering killers in the woods.

"Okay, Mom, maybe I'll sit with you a little while."

For the next hour or so, I snuggle under a quilt on the old velour couch in Nikki Jo's den. Roger stores his gun, then joins us to watch cooking shows and drink strong coffee. By the time Thomas returns for me, I've repressed my shock enough to walk back to the cottage with him.

Petey apologizes profusely for setting an effective bear-trap.

I try to reassure him, although he's going to have to do something about those traps. Who knows what other animals are lurking around here?

All the way down the gravel path, I avoid looking at the now-vacated hole. Once we're inside, I turn on every single light and pour a hot bath. For some reason, it irks me that Thomas doesn't pour the bath for me. Sometimes I notice weird things like that—things my Prince Charming would have thought of without being asked.

I'm just sinking into the water when Thomas knocks on the door. "Tess? Miranda's on your cell phone."

Seriously? He picked up my cell?

"One minute." My pineapple-colored towel fails to cheer me like it usually does. That shot of yellow does wonders in our windowless bathroom.

My soppy footprints mush into the rug as I wrap the towel around me and open the door. I ignore Thomas' suggestive looks as he hands me the phone.

"Miranda?"

"Hello there. Sorry to call so late, but something told me you'd be awake."

How right she is. "No problem—what is it? Are we still on for tomorrow?"

Miranda clears her throat. "Well, I was calling about that. Paul invited us over to his house. Would you be willing to come along? I know you weren't too thrilled with him last time."

Did I hide my feelings so poorly? "Okay, but are *you* okay with that? I know you didn't want to see Rose's house again…"

"I've been thinking on that. Rose is long gone, and it's Paul's house now. I should be able to handle it."

"Then of course I'll go with you. What are the directions?"

"Just come to The Haven at one—he'll meet us here."

"It's a plan." I just wish it were my plan, not Paul's.

When I hang up, ready to scurry back into my warm bath, Thomas stops me at the door. He's wearing his favorite four-leaf clover boxers and smiling like a deranged leprechaun.

"My dear girl. Have I mentioned how lovely you looked tonight?"

Wow. Such a deeply-pondered compliment. I push him aside. "I'm freezing. I need to get warmed up."

His dark eyes get serious. "Look, I came close to doing something stupid tonight to that florist. It could've messed up my career. So I appreciate your stepping in, even though I hated it at the time."

Appreciation. An effective tactic. I ruffle his hair. "Do continue."

He traces my cheek. "You honestly have no idea how drop-dead gorgeous you are, do you? Your soft skin, the way you arch your eyebrow when you're serious, and your perfect cupid's bow...Axel's not the only guy who'd probably knock my lights out to get to you for one second."

The whole day flashes past, from Axel's greeting, to Rosemary's swinging hips, to the blow-darted bear. Suddenly, I'm just glad to be standing next to my good-smelling, smooth-talking husband.

I wrap my arms around his shoulders. "Date night isn't over yet."

13

The more Pastor Cliff wanted to talk things out, the more I clammed up. After telling him all my dark secrets, I had nothing left to give. Emptiness filled me, substantial and relentless, like a sandstone rockslide.

Cliff knew the Bible like it was his best friend. He had a verse for every issue I mentioned. One of the hardest things was when he told me I couldn't forsake assembling with other Christians. I tried to explain the impossibility of it all.

"There's no way on earth Paul will let me go to church. You're the only Christian fellowship I can have now—you have to accept that."

Cliff frowned. "You can't grow if you're not challenged, Rose. The whole church body has to work together. I can't fill that huge void in your life. You need to stand up to him in this area."

"But what if he beats me for it? So far it's only been a punch or smack here and there. Who's going to stop him if he

gets really angry? And don't tell me 'God,' Cliff. God didn't stop those first hits."

The way Cliff looked at me, with no hatred or vengeance in those green eyes, you'd think he was some kind of peace-loving monk. But his answer flew in the face of this misperception.

"Who will stop him? You will, Rose. You're far from cowardly."

He sat in my favorite chair, a golden brocade-covered wingback. I swear the light from heaven lit his red hair aflame. In reality, the sun was just bearing down through my living room window.

It was a revelation. I wasn't helpless—even before I put my plan into effect. I could try to make my life work.

I jumped up and hugged Cliff, and his eyes met mine. Recognition shot through both of us, and I dropped my arms.

Another complication.

We linger over bagels and cream cheese before Thomas leaves for work. He's more alert this morning, and winks at me no less than five times. Once I kiss him goodbye, I jump on the stationary bike, determined to burn off my excess energy. I need to get rid of any hostility, so I can be kind, no matter how obnoxious Paul acts.

A cramp hits my stomach mid-stride. Maybe Nikki Jo was right when she told me to take it easy on the exercise while I'm pregnant. Even with last night's protective feelings toward the baby, it's so hard to believe I'm going to be a mother.

Before walking out the door, I put on a hearty coating of my favorite crimson lipstick. It somehow makes me feel more powerful. Mr. Paul Campbell might look skinny and harmless, but I don't trust him or his motivations with Miranda.

My knife clips easily onto my chinos' slant pocket. As I settle into the SUV driver's seat, the empty bear-pit draws my attention. No flip-out knife would've protected me from *that*. What if I'd been alone on the porch when that bear wandered up?

I shove it out of my mind. *What ifs* drive people mad. I've worked my way through lots of them, like *What if I'd been a boy? Would Dad have stuck around? What if I'd gone to a local college? Would Mom have stayed away from the pills?*

The important *what ifs* are the ones I can do something about. Like *what if* Paul's a murderer? *What if* Rosemary's lying?

By the time I pull into The Haven, I'm mentally pumped up. Miranda rolls her wheelchair off the front porch ramp, down the sidewalk to meet me. She's beaming.

"We have so much catching up to do, girlie! Paul will be here soon."

The wind picks up, rattling the dead leaves. I wheel Miranda back up to the sheltered porch, where she tucks a small fleece blanket over her thin legs. Doc Cole strides out the front door, obviously in a hurry.

He turns to us. "Tess! Good to see you. Miranda, I'll be checking in same time next week. Keep the excitement minimal."

As he runs to his car, I note his straight-leg dress pants. I want to get some of those for Thomas. I turn to Miranda, who's also focused on the Good Doctor, an inscrutable look on her face.

"And what's Doc Cole talking about? Excitement? Did you get another note?"

"Nothing like that, sweetie. That's what I wanted to tell you. Paul proposed to me yesterday. I...just wanted to share it with you in person."

I swallow several times, vainly trying to wet my dry throat. "And you accepted?"

"Why shouldn't I?" Miranda smiles, highlighting her still-striking bone structure and shining eyes.

What would Russell want me to do? What would her first and beloved husband think of this engagement? Should I say something? Or feign excitement, despite my numerous misgivings?

"Wow!" It's all I can manage.

Miranda watches the parking lot, no doubt waiting for her fiancé. The charming knight, ready to sweep the handicapped elderly woman off her feet...

"I need to ask a couple of questions," I say.

Miranda squeezes my hand. "Go right ahead."

There's no polite way to phrase it. "I know this may seem nosy, but it's important. How much money did Rose leave you?"

"Let me study on it a minute." Miranda looks to the gray sky, ticking off numbers on her fingers. "Hm. All in all, I'd say it's about five hundred. Yes, about five hundred thousand."

Enough to change someone's life. "You said it *is* that much? Have you spent any of it?"

This is why I love Miranda—she doesn't say, "Well, aren't

you curious?" She trusts I'm going somewhere important with this.

"I used some of it for Rose's funeral—Paul couldn't cover it. But other than that, no. I didn't need it. My Russell worked hard all his life, and he made sure I was well taken care of."

I play a hunch. "Doc Cole's an interesting guy. He's not married, is he?"

Miranda shakes her head. "No. But he's made a good living. He did move to Arizona for a while, after Rose—" She shoots me a guilty look and stops.

"Those two were involved, weren't they? I was pretty sure of that," I say. "You can tell just talking to him. Did Paul know?"

"No. And Rose didn't talk about it. But watching Bartholomew at the dinner table—that man was smitten. Hush up!" She puts a hand on my arm as Paul parks his car—an old two-tone Ford Aerostar van. I had no idea those were still on the road.

Something Miranda said simmers in the back of my mind, but I have to focus on the task at hand—getting through the day with a smile on my face. A smile for my best friend's fiancé.

Paul's tightly-belted jeans slide up his thin torso, showing off his white sport socks. He offers me his hand, but doesn't quite look me in the eye. "Howdy, Miss Tess, guess you've heard our news?"

"Yes indeed." Since I can't think of anything nice to add, I wheel Miranda down the sidewalk.

"Oh, no—allow me." In a forced show of chivalry, Paul takes the handles and steers her toward his hot ride.

I firmly remind myself that appearances mean nothing. The

man is poor—he can't help that. His wife left him with nothing but his house, which is probably in horrible shape if he has no income for upkeep. Didn't Paul get some kind of retirement package? Does he work at all now? Has Miranda asked herself any of these questions? What kind of life is she stepping—

"Tess? Could you help me?" Miranda rescues me from my black thoughts, holding my arm and trying to stand on her wobbly legs.

I grab her around the waist. "Of course." Paul's left us to our own devices on the passenger side. Maybe he thinks it's too personal to hoist Miranda's frail body into the van. The passenger seat looks about five feet high as I try to manipulate the Grande Dame into it while keeping her dignity intact.

Paul keeps his eyes averted as Miranda straightens her pants before hooking her seatbelt. Maybe he's not so bad. Maybe Rose really did commit suicide and it had nothing to do with him.

It seems more likely her suicide was connected with the Doctor, since they were having an affair. My niggling thought surges to the forefront. Miranda said Doc Cole went to Arizona after Rose's death.

Miranda's warning note came from *Arizona*. It would've been easy enough for him to have a friend mail it.

Maybe the Good Doctor hated Paul. At the library, Doc Cole came to me with questions about Paul...or was he planting suspicions?

"And so I thought, what better time to be married than New Year's Day?" Miranda turns sideways to observe me, her body barely larger than a skinny eleven-year old's. If this van had airbags, Miranda's probably wouldn't activate.

New Year's Day. I have only three months to figure out if the warning note was a threat to Miranda or Paul. One of my favorite verses from youth group springs to mind—something about being wise as a serpent and innocent as a dove. I observe my beautiful, handicapped friend, smiling to herself in the front seat.

If anyone lays a hand on Miranda Michaels, this viper is going to strike.

14

I mixed the ground cloves and cinnamon into Paul's favorite gingerbread. He loved spicy foods. But I was making this gingerbread for Cliff.

As I pressed the batter into the pan, I visualized him. The red stubble over his lip. The way his eyes crinkled when he laughed. His rough-hewn muscles, so different from Paul's thin, wiry build.

But it was the light that drew me to him. He was lit from within. Every word he said meant something. I'd never talked with Paul like that. Or even with Bartholomew.

Bartholomew had loved me when I seemed weak and unprotected. When I'd stood up to him, he'd decided to end things. I didn't blame him. I was a loose cannon rolling all over his perfectly ordered ship, ready to blast off at any time.

I clung to Pastor Cliff's words. He planned to come today, after lunch. Nervousness threatened to undo my happiness. What if Paul came home early from work? To be safe, I hid all *his guns—all the ones I could find.*

As soon as I heard the familiar cherry-bomb muffler on Cliff's truck, I relaxed. He brought some kind of peace with him. I wanted more of it.

Snow still lay on parts of the grass, but most of it had melted into our dirt driveway, churning it up like a muddy pigsty. I knew I'd have to go out and flatten the mud with a shovel, once Cliff left.

I should've canceled our meeting. I knew it would be cutting it close. But I was selfish.

Cliff never touched a bite of that gingerbread.

Paul's dirt driveway winds halfway up the side of a mountain, miles from anyone else. I wonder how he gets out in the winter. He seems to sense my question.

"Had to get myself a tractor, years ago. State don't plow these back roads. Got a generator, too, in case I have to hole up for awhile. It's come in handy a few times, let me tell you. Especially in that windstorm last year."

None of us will soon forget the derecho of 2012—that wall of wind that took down trees like toothpicks and barely left a yard unscathed. In those hundred-degree temperatures, our power had been out for five days. After that, Roger went out and bought four generators, just in case.

Sunlight barely filters through the thick pines, but then a low green hill bursts into view. The craftsman house sitting atop it seems to fit perfectly. Somehow it resembles the magic gingerbread house in fairy tales: its windows, stonework, and dark siding meeting at various unexpected angles.

Miranda takes a deep breath, like she's preparing to dive underwater. In a way, she is. The last time she saw her friend alive was probably in this house.

Paul reaches over and holds her hand. Maybe that's what she gets from him—a physical connection. Ever since I've known the Grande Dame, she's always been a hugger. She must feel stranded without a husband and no family nearby.

Paul pulls into the circular drive, right next to the front porch. I immediately notice the six steps leading up to the front door. Miranda's supposed to live here?

Again, Paul senses my thoughts, which totally freaks me out. "I'm building a ramp on the side of the porch. That way it'll be easier for Miranda. I plan to find a van that's easier for wheelchairs, too."

He smiles. Something deep inside me recoils. He's hiding the truth; I know it. But what *is* the truth here? We both know the only way Paul can afford a new van is with Miranda's money. And a great deal of Miranda's money is Rose's. I imagine a dog licking its chops, hungry for the food in hand. The Grande Dame needs to grip it tighter, not drop it to the ground for Paul.

My lips crack as I return a tight smile. It's time for a little on-the-spot research. This used to be Rose's house, after all. I'm sure Paul didn't get rid of all her stuff.

Paul picks Miranda up and shuffles toward the stairs. Instead of bringing the wheelchair along, I stand at the base of the steps, arms outstretched, in case the thin man drops her. Once he safely reaches the porch landing, I grab the heavy wheelchair and haul it up the stairs in about three seconds. Paul shoots me an inscrutable grin.

While Paul settles Miranda in her chair, I wander to the side of the half-wraparound porch. The back yard stretches below us with so many flowerbeds, I can't count them. The yellowed summer stalks lie on the ground, blurring the sharp brick boundaries of the beds. Rows of unkempt boxwoods flank an arching white wicker arbor. Lush grass is visible just beyond it, hinting at even more cultivated space.

"Never have been able to keep up with the flowers. Rosey had a knack with them. Especially the rosebushes." Paul's standing right behind me.

I glance behind him for Miranda, but she's not on the porch. Must've gone inside.

"I heard she loved to garden." My neck hair prickles as I force myself to focus on the flowerbeds again. I'm casual. I'm not worried about who's standing behind me.

"I'm going to fix us some coffee." Paul turns back toward the house. "Feel free to walk around."

Too happy to oblige, I power-walk down the steps, into the back yard. Though Paul's not in sight, I still feel watched. There's a presence here—it has to be Rose. I don't give much credence to ghosts communicating with the living. But I can't help wonder, what would she try to tell me?

I wish Nikki Jo were here, so she could point to each dead plant and tell me what it was. One thing I do know—there aren't any roses here. But Paul had mentioned rose bushes. As I pass under the looming arbor, a hidden garden takes my breath away.

Unpruned rose bushes twine into each other, forming a

thorny labyrinth. From the faded blooms on the branches, I can tell Rose had every color of the rainbow—butter yellows, raspberry pinks, icy whites—everything.

Any income she had must have gone into these bushes. And probably intense physical effort. When I examine the base of the bushes, thin black pipes of a watering system protrude slightly under the disintegrated mulch chips.

Tucked under a red rosebush, a small pile of quartz chunks catches my eye. Maybe a burial spot for a favorite animal? But what an odd place for it. I turn one over, surprised to see words written in faded permanent marker.

It says "*Mene.*" Strange name for a pet.

I turn over another. "*Mene,*" again. Another language? Thomas said Rose's dad was French. I shift the pile of rocks around, poking my finger in the soft dirt beneath. A glint of metal, maybe a pop can tab, loops into the ground.

Paul calls from the front porch. "Coffee! And cake!"

I grab a nearby stick, determined to dislodge the tab. With a plink, a dirt-encrusted white gold ring lands near my foot. When I wipe it off, a little rose etched inside shouts to me like a voice from the grave.

Rose buried her wedding ring.

The weather shifts, wind ripping at the legs of my chinos and rearranging my bangs, like it's got a personal vendetta. Blue-gray clouds hang low in a hazy white sky. For late fall, the day's oddly warm. A weather front moving in...a change we weren't prepared for...

I shove the ring in my pocket, figuring Paul doesn't need to see it yet. I've seen those words on the rocks before, in church. Once I get home, maybe I'll pull out my Bible or ask Nikki Jo about them.

Now it's time to go into the gingerbread house. Such a cheery house on the outside. Why do I suspect that evil will emanate from within?

15

We talked about heavy things that day, like how my mother pushed me to marry Paul. Over and over, she'd repeated the chorus "He's such a nice young man." To the day she died, she'd covered for Paul's overbearing ways, telling everyone I was some kind of shy recluse. She seemed to think that Paul's hovering, oppressive demeanor trumped my father's absentee lifestyle.

Cliff asked about Bartholomew. I couldn't explain how much, yet how little he meant to me. Yes, I missed his protection, his willingness to defend me at our dinner parties. I missed the feel of his long, tan fingers as they traced the hollow under my neck. I couldn't walk under my arbor without imagining his spicy scent, lingering in the air.

But he'd refused to support me when it counted. So I'd convinced myself he didn't really love me, not the way I needed to be loved.

I wondered how Cliff would counsel me—to forget about

Bartholomew and focus on my husband? The husband who wouldn't share my bed? The husband who snarled like a wolf when he didn't get his way?

Or did Cliff care too much about me? Did he want me for himself?

I never found out. Paul came home early.

Paul's hands tremble as he pours the coffee into navy WVU mugs. They're so chipped, it's entirely possible he bought them the year the University was founded. As he sets them on the kitchen table, he gives us an apologetic glance.

"I wasn't able to keep Rose's china, so these will have to do."

Miranda smiles. "Oh, I'd forgotten! She had the *Old Country Roses* pattern. I remember using it all the times we got together. She didn't worry about chipping her dishes. 'Might as well use our pretty things while we can,' she'd say. I'd always tell her she was too bleak...I guess she was right after all." Miranda ducks her head for a sip of coffee. She'd prefer tea, but Paul doesn't know that.

The store-bought carrot cake crumbles in my mouth, like it was made a week ago. I start planning my escape after one drink of the watery coffee.

At least Paul didn't get rid of the furniture. The house is chock-full of ornate mahogany pieces that would probably be worth a small fortune. Why would he hold onto them? Or to this big house? Has he been gunning for Miranda all along, hoping to have something to offer her?

A crumb lodges in my throat, starting up a fully-fledged coughing spasm.

"Tess honey, you okay?" Miranda reaches for me across the table.

I point to the nearby bathroom and rush out, hacking as I go. The crumb's long gone, but I'm buying some time. When I came in, I noticed the bathroom had a back door. Maybe it opens into the master bedroom? If not, I can always sneak out and upstairs for a little spying.

Sequestered in the bathroom, I check the old aqua medicine cabinet. My controlled substance pill-spotting abilities are keen, since Mom was addicted to painkillers. There's nothing in the cabinet besides regular old-person medications: eyedrops, laxatives, vitamins, and heart pills. But the heart pills are Rose's prescription. I pull out the bottle—sure enough, it's Digoxin, exactly what Doc Cole said she overdosed on. Surely Paul didn't keep the bottle? How twisted would that be?

I test the loose knob on the back bathroom door. It opens into a dark-paneled room. Once my eyes adjust, I can make out bookshelves lining the walls. A library. The thick dust nearly chokes me, bringing on a sneeze I barely manage to stifle.

Obviously, Paul hasn't been in here much, if at all, in the forty years since Rose died. *If I were Rose, where would I hide something?* She was a recluse who loved flowers and gardening. If only she'd had a potting shed—you always find evidence in potting sheds in Agatha Christie books.

The library would be the next obvious place. If she hid something in the kitchen or bedroom, Paul would likely go through it when she died. And, assuming she committed suicide, she knew she was going to die. Maybe she needed to hide something personal.

I look at the worn bindings, wiping some with my finger to read the titles. Encyclopedias; classics; cookbooks. I drag the step-stool over to reach the top shelf, admiring the hand-carved built-ins. If someone polished up the wood, these burled-wood shelves would be amazing.

One large book spine sticks out from the rest. *The Language of Flowers.* I tug at a couple books near it: *Care and Maintenance of Roses. Rose Pests.*

I don't know why I'm so certain Rose hid something, but I feel connected to her somehow. The more superstitious part of me says it's her ring in my pocket. Yet if I'm honest, all I know about her is that she was friends with Miranda, she was married to a guy I can't stand, and she had an affair with a handsome doctor.

The Language of Flowers seems the best place to start. I pull it all the way out, flipping through the pages. Several corners are turned down, but I need to hurry, so I set it down and go back to rummaging.

One small red book catches my eye, so I take it down. There's a skull and crossbones on the cover, entwined with flower vines. The cursive title reads: *Deadly Blooms: Flowers that Kill.*

My stomach clenches. Or is it the baby? I have no idea what the baby's kicks and movements are supposed to feel like at this stage.

I take the books and sneak back into the bathroom, coughing a little for effect. Where on earth can I hide them? They won't fit under my shirt and I didn't bring a jacket. The cabinet under the sink looks hopeful. Sure enough, it's full of towels. I arrange the books between two ratty, avocado-green wonders. Miranda's used to fresh, super fluffed towels, and this is what Paul has to offer? This impending marriage is heading for an epic fail.

The kitchen's been evacuated by the time I get back. Miranda's laughter carries in from the living room, so I follow it. She's sitting by the stonework fireplace, holding a glass framed picture.

The sunlight picks out the whites in her salt-and-pepper hair. "Good gracious, dear, I wondered what happened to you! I almost asked Paul to go knock on the door, but we both agreed that wasn't good manners."

"So sorry! Just took a lot of coughing to clear my throat for some reason. What's that picture you have?"

"Oh honey, it's an old one of Rose and me, at a dinner party a long time ago. Look at how we were standing—didn't we just think we were the *stuff*?"

My eyes range over the young Miranda first. Hands on her hips, chin set, snazzy tweed pants and vest, she looked like a Hollywood glamour girl.

But once I see Rose, I nearly drop the heavy Waterford frame. Full lips, full hips, and huge wide-set eyes. Creamy skin with peachy undertones. Long strawberry-blonde hair. I've seen this woman before.

It's the waitress, Rosemary.

16

The minute I heard Paul's car coming up the driveway, I told Cliff to hide. Of course, it was foolish. His orange truck sat square in the middle of the drive. Even traveling salesmen never came up that far.

"Tell him it was an emergency of some kind," I begged Cliff. But what? My parents were dead. "A miscarriage. Tell him I had a miscarriage."

"Have you even been with him lately?" Once again, Cliff knew me better than I thought. He was right, Paul would never buy that.

"Okay. We'll say...I wanted to get baptized. You had to nail down the date and talk through my decision. Surely he can't oppose a baptism?"

"A baptism it is. Someday, you're going to have to stand up to him, though. And I'll be there to back you up. I'm sure Bartholomew will help, too."

The front door opened and slammed into the wall. Things

moved in slow motion as Paul strode over to the couch where I sat.

"And what have we here?" He didn't even look at Cliff as his eyes fixed on mine. A flush started at my chest, but I tried to repress it. I had to believe my lie.

"Paul, this is Pastor Cliff, from church. I've been thinking about things, and I decided I need to get baptized. He came over to talk about it and get the details ironed out."

Paul rotated his head slowly to Cliff, who looked relaxed in the golden chair. My husband extended his hand. "Well, right nice to have you, Pastor."

A fake smile spread across Paul's face. Hypocrite. Maybe my mother fell for that smile, but Cliff wouldn't.

The pastor stood a good five inches taller than Paul. "Appreciate this chance to talk about spiritual things with your wife, Paul. We'd love to have her in church every Sunday." Cliff's words meant nothing to me—it was his tone that spoke volumes. It was the tone a leader uses, or a king. Someone who would be obeyed. I wanted to follow that leader to his truck and ride away from my house and my empty marriage forever.

Paul's smile froze, exposing only his upper teeth. I hated those teeth. I wanted to smash them with a baseball bat. I wanted to—

"I'll think on that, Pastor. In the meantime, if you don't mind, I'd like to get my supper."

It was only four o'clock in the afternoon, and Paul knew full well I didn't have supper ready at this hour. He was going to throttle me. With my eyes, I begged Cliff not to leave me alone.

But even though Cliff could practically read my mind, he didn't stay. He didn't ask me to join him. He simply said,

"Alrighty then. See you at church sometime, Rose."

I couldn't tear my eyes from Cliff's red hair and plaid shirt as he walked out the door. He was leaving me alone with my husband.

His loud muffler roared to life, and I listened as it faded into the distance. Paul would definitely wait until the Pastor was gone to start hitting me. I turned to see where he was standing, so I could get a head start. I would run up the long drive, deep into the woods, anywhere to get away this time.

But Paul was gone. Maybe he was looking for his guns? Or a knife in the kitchen. I stood, frozen like a stalked deer. Cowardice flowed through me, and I loathed myself.

The sound of car tires sliding in the muddy drive brought me to life. Paul was leaving. Why? In jerks and starts, Paul's car headed all the way out the driveway, then vanished from view.

I put on my warmest coat and gloves and hid in the woods for two hours, watching the house. The car didn't return. Finally, cold and mentally drained, I trudged back. Paul's pistol was waiting where I'd hid it, so I loaded it and stashed it under my pillow. I didn't expect him to come to my room, but if he did, I was ready.

After a sleepless night, I went downstairs at sunrise to pack Paul's lunch. He was sitting at the table, sipping coffee. He looked up from his paper with a smile.

A creeping premonition came over me—something that tasted like bile in my mouth. He was never happy, unless he knew I was unhappy. So he must know something...where did he go in that car? As I puttered around the kitchen, I couldn't bring myself to ask.

After he left, I sat by the phone and waited. I called the church, but no one answered. Finally, at three o'clock, the phone rang, yanking me from my unwelcome nap.

"Rose?" I recognized Cliff's mother's voice, with its hint of brogue.

"Yes, it's me."

Her voice cracked. "There's been an accident. I wouldn't have called you, but I saw on Cliff's calendar he was supposed to meet with you today."

"Oh, it's okay—I understand he has to help out. Who had the accident?"

"Dearie...Cliff had the accident; that's what I'm calling about. His truck went over the ravine—out your road, actually. They just found him this afternoon, when a driver saw the tire marks—"

I dropped the phone and ran to the bathroom. Dry heaves wracked my body. I couldn't think what to do. I poured a deep bath and climbed in. Drowning had never occurred to me as an option, but it seemed an attractive way to go.

Underwater, I instinctively held my breath and watched strands of long blonde hair float and tangle over my face. But it only took a couple of moments for my mind to clear. I jerked my head up and took a gasping breath.

Paul had killed Pastor Cliff—I had no doubt he'd run him off the slick road. I imagined he'd probably made sure Cliff was dead somehow...maybe he bashed him in the head with a rock. Maybe he held his jacket over his head when Cliff was too weak or injured to struggle. How could anyone know what happened in a car wreck?

Well, I knew. And I knew something else. Paul would pay

with his life.

I hand Miranda the picture, then decide to play the pregnancy card.

"Paul, it's been so lovely. I'm just feeling a little chilled and sick. Probably pregnancy stuff, but would you mind taking me back to The Haven? And do you have some kind of jacket I could borrow?"

Paul scurries off to find a jacket, while Miranda fixes me with one of her intense stares. She knows I'm up to something. Thankfully, she says nothing and rolls her wheelchair toward the front door.

Once Paul hands me the old jean jacket, I grab my stomach and rush into the bathroom. I stick my finger in my throat to generate several convincing gagging noises, then flush the toilet repeatedly. The jacket buttons up a little loosely, but I stick the two books underneath, holding them to me while gripping my stomach. Pretty stinking resourceful, Tess Spencer.

Miranda's already in the van by the time I get back. The thought of Paul lifting her down the steps and into the van makes me angrier than the thought of him leaving the job for me.

A few coughing and sighing spells later, and we're at The Haven. I thank Paul again and help Miranda into her chair, wheeling her toward the porch before Paul can walk around to say goodbye. I can't handle watching him kiss her.

We zoom past the Rec room, where the residents turn from the TV to watch us. I have a feeling they weren't entranced with *Dora the Explorer*, anyway.

Outside Miranda's room, her neighbor Nettie stands in the middle of the hall, wearing nothing but a snap-up cotton robe. She's clutching a worn baby doll. Nettie will probably be downgraded from this assisted living facility to an actual nursing home soon. I go over and squeeze her hand, though the smell of her unwashed body makes my stomach lurch. She looks at me with agitated, watery blue eyes and says, "Have you seen Laura? Where's Laura?"

I glance at Miranda, who ever-so-slightly shakes her head. Does that mean there isn't a Laura? Or that I'm not supposed to play along and encourage Nettie?

"No, honey, I haven't seen her," I finally say, patting her hand. If I were an old woman, looking for my baby or mother or whoever Nettie's looking for, I'm sure I'd want someone to acknowledge that the person existed.

Nettie nods and shuffles off. Miranda fumbles to turn the lock on her door with the one key on her keychain. "Poor Nettie, her mind was gone a long time ago. It's a wonder they let her stay here this long…why doesn't this thing ever work right? Wait a minute, was it already unlocked?"

I pull Miranda back, then walk in ahead of her to survey the suite. After throwing a quick glance under the couch, I toss the jean jacket and books onto a cushion. Then I check under Miranda's low four-poster bed. Everything looks okay, until I get to the kitchen.

There sits another handwritten note. No envelope. I read it before passing it on to Miranda.

Dear Miranda,
I did warn you to stop seeing Paul Campbell. Now you're even more involved. I'm afraid I'll have to stop this.
Because I am, and always will be, a FRIEND.

This note seems more personal. A *friend*. Miranda's talking to someone in the hallway. I peep out—it's the Good Doctor. He must do rounds here twice a day. I wait until he's gone, then I walk over to the Grande Dame, dreading my mission. She holds a hand up to me.

"Just a second, dear. Thank goodness Doc Cole was around. He just brought me my new heart pills. I've been having the flutters since I saw Rose's house again. Could you get me a little glass of water?"

I nod, stuffing the note in my side pocket as I turn away from her. She shouldn't read it now, in her state. Once I bring her water in a juice glass, she sips at it daintily and swallows her pill. I glance into the hallway, hoping to flag down a caregiver.

I turn back to wheel Miranda to her bed, but she's clutching her chest, gasping for breath. Her lips look stiff.

"HELP!" I scream. Good God in heaven, if you're there, help my best friend *now*!

17

Miranda came to visit me the day after Cliff's death. She didn't know I'd been seeing him, but she knew the accident happened near our house and wanted to talk about it. I did not.

As she ate a piece of the gingerbread I'd never touched—the gingerbread that should've been for Cliff—she rocked Charlotte. The baby had the softest-looking cloud of dark hair I'd ever seen, a regular swirl of loose curls. Miranda offered to let me hold her.

"No, I honestly don't know how," I said.

"Of course you do! What's the worst she can do? Cry? She does that all the time for me, and I'm her mother!"

I let Miranda snuggle the powdery bundle into my cradling arms. Lake-blue eyes looked up and took a moment to focus on my face. Then Charlotte pursed her rosy little lips and blew a bubble at me.

Something inside me stirred, something deep and maternal. Something that whispered my mother had loved me all along—

every time she fixed my hair and got me ready for church. Every time she defended my willfulness to my father. Every time she had to tell me Father wouldn't be home that night.

Gratefulness for Miranda filled me. I knew what I had to do, but I would never forget her calm faith in me.

The ambulance comes so quickly, I suspect it routinely circles The Haven, waiting for emergencies.

I half-sit on the blue couch, unsure of what to do. They wouldn't let me join Miranda in the ambulance, since Paul's the one listed on her paperwork. I pull out my phone and dial Thomas.

"Hey, hotness, looking for a good time?"

I sure hope he's in his own office.

"It's Miranda. I saw her…they took her to the hospital. Something's wrong and I think someone may've poisoned her but the only person who could've done it was the Good Doctor and what if he comes back here?"

"Whoa. Slow down. Miranda's in the hospital? And some doctor is trying to kill people?"

I explain things, slower and in more detail. While I talk, I hear a small clicking in the background. Finally, it dawns on me what it is.

"Thomas, are you typing while I'm telling you all this!?"

"Yes, but I have to—"

I hang up. *No way* is he ignoring me when something this traumatic just happened. My best friend's in the hospital. I can't think what I need to do next.

I pull the wrinkled note out of my pocket. Blast you, whoever you are. Guess what? I'm not even going to share your little warning with Miranda. Because I am going to hunt you down first.

The jean jacket and Rose's flower books lie scattered where I dropped them on the couch. I pick everything up and head for the door. I'll wait for news of Miranda at home, where I can think. And where I don't have to worry about the Good Doctor showing up.

I leave my name and number with the young caregiver at the desk, promising Christmas goodies for all if they call me immediately with any news. The girl, twenty at most, pops her bubble gum and shoves her blue-streaked hair behind her ears. "Well, you could ask that dude right there," she says, pointing behind me.

I sense him before I see him. The spicy scent, the intense gaze…the Good Doctor.

As I turn, I have the impulse to knock him to the floor and punch him in that classically proportioned face. Instead, bluntness overtakes me.

"Miranda's in the hospital. You gave her those pills. I saw you."

The Good Doctor takes a step forward, clasping my shoulders. If his eyes weren't so earnestly confused, I'd probably yell.

"I have no idea what happened. I picked up her Digoxin refill from the medical closet here. The pharmacists send the refills directly to The Haven. Maybe someone tampered with it? Or they refilled it incorrectly? I'll get the bottle and send it for testing. I want to know who did this, too, Tess."

My gut tells me he's not lying. But I'm not ready to let him off the hook that easily. "Too late. They already took the bottle—to the *police*. I told them to."

"Good." He looks genuinely relieved. But maybe he's just thankful I'm not smacking him with a malpractice suit.

I walk out the heavy oak doors without another word. I'm sick of talking with men today. Paul, Thomas, and Doctor Cole. Men get in my way. I'm going home to be alone with Rose's flower books and a cup of hot, strong coffee.

The short drive home turns out to be all the privacy I'm allotted. As I pull down the drive, Nikki Jo bolts out her front door to meet my SUV. I roll down my window, feeling all my weariness weighing on my eyelids.

"Oh, good *lands*, darlin'! I heard about Miranda on the prayer chain! Weren't you with her today? Is she all right?"

"I don't know. I'm waiting to hear. Some sort of heart problem, they thought." I don't want to talk about the Doctor or the pills.

Nikki Jo wrings her hands so hard, one of her manicured tips might pop off. "Now listen, I put a steaming pot of chicken noodle soup on your stove, and a loaf of bread on your counter. You just go home and rest. Let me know when you hear anything about Miranda, okay?"

A blonde angel of mercy, that's what my mother-in-law is. How'd I get so lucky?

I reach out and pat her arm. "I'll call you first thing."

Inside, I slide onto the couch, staring at the gold-flecked ceiling tiles. This has gotten more serious than I thought. Am I making things worse? Asking the wrong people the right questions?

I don't know if I need a long bath or a hot meal. What can I do? I can't help the Grande Dame. So I guess I'll try to help myself.

I pull on my favorite bomber jacket, sliding the Glock into one of the deep patch pockets and my phone in the other. On the porch, the air's pregnant with rain. Thomas says I have extra-sensory rain radar.

My favorite cliffs lie deep in our back woods. I hope Petey didn't booby trap those, too. I can just imagine buckets of tar or water falling on some unwitting bear's head. I'll have to keep my eyes open.

I love the tactile experience of walking in the woods. Its muted browns, grays, and greens comfort me. The moss and leaves give softly under my boots. Large, scattered rocks feel permanent and unshakable. The pull of the mountain is like gravity for my soul.

My cliffs consist of rock overhangs with little hollows underneath. I sit on my favorite: a rectangular rock next to a tree with a long vine trailing from it. I fight the familiar and completely irrational temptation to jump and swing on the vine, Tarzan-style.

I close my eyes, feet dangling over the edge. The pieces still don't fit, and I can't force them to. I don't think the Good Doctor gave Miranda the wrong medicine—but if he didn't, who did?

And the more I know Paul, the more I think he might actually care for Miranda, in his own inept way.

My *Doctor Who* ringtone sounds, and I yank my phone from my non-gun pocket.

"It's me." Thomas sounds stricken. "I *was* listening to you. I just had to finish a document before I could leave early. I'm at the house; where are you?"

He took off work early for me? I mouth *thank you* into the phone. But I won't say it out loud, since I'm still a little ticked.

"In the woods. But if you come out, watch for Petey's traps. Oh, and I've got the Glock with me."

"Good girl. I'm on my way."

Sometimes, Thomas comes through for me. Today is one of those days. I pat my stomach. "You've got quite a daddy, little one."

18

After Cliff died, I stopped talking to Paul. My hatred grew in tandem with my certainty that Paul had run the Pastor off the road.

I broke down and asked Miranda to take me to Cliff's funeral. As I fingered the dark wood of his closed casket, I wished light should shoot from the seams, wrapping me in his warmth again.

On the way home, Miranda asked me point-blank what I'd felt for Cliff. Since nothing mattered anymore, I didn't lie.

"He believed in me. I loved him for it," I said.

Her bluntness shocked me. "I knew you'd been seeing someone, only I didn't think it was the Pastor." She set her jaw, her back rail-straight against the seat. "Does Paul know?"

"Why are you so upset? He's not your husband."

"No, but if he were, I wouldn't be running around on him." She flexed her hands on the wheel.

"Because Paul's so wonderful? Why don't you come and live with him for a while? And I hardly run anywhere, Miranda. You don't know what you're talking about."

"I'm not as blind as you think." Miranda pulled up our driveway too fast, then slammed the brakes. *"You watch yourself."* She turned her unwavering blue gaze on me, judging me.

And with that, I stopped talking to Miranda, too.

The call comes that night, after we're in bed. I'm not sleeping, so I throw my slippers on and rush downstairs to grab the phone.

It's the negligibly Good Doctor. "She's stable."

"Thank you." I squint in the dark room, as if I could see the Doctor better that way.

"Her prescription wasn't filled as per my orders, as I suspected. The dosage was too high. Thankfully, she only took one pill and they got to her in time."

I slide to the floor, letting it sink in. Miranda will live.

The rich voice sounds on the phone, which I still hold loosely at my ear. "Believe it or not, Tess, I care very deeply for Miranda. She's always been a bold woman, and I admire that."

Bold? I don't always see this side of Miranda, but the Doctor's right. Maybe my friend knows more than she's told me. Or maybe she doesn't know *what* she knows.

"Perhaps we should continue this conversation later," he

says. "I'm booked solid this week, but how about next week sometime?"

I close my eyes. I'm in a bad place, hunting around for a killer with no backup. But my best friend is inextricably involved, and she can't afford another accident.

What if the Doctor is lying? What if I'm next on his list? Then again, what if he's the best ally I've got?

We'll meet somewhere public. I wonder if the Doctor has seen Rosemary before?

"How about the Bistro Americain, in Point Pleasant?" I ask.

Once we agree on a time, I hang up and flick on the fluorescent light over the cabinet. I can't sleep. Tomorrow's my first obstetrician appointment. I put my hand on my stomach, wishing I had Superman X-ray vision and could see what's inside. Why can't I get more excited about this baby? What's wrong with me?

Thanksgiving is this week, too. Andrew will be in from college, no doubt towing along his latest girlfriend. We'll have Spencer family-time galore. I wish I could have my family over, but it consists solely of my mom, and she'll be eating her turkey in prison this year.

I open the *Deadly Blooms* book, wondering how Rose got her hands on such a thing. Beautiful, guileless-looking Rose. What would she want with this?

No pages are marked, but there's a coffee stain on the foxglove page and it's pushed down, like it was referred to often. Maybe Rose just grew foxgloves and needed to know how to handle them. I skim down the page. Even the pollen from the plant can cause hives and allergic reactions. But the interesting thing is that foxglove leaves are used for Digoxin.

Rose overdosed on Digoxin. Someone just mis-dosed Miranda on it.

Coincidence? I think not. Digoxin's our poisoner's drug of choice.

By the time I finally close the book, it's almost two in the morning. I'll be lucky if I wake early enough to say goodbye to Thomas. I pull my coral faux pashmina throw over my legs, registering that it's too light for this weather. But I'm too tired to hunt down a different blanket.

Warped dreams hound me. I'm Gretel, going into the witch's cottage. Where's Hansel? I can't avoid the oven without him...

Then I'm with Doctor Who, whisking off in the TARDIS. Stars and black holes zip by...until I realize my phone is ringing next to my head.

I sit up, disoriented by the morning light. The cell rings on the coffee table behind me. I try not to drop it as I pick up.

"Yes?"

"Hey baby girl, you ready to go?" Nikki Jo is chipper as Pollyanna.

Go? Oh, shoot! The appointment! I pull the phone back and look at the time. I have fifteen minutes.

"Running late, Mom. I'll drive up in a minute."

"Okay!"

I throw on some dark straight-leg jeans and a flowing pink paisley top. My brown motorcycle boots and purple hobo bag complete the ensemble. I always admire women who are all put-together, from their earrings down to their shoes. I'm most definitely *not* one of them.

Nikki Jo is, however. When I pick her up at her front porch, she's wearing her cherry-red Chico's sweater, along with her favorite gold necklace and earrings. Her tailored black pants and kitten heels seem to put the "trailer" in my "trailer park." It's a good thing I love her so much or I might have to despise her.

"I heard on the prayer chain that Miranda's being released tomorrow." She settles into her seat. "Now, don't worry if you knew it already. I figured no one knew till late last night."

I'd forgotten to call Nikki Jo back when the Doctor called— too wrapped up in unmasking a murderer, I guess.

"Let me know when you're going over and I'll send something along," she continues.

We sit in congenial anticipation until we reach the doctor's office in Point Pleasant. It's a quaint wood house with tiger-lily orange awnings.

The secretary seems to have missed her calling as a hard-hitting drill sergeant. She gruffly lets me know that if I don't have insurance or Medicaid, I can't have this baby with them. How long will it take to sign up for welfare? Then how long until I can schedule another appointment?

I'm on the verge of shameful tears when Nikki Jo steps up, brandishing her nails in the secretary's face.

"Now, look here. This birth will be paid for, start to finish, by us. *Roger and Nikki Jo Spencer*." She pulls out a gold credit card and slams it on the counter. "You got that? Now, you give Tess her urine cup and get this show on the road. We didn't drive all this way to get harassed. You ought to be ashamed, treating a new mother this way."

My appointment moves very quickly after that.

Once we're settled in the cozy, amber-hued room, the

doctor comes in. She's middle-aged and very apologetic.

"So glad to meet you, Mrs. Spencer. Sorry for the misunderstanding about payments. Now, let's take a listen to this baby, shall we?"

After spreading warm gel around, she slides a monitor over my stomach that looks like the library check-out device. I catch my breath when a whooshing, thumping sound fills the room.

Nikki Jo's eyes well up. The doctor smiles. All my tightly-held control flies to the four winds and I start crying—great, gasping sobs.

This is for real. I'm going to be a mom.

19

The first time my mother's ghost appeared, I was working in my flowerbed.

Gloves and a mask were my typical attire, especially when I worked with poisonous plants like foxglove. I'd heard some stories about people inhaling the pollen and getting sick.

The now-familiar light flickered in our woods. At first, I thought I was seeing things, that my mask was clouding my vision. Then her voice drifted over on the dry winter air.

"Rose?"

Plain as day, just like that. It was my dead mother's voice. I didn't know if I should hide in the house or answer her.

Finally, I pulled down the mask and shouted toward the light.

"What do you want?"

The light moved toward me, but I held my ground. I could see her face, shimmering in the sunrays.

"Justice."

How did she know what Paul had done? Did she finally believe how hateful he'd been to me?

"How, Mother?"

The translucent entity darted toward me, and I fell on the ground. It hovered over my flowers.

It was as if the ghost read my mind. I'd known for so long that foxglove was the key to my freedom. Now I had the supernatural approval I needed.

It was time to act.

Copious amounts of sunlight and unusually warm temperatures short-circuit my hunt for a murderer until Wednesday. Nikki Jo's been gearing up for the Thanksgiving feast for at least a month now, and all her preparations are starting to fall into place. I bring my meager candied walnuts over to add to her storehouse of foods.

Five cheesecakes cool on the granite-topped island in the kitchen. I don't even try to compete. Tomorrow, I'll bring my defrosted éclairs and crème puffs from Sam's Club, and regardless of my lack of effort, everyone will tell me how delicious they are. The Spencers are a grateful lot.

When Miranda called yesterday, I was so overjoyed to hear her familiar voice, I hardly caught a word she said. She agreed to come to Thanksgiving dinner here. With her birdlike eating habits, she'll hardly make a dent in our banquet.

Nikki Jo bangs around upstairs, probably vacuuming and changing sheets. I sneak out of the house so I don't distract her.

Roger's outside with pruning shears, attacking a boxwood. It's questionable if what's left of it will even look vaguely symmetrical. He waves.

"Never pays to be inside during Thanksgiving week." He winks at me.

I laugh. "Tell her to call if she needs me."

"Will do. Only women can get this stuff right. I tried readjusting the centerpiece on the dining room table one year. Never got over that experience."

It strikes me how much Thomas is like his dad. Not only do both have the same strong jaw and lean-muscled build, but they also share a mischievous sense of humor.

As I walk down the path, my hand automatically covers my stomach. Wonder if this is another Spencer boy, to carry on the family name?

Petey skitters out of a mulched flowerbed, practically running into me. He's holding a shovel. Thor yips from the side of the yard.

"Dad said I had to fill in the trap holes. He was pretty ticked about the bear thing. I had to tie up Thor so he wouldn't follow me." He throws a rueful glance over his shoulder.

"I appreciate that, Petey. When's Andrew getting here?"

"Mom said later today. Said he's bringing some big-city girl with him."

"You don't say."

"Course, she's gonna stay with a lady in church, not us. But she'll be here for dinner tonight."

Petey's eyes gleam. Big-city girls are somewhat of an alien species around here.

"See you tomorrow, then. Be careful disarming your traps."

A smile wrinkles his nose. Suddenly it hits me that this intrepid little redhead is as much my brother as he is Thomas'.

The possibility of squeezing in a little research presents a strong temptation. I know I have to be careful after what happened to Miranda. But I had a brainstorm last night. I could ask Axel who sent my yellow begonia.

I've tried calling Fabled Flowers, but a woman always answers. If I just show up, Axel might look it up for me.

It's more than a possibility that the same person who sent me those flowers sent Miranda her notes. I feel like I'm closing in on a stalker…if not a killer from forty years ago. How could I *not* go check into this? I stride in the house, determined to take a trip to town.

As I put on my forest eyeliner and a couple coats of mascara, I'm thankful for my time selling Mary Kay in college. Not only did it bring in a little extra cash, it also taught me how to make the most of my assets. Heart-shaped face, clear blue eyes, dark brows, and wide bowed lips. Thomas says I'm prettiest without makeup, but today I'm not getting ready for Thomas. I need to catch Axel off guard, to make sure he'll talk.

By the time I find my purse and put on my heeled ankle boots, I'm ready for war. Once I'm on the main road, I find the loudest radio station and blast it. College memories tumble through my head the entire trip to Point Pleasant, but I keep shoving them back. No one tries to kill my best friend and gets away with it.

20

Bartholomew came to see me. Having him in my proximity again brought back a flood of memories. But instead of falling for his magnetic charm, I flew off the handle. I screamed at him like a deranged banshee, beating his chest with my fists. He stood still as a statue and took it.

When I stopped, he wrapped his long fingers around one of my still-clenched fists. He moved close to me, his sheer presence overwhelming.

"I can't bear to see you like this. What's happened? Has Paul done something?"

Pastor Cliff's death was too fresh. I could close my eyes and hear him saying he and Bartholomew would get me away from Paul. Should I take this chance, telling Bartholomew everything?

Was it the easy way out? Or the hardest?

His hands, always gentle, stroked the hair from my face. When he leaned in to kiss me, the future swirled before me, bright as sunlight on creek water.

I told him almost everything.

After fortifying myself at Kelly's Coffee with a grande cinnamon-vanilla swirl, I make the quick half-block walk to Fabled Flowers. Knowing better than to get close to the display window, I push the door open, clanking the cowbell.

The intoxicating smell of eucalyptus fills the shop. Exotic ferns form a semicircle around a water feature in the back. Its light, gurgling sounds remind me of the creek. The tension in my shoulders unwittingly slides away.

Oddly enough, some of my favorite flowers are on display in the coolers. Full white hydrangeas riot with double burgundy roses. Crisp off-white calla lilies and orange daisies make an unusual pair.

As I'm trying to figure out how they got hydrangeas this time of year, someone walks up quietly behind me. I turn to see a lovely Asian girl, with striking cheekbones and a quick smile. "What can I help you with today?"

Axel isn't in sight. Should I stall or tell the truth?

"Um…yes. I mean, I think you could help. I'm looking for Axel Becker. Does he work here?"

"Yes ma'am, he owns the shop. He's not here right now—probably walking down by the river. He does that every day."

"Oh, okay." I contemplate. Should I hunt him down? Wouldn't that look desperate? But maybe I am desperate. I give the girl a warm smile. "Thanks so much. I'll find him."

Once I'm outside, I follow a hunch and walk toward the amphitheater. The bright cornflower sky is full of conflicted clouds—white and puffy on top, gray and flat underneath. Cumulus? Cumulo-nimbus? Scientific terminology has always thrilled me.

"Ooch!" My head comes out of the clouds when I step on someone's foot. A very long foot.

"Hallo." Axel gives me an amused smile, flexing his foot. "You are in town today?" His German accent flows without much American restraint today.

"I came to find you. We need to talk." I fall into step beside him, taking two steps to every one of his. "I need to know who sent me the plant."

"Yellow begonia. Ja. I had no name."

"But you might have the order record? Maybe the credit card links to an address."

His pale eyes widen, as if he'd never thought of that option. "I should." The strong jaw flexes, like He-Man bracing to kill a mastodon.

Why on earth does a dude like this own a flower shop? Axel's about as über-masculine as it gets.

We go back into the shop. I stifle a laugh when the secretary gives a short bow to Axel before giving him the phone messages. Like the king of the pride, he dominates the entire shop with his presence.

He leads me into a back room, which doesn't alarm me as much as it possibly should. There's an old wooden file cabinet against the back wall. He rifles through folders until he finds the right one. He hands me the receipt, which says:

For Nov 1ˢᵗ. One potted YELLOW begonia.
To: Tess Spencer, 2 Spencer Hill Road, Buckneck, WV
From: Anonymous (phone ID Sedona, AZ), payment in full
with Visa last numbers 3026

The pink receipt rattles in my hand. Arizona. The Doctor lived in Arizona. Miranda's note was postmarked from Arizona.

"You are having thoughts on this?" He stands near his desk, a respectful distance from me.

"I am." I don't try to explain things to Axel. I'm not even sure how much he'd understand. Though his vocabulary seems limited, he does have intelligent eyes. However, those sharp eyes are currently roving over my body.

"You are with child?" He seems surprised.

"Yes, I'm married—*verheiratet.*" My high school German washes over me when I visualize Frau Hansen writing words on the board.

His features soften as I speak his language. "*Viel Segen.*"

I don't know what that means, but it sounds slightly off-color coming from Axel's mouth.

I pull my purse tight, backing toward the door. "I have to go. Thank you. Many *danke.*"

He quickly walks in front of me, and I picture him blocking the door, leaning in to steal another kiss. Instead, he opens the door and beams at me.

"*Auf wiedersehen*, Tess Spencer!"

As I walk back to my SUV, raindrops lightly patter on my face. I cozy into my car seat, drinking my cold cinnamon coffee and trying to understand.

Why do I trust the Good Doctor, when everything points back to him? Miranda's wrong dosage, her warning letter, and now the anonymous begonia delivery from Arizona. Not to mention his involvement with Rose. Maybe he assumed she'd leave her money to him, and he's bitter that Miranda got it.

There's nothing for it but to ask him point-blank what he's holding back. I pull out an abominably high gas receipt and scrawl my questions for the Doctor.

My stomach rumbles. When was the last time I ate? Those orange-glazed scones in the coffee shop looked so good. I turn the key, ready to go home. When I look up, I can't believe my eyes.

Andrew's restored turquoise Karmann Ghia is unmistakable as it races into the municipal parking lot and jerks to a halt. Thomas' younger brother steps out, producing the usual effect. Women walking by on the street point and wave, convinced Brad Pitt is in town. With his longer hair and trimmed blond beard, he's a dead ringer. Unfortunately, he knows it. He stands and yawns, leaving his girlfriend to open her own door.

Oh, mercy. The poor girl wears a parka and snow boots, all ready for a blizzard in our sixty-degree weather. With her gaunt build, she looks to be about fourteen, but I know she's in college.

Andrew turns and shields his eyes—from what, I have no idea, since the sun's behind those cumulo-nimbus clouds. He waves and rushes to my car, leaving his girlfriend in the dust.

"Tess! I can't believe it! What're you doing in Point Pleasant, woman?"

I suppress a smile. "As you know, I don't live too far away. You on your way home? Don't eat anything—your momma has tons of food waiting."

Andrew smiles exactly the same smile as Thomas. His girlfriend segues over to our car, just taking her time, as if she wasn't left behind by her boyfriend.

Andrew notices her. "Tess, allow me to introduce Kelsey Brighton. Kels, Tess is my brother's wife. She's pregnant."

He peers at my stomach, obviously disappointed there isn't more to see.

"I'm not *that* pregnant yet, you silly. I have to get home because I'm starving. You want me to call your mom?"

"No way. We're going to surprise her. She wasn't expecting us till tonight. It'll be epic."

I shake Kelsey's hand, fully realizing I'll forget her name by the time I get home. Kelsey, Kendra, Kayla, Kendall...trendy names fly right past me. I need book or TV characters to ground them for me.

Thomas calls as I'm speeding over the mountain. After living in Buckneck a couple of years, I feel like I know every curve by heart. Sometimes I think I could drive it at night, with no lights on.

Thomas sounds perky. "Hey babe, what's going on?"

"Just did a little research in Point Pleasant, and guess who I ran into?"

"Tell me it's not that hulking German."

I won't tell him, then. "Your brother Andrew and his new girlfriend, Kendall or something."

"Did she seem any better than the last one?"

"Well, she's...more humble. But she trails around after him like an orphan puppy, just like all the others."

Thomas sighs, then affects an Irish accent. "He's a blemish

on the bonnie Spencer name."

I laugh so hard, the phone slips out of my hand and into the tissue box. I fish around for it, wiping my eyes. Thomas' accents kill me, even if the word "bonnie" is more Scottish than Irish.

As I finally pull the phone to my ear, Thomas shouts at me. "Tess!"

"I'm here!"

"Listen, I gotta run, babe. But I've found some information about Rose's will. It's a bit odd."

What's one more bit of odd information? I'm in deep now. Bring it.

21

Many days, I sat in the living room, waiting until the sun hit the gold chair just right. The dust would light up like so many tiny crystals—even tears—rising to the sky. I imagined Cliff looking down on me, fully approving what I was planning. After all, my mother did.

I hadn't told Bartholomew about the ghost. Having such a logical doctor's mind, he wouldn't understand. At least that's what I told myself.

Paul started avoiding me. Did my anger brand me, like a giant scarlet letter? I feared he saw more than he let on. What would the punishment be, if he knew about Bartholomew?

One night, long after Paul went to sleep, I went outside, drawn to the thin light of the half-moon. I stood barefoot beneath my wisteria arbor. The dark vines twined around the wood like snakes. I raised my hands, summoning a ghostly appearance. I doubted it would work, but I craved that peculiar closeness with my mother.

Out of the corner of my eye, I caught a hollow-looking light. It shot up to me and hovered, as before. I tried to watch it, but it was like a star. The more you stared directly at it, the more it disappeared.

"Mother. I know you loved me. I want to tell you that."

The light flickered.

"I also want—"

"Rose? Who you talking to out there?"

The light died as I turned around. Paul ran up to me, wearing his boxers, V-neck white tee, and dirty black boots. He grabbed me by the shoulders, shaking me.

"You're out here on the frozen ground, standing barefooted? Confound it all, I don't know what's gotten into you lately!"

I smiled. Paul took a step back. I had tapped into a power bigger than myself, something that carried me through, until all the pieces were in place.

Around six, Nikki Jo sends Petey over with two hot homemade meatball subs. She probably made enough for an army, unsure of how much Andrew's girlfriend would scarf down. His last girlfriend ate like a horse and weighed in at a whopping 110 pounds.

Petey gives me the lowdown. "Kelsey has a tattoo on her neck. And a tongue ring. Mom said, 'Hope she'll wear a turtleneck and keep her mouth shut in church on Sunday!'"

I laugh. I'm sure Nikki Jo didn't want that comment spread

around. The Baptist church here tends to look down on jeans, long hair, and body art. Andrew and his girlfriend will probably knock it out of the ballpark in terms of looking like total heathen.

Petey looks pensive. "Still, she seems nice. I showed her all my traps—at least, where they used to be. And she plays Xbox."

I frown. "Hey, I play Xbox too, little bro."

"I know you *try* to. But you don't get out there and shoot people! You just—"

I flick my dish towel, shooing him out of the house. "Hey, no hating on my game-playing skills."

Petey and I have been known to while away an entire afternoon on one of his shooter video games. I'll hide somewhere on the game-board, waiting for him to come to me. He'll taunt me to come out in the open. Usually, once the clock ticks down far enough, he gets desperate to rake up some kills and I pick him off with my sniper rifle.

"Stalker!" He grins, walking backward up our pathway.

"Good-night, you foolhardy young 'un! Good things come to those who wait!"

"Or they just get old!" He shouts this parting insult.

God knew what He was doing when He put me in the Spencer family. I turn our creaky doorknob, filled with affectionate warmth for my in-laws. The day I said yes to Thomas was the day God restored my hopes of having a normal family.

In a routine that's getting way too familiar, Thomas doesn't call to let me know when he'll be home. I give in to my cravings for the luscious-smelling sub and dig in. At 9:20, when Thomas finally opens the door, I've also gone through a bag of popcorn and a Fudge Round, and I'm on my third episode of *Star Trek*. Doesn't anyone notice some of those outfits are totally impractical for exploring the universe?

Thomas heads straight for the fridge, rummaging around even though he's still wearing his dress shirt. Not a good sign. I really want to hear about Rose's will.

"Meatball sub's on the stove. There's some pasta salad in the fridge." I turn the volume up on the TV again. It'll take him a while to decompress. If there's one thing I've learned from Nikki Jo, it's the importance of man-cave and chow time before I start peppering Thomas with questions.

But he volunteers information while he's heating his sub. "About Rose's will. You're never going to believe it."

I jump up, dropping some errant popcorn kernels. "Wait, wait!" I run into the kitchen.

He takes the sub out of the microwave, bows his head for a quick prayer, then takes a bite. Being of the gentry class, he fully chews it before speaking. Amazing. I hold my stomach, as if the baby might drop out with any shocking news.

"Okay." He wipes his lips with a paper towel. Really?

"Just talk already."

He winks. "Patience, my dear. Rose did indeed leave everything to Miranda. However, there was a stipulation clause. If Rose had a child, the money would be left untouched until the child's twentieth birthday. Strange, huh?"

"Yeah, especially since Rose didn't have children. Why would she put that in there? Did you ask Royston?"

"No way, Tess. I was totally covert about this research. Under the radar, if you will. Black Ops." He grins conspiratorially and takes another bite.

I smile. Thomas and Petey have both thrown themselves into helping me out with this case. *Case?* What am I, Nancy Drew? Ah, well, it's nice to have some masculine backup. Even Nancy had her Ned.

Thomas spreads his fingers over my stomach. "Any movement yet?"

"I think not. But I do feel like this babe is taking up more space."

We've barely talked about my first doctor's appointment. I feel silly admitting I cried when I heard the heartbeat. Maybe next time I'll drag Thomas along and see how *he* reacts.

Rain starts pattering on our metal roof, putting me in a snuggly mood. I set out my éclairs and crème puffs for tomorrow's grand feast. Then I whip up some decaf in the French press and hang out with my very best friend until midnight, when we finally trudge upstairs for bed.

Ever since I've been pregnant, I've been having the most intense dreams. But my dream tonight takes the cake. Rose stands in her garden, long red-blonde hair blowing in the wind, looking completely ethereal. She's pregnant—hugely pregnant. She bends to touch a flower with purple bells, one I know instinctively to be foxglove. I scream at her, waking myself up.

Thomas snorts, then reaches over and absently puts his hand on my head. I lie awake, eyes wide open in the blackness. I feel like Rose is watching me, moving me to help.

What can I do? I close my eyes and relive the dream. Someone else was there, someone I could barely see, peeking from behind the arbor. The dark hair, the red lipstick...Miranda. Is she holding out on me?

22

I celebrated Thanksgiving alone. Paul had to haul coal down in Mercer County. Miranda had made it clear I wasn't good enough for her. Bartholomew had flown to Arizona to visit his sister.

My turkey sandwich on rye seemed a poor substitute for a feast. Still, I used the time to make notes on the red book I'd kept from the library for about half a year. It probably showed up on Miranda's account as a missing book. To her credit, she'd never mentioned it. Maybe she paid all the fines herself.

I turned to one of my dog-eared pages. Belladonna. Italian for "beautiful lady." Better known around here as "devil's berries." How odd that the most poisonous plants also had some of the strongest benefits. They used it in the 1900s to put women into a "twilight sleep" during childbirth. And yet eating just a few berries could be toxic.

The phone jangled my senses. I felt as if my nerve endings were scraped raw. "Yes?"

"Rose. It's Claire Hogan."

Cliff's mother. Why was she calling me again?

"I...I don't know how to talk about this on the phone. Would you mind if I came to visit sometime? I know you don't get out much, dear. I'll bring those hot cross buns you used to love as a child."

I closed my eyes and almost smelled the yeasty, glazed goodness of Mrs. Hogan's raisin-filled rolls.

"Please do. How about tomorrow?"

Since I stayed up half the night dreaming and worrying, Thomas offers to pick up the Grande Dame for the Thanksgiving meal. I finally acquiesce, determined to take a shower, curl my hair, and put on my favorite clothes. Why shouldn't I enjoy family time with the only family I have?

Once I'm all fancied up, I scrounge around the kitchen for something to put my pastries on. Shoot. The only fancy tray I have is a silver-leaf number that might have been purchased at the Dollar Tree. It's entirely possible that Nikki Jo will re-plate the éclairs and crème puffs if she deems the tray subpar. I should probably take offense at this, but I really don't. Anyone who owns enough china and crystal to fill four china cabinets should get first dibs on her table accessories.

Halfway up the path, dessert tray in hand, I find myself wishing I'd donned a coat. My brick-red turtleneck covers me thoroughly, but it's not thick enough. Thor runs down the path to meet me—all the more reason to keep moving. I don't want this tray to go flying, any more than I want his black hair rubbed all over my pale chinos.

I almost lose my footing on the porch steps when the little dog starts circling my heels. "Get out of the way, you crazy runt!" Holding the tray aloft, I use my elbow to ring the doorbell.

Roger opens it immediately, as if he's been told to keep post by the door. He's wearing a royal blue pullover and a muted-check oxford shirt. There's not a wrinkle in his clothing, unlike mine.

The smell of homemade yeast rolls fills the house, along with the heavier smell of brined turkey.

A huge smile spreads across his face. "Been waiting for you! Thomas said he's on his way with Miranda. I'll take those. Let's head to the kitchen."

Roger's gentlemanly manners have always impressed me. He'd never let a woman who was carrying anything walk by him without asking to carry it for her.

Petey slides halfway down the stair railing, until Roger's death glare stops him short. He hops off and runs the rest of the way down. Unlike his father, his plaid shirt is crinkled, like he pulled it off the closet floor.

"Tess! Andrew and Kelsey are playing chess in the living room. I told Andrew you could kick his hiney. I don't think either one of them knows what they're doing. They've been in there for an hour."

I wonder if the door's been shut while they were in there? Suspicious mind, Tess. Knock it off.

"I've got to help your mom with the food first. I'll play him later if you want."

Roger marches us through the dining room. Nikki Jo has set the table with her favorite Spode china. The plates have peacocks in the middle, with swirling blues, oranges, and golds around the rims. Classy but loud. In your face but pretty. Much like my mother-in-law.

Nikki Jo turns as we come in, a hand-mixer dangling over the mashed potatoes. From her taupe-pink lipstick to her kitten heels, she's the picture of the hostess who inspires jealousy in many. But I know this perfect woman. She's willing to dig around in dusty bookshelves for me. She's ready to take on the fiercest OB receptionist to make sure our baby gets proper care.

I walk over and give her a hug, unexpected tears welling in my eyes.

She looks at me closer. "You feeling okay, honey? Everything good with the baby?"

"Everything's just right, Mom. What you need me to do?"

By the time everything's on the table, from the rice pilaf to the green bean casserole, Thomas opens the door and rolls Miranda in. I run over and cling to her neck like she's going to vanish right in front of me.

"Oh my word. I thought…I saw you—"

She puts a finger to my lips. "Hush up. I'm here now, thank the Good Lord above. Now, where's that delicious food I'm smelling?"

After joining hands for prayer, we arrange ourselves at the table, according to the gold-edged place cards Nikki Jo set out. I'm on one side of Mom, with Andrew's girlfriend directly opposite me. Nikki Jo probably wants to keep an eye on her.

Thomas and Andrew, their back-slapping hellos out of the way, sit across from each other, still talking at top volume across the table. It's quite possible they're trying to one-up each other.

Andrew, charming in a navy striped sweater, grins at his big brother. "I'm getting an internship next year with Glaxo. Clinical trials; all that." Andrew's gearing up to be a doctor. We all wonder if he's realized how many years of school that entails.

Thomas, equally charming in his gray turtleneck, fires back. "I just closed a deal for the Kanawha County Public Library."

Ooh, really—Charleston, West Virginia? That's all you got, Thomas? Andrew doesn't have to speak; the thoughts are written all over his face.

I smile at Kelsey, thrilled I've remembered her name. "So, Kelsey, what are you studying in college?"

She looks at me, apparently shocked a married woman is speaking to her. "Art History."

Wonders never cease. One of my favorite electives in college. "So, who's your favorite artist?"

She leans in toward me. "I'm crazy about Klee, but Andrew hates him."

"I'm okay with Klee. I like Redon and El Greco better. But my favorite would have to be Chirico."

"Oh, I know—the shadows! So mysterious. Reminds me of that Hopper—have you seen it? The one of the house by the railroad? You know they based *The Addams Family* house on that one?"

We're still passing foods around the table, but my plate's already overflowing and so is my side dish. I smile at Nikki Jo as I hand her the butter, and she winks.

"Sounds like you gals have lots in common. Glad to see

that. Tess is like the daughter I never had."

No pressure there.

Miranda chimes in from her place next to Thomas. "She's the most determined, protective little lady I've ever met." She elbows Thomas. "You're one lucky fella."

I pick up my fork, playing with my fruit salad. My cheeks flame.

Andrew notices. "Thomas, you don't compliment your woman enough. Here she is, as gorgeous as a Victoria's—um, as a model, and Mom tells me you're working all the time. "

Thomas' smile fades. I turn to Nikki Jo, blocking out my husband's response.

"The turkey's perfect—melts in my mouth! I don't know how you get it that way."

We literally talk turkey for a while. Nikki Jo shares that for some mysterious reason, in 2007, Marie O'Dell drenched the church Thanksgiving turkey in lemon juice. "Honey, ain't no one wants lemonade turkey, I can tell you that."

By the time the conversation moves around to Miranda, I've sampled about ten different dishes. I force myself to stop eating so I'll have room for dessert.

"How you feelin' these days, sweet gal?" Nikki Jo shouts down to Miranda.

Miranda dabs her lips with the linen napkin, losing some of her lipstick. "Pretty much back to normal. Switch-up with the pills, they said. Happens all the time, I guess."

"Well, that's scary to know," Roger says.

"Doc Cole's stopped by every single day to check on me, bless him."

"Bartholomew's always been thoughtful," Nikki Jo says.

"My momma said he handled everything when Rose Campbell died. Wasn't Paul in shock or something?"

Miranda lightly clears her throat. "Sure was. Grieved something awful for at least a couple years." She talks like he's a saint. I suppose she's still bowled over by the skinny widower's intentions to marry her. I really want to like him, but something keeps holding me back.

Nikki Jo and I clear the table. Kelsey sits planted in her seat. She probably doesn't feel comfortable enough to hang with us in the kitchen yet. Either that or she's just lazy.

We take orders for cheesecake flavors and serve it up. I make sure to cut myself a generous piece of my favorite, caramel praline. I brew up some Earl Grey for Miranda, knowing she's tired and probably ready to go home.

She rolls into the kitchen, offering to help. I'm surprised when Nikki Jo hands her a dish towel and some silverware to dry. Then I realize it's the mountain way—at least it used to be. Mountain people didn't wait around for hand-outs. They took pride in doing things for themselves.

I ponder those earlier days. Rose grew up same as me, in the mountains. Did she go running in the woods to get away from her life, like I did? Did she learn to shield herself from unhappiness? Or did she have an idyllic childhood in a big house?

Nikki Jo lounges against the counter, blowing on her black coffee before taking little sips. "I hear the Methodist church is doing a joint service with that little independent church—you know, Miranda, the one Cliff Hogan pastored way back when? You and Rose both knew him, didn't you? I swan if I didn't think he was the handsomest thing I'd ever seen, with that fiery hair."

Miranda looks up from drying a bowl, a sad look on her face. "Yes, she—we—knew him."

That look and those words confirm my dream. Miranda hasn't told me everything. And for her own sake, she needs to spill it all. Who knows what that anonymous note-sender will do next?

23

When Cliff's mother came the next day, I seated her in the same chair her son had used, all those times he'd tried to help me. We both had a couple hot cross buns, which were as mouth-watering as I'd remembered.

What I hadn't remembered from her childhood visits with my mother was her strong personality. Claire Hogan didn't mince words.

"It didn't take much sifting through Cliff's things to realize he'd been coming to visit you quite frequently. And then I saw you at the funeral—standing there bawling your eyes out, worse than his own sister."

Claire set her coffee cup on the rickety fern table next to her and leaned forward. As she dropped her voice to a whisper, her broguish accent took over. "Ye know, Rose, I've helped me mother for years with birthin' babies. I can tell right off if a girlie is carrying a wee babe, and dearie, ye are."

Her clear green eyes, so earnest, and so like her son's,

spurred an unwanted torrent of sobs. She took this as a confirmation of her diagnosis.

"We'll get through this together. I know Cliff was always attracted to ye, just like every other man in town. Your husband need never know."

My plans started crumbling when she said that. But my mind rushed to construct a new plan, one which could include both Bartholomew and Claire Hogan. Maybe my mother had sent me an earthly angel to save me from my marriage.

Now's not the time or place to cross-question the Grande Dame, who's looking exhausted. I make one more round through the dining room, offering refills with the fresh coffee. Thomas grabs me around the waist and pulls me to his lap, whispering in my ear.

"Come sit with me. I feel like I haven't seen you all day."

Andrew shouts, "Hey, bro, keep it kosher!"

Petey comes to our rescue. "Aw, man, lay off."

Andrew reaches over and rubs Petey's red hair until it's in total disarray. "What's wrong, little bro? Looking out for your girl?"

"Aw, shut it!"

Thomas doesn't budge, keeping me firmly planted in his lap. "Get him, Petey! He's too big for his britches!"

In the boyish ruckus that ensues, Kelsey shoots me several desperate glances. I decide to rescue her.

"Want to play chess? I heard you like to play."

"Sure, love to." As she says *love*, I notice the tongue ring for the first time.

I kiss Thomas' cheek to distract him, then slip from his grasp. "We'll be in the den, babe."

"Aw." He turns to his fighting brothers, ready to rejoin the fray.

Kelsey and I are in the hall when Nikki Jo rushes out, her kitten heels long since exchanged for embroidered house slippers. "Tess, I think Miranda needs to get home. She's a little short of breath, but she won't stop working around the kitchen. I'm worried about her."

"No problem, Mom. Sorry, Kelsey. I'd better get her home."

"Sure." Kelsey looks bewildered as to what to do next.

"I'm sure Petey would love to play some Xbox with you," I add.

"Yeah, sounds good." She saunters back to the dining room. I'm not sure if she was being serious or facetious about playing with Petey.

Nikki Jo speaks behind her hand. "I swan, I don't know what to make of that one. She's quiet as a mouse. I don't know what Andrew sees in her."

I try to be diplomatic. After all, I was once a girlfriend under Spencer scrutiny. "Maybe he needs someone quiet like that. I mean, you know Andrew."

Nikki Jo nods thoughtfully before going to retrieve Miranda for me.

When Nikki Jo rolls her in, the Grande Dame is so pale, her perfectly-matched ivory makeup sits like a tan mask on her face. Why didn't I get her out of here sooner? Why didn't I notice?

"I know what you're thinking, girlie. Don't you worry one bit. Just bundle me back home and one of those little caregivers will make sure everything's okay. Or maybe Doc Cole will be around."

Every time Miranda says *Doc Cole*, my stomach clenches. Too many coincidences surround him. I wish I could move into Miranda's suite, until we figure out who's sending the notes. I remember I still haven't showed her the second note. I don't think I ever will.

Nikki Jo and I drape Miranda's mink-trimmed black coat around her arms, wedging it against her chair. Thomas joins us, ready to carry the wheelchair down the front steps.

As he picks it up, his triceps flex in his fitted shirt, destroying my morbid train of thought. I can totally picture the light blond hairs on those tan arms. He catches my wandering eye and winks.

Jeepers. Sometimes I'm way too transparent.

Once we're settled in the SUV, Miranda sighs.

I adjust my seat, since it's pulled all the way back for Thomas. "Sorry if this tired you out today."

"Oh, no, honey. It's not that. It's just memories." She sighs again. Something's weighing on her.

"You want to share?" I fight the urge to fire off twenty questions.

"Nikki Jo was talking about Pastor Cliff. He was a good man—died young, you know."

Sometimes Miranda talks to me like I'm her age. I take this as a compliment.

She pulls a handkerchief from her beaded 1960s-era clutch and dabs her eyes. "So sorry, I still get emotional after all these years. I took Rose to his funeral. He was no older than we were. One of the sweetest souls God put upon this earth."

"What happened?"

"Winter roads on the mountain, that's what happened. He had an old truck—they said the tread was gone. Slid right over the bank, not far from Rose's house."

"That's a pretty secluded road."

She shoots me a sharp glance. "You don't miss a thing, do you? You're right—he'd been out visiting with Rose."

Her blue gaze doesn't waver from my face. She either suspects or *knows* there was something between the pastor and Rose. She's just too much of a lady to come out and tell me.

For a housebound woman, Rose sure got around. The more I uncover about her, the more compassion I feel for Paul. How much did he know?

Reading my mind, Miranda speaks up. "Paul had no idea what was going on."

So she thinks. But have they even discussed Rose's love life? Seems to me, if I were a husband who found out, I'd be tempted to hurt my wife's lovers. And Pastor Cliff died right near the Campbells' house.

Miranda leans her head back into the seat and closes her eyes. I drive as fast as I can around the switchbacks. If she has an attack, I have no idea how to help her.

By the time we pull into The Haven, I've called ahead and a caregiver rushes out to help Miranda out of the SUV. I look closely at his build. He's the gutter-cleaning stalker guy.

"Hey!" I jump down from my seat and run around the car. "Hey! Who are you?"

He steps back, wincing a bit. I guess he remembers me

whapping the chair into his leg. Good. I like to give off a slightly terrifying vibe.

"Look, lady, I don't know you."

"I know you don't. But I might just know something about *you*." Miranda's still fumbling with her seatbelt. "I think you were watching us for some reason. Are you working for someone?"

"Yeah, lady." He points to the logo on his shirt, giving me a smug grin. "I work at *The Haven.* They're my *employers.*"

Oh, no. You did *not* just get all snarky with the pregnant woman. I grab his shirt in my fist, judo moves from college replaying in my mind. I pull him inches from my face.

"*Get this. IF* you touch one hair on this woman's head, I will hunt you down and kill you myself, in a very medieval, torturous way. So if you know something, now's the time to come clean." I feel my eyelids frozen in a wide-open position, no doubt adding to my deranged demeanor.

To my utter amazement, he answers, twisting back from my grip.

"Okay, okay! Listen, this chick wanted me to watch Mrs. Michaels. She wanted me to listen if she mentioned her old friend Rose. So when you two were outside talking, it was easy."

"What did she look like?" I glance at the SUV. Miranda sits close to the window, her breath fogging it up. I can barely make out the quizzical look on her face.

"Maybe forties? Blondish hair. Hot."

Men.

"Did you tell her anything?"

"Just that Mrs. Michaels has some pictures of Rose. That

was all I caught."

"Where did you meet?"

"Right here, lady. She works here on weekends. She's a volunteer."

24

December came in like a lion that year, outside and inside. One day, three feet of snow blocked Paul into our driveway. My skin crawled when I was around him, so I hid in my room all morning. Finally, around noon, I tried to sneak downstairs to grab something to eat.

He was sitting in my favorite chair, looking at my little red book.

I turned, ready to bolt up the stairs and lock my door.

He shouted at me. "Rose! What in the tarnations are you doing reading this thing? Where'd you get it? Looks like a library book?"

I swallowed several times. "It is. Miranda picked it up for me by accident."

"It's stamped three months ago. And why are all these pages folded down?"

I glared at him, trying to believe my own answers. "I have no idea. Where'd you find it? I thought I'd lost it."

He stood, dropping the book to the chair. He pointed to my side table. "It was sitting right on this blessed table, Rose. You okay?"

The urge to scream almost overwhelmed me. Instead, I ran up to my room to hide. It seemed like all I ever did. Lie and hide.

My mother was waiting near my closet.

"I know, Mother. I'm going to do something about this, really soon."

Paul's sharp rap on my door made her disappear. "Who you talking to, Rose?"

The caregiver, who finally admits his name is Anthony, maneuvers Miranda out of the car, into her wheelchair, and down the hall to her suite in an admittedly gentle manner. He then books it out of her room, presumably to get a nurse.

Miranda doesn't ask any questions about my shirt-grabbing interrogation technique. Her eyelids are drooping and she seems utterly depleted. She grabs my hand and squeezes it before the overly cheery nurse whisks her into her room.

What did Anthony hear? I replay our conversation at that metal table. Miranda watching the tree, distracted. The gutter cleaning farce. Then, *"You want a picture of Rose? I've got a whole album of them."*

I need to find that album and get it to a safe place before the hot blonde volunteer finds it. After all, that last note had no envelope, so it had to be an inside drop job. She would've had access—they keep a master key for each room in the main office. Would she have been able to switch Miranda's meds, too?

Sidling up to the buffet drawers, I open one and glance in while the nurse works in the other room. How easy would it be for someone to walk in Miranda's suite door? Half the time it's not locked.

Finally, I lean over the couch to check a crowded bookshelf. I spot a black-bound album at the very bottom. When I walk around to pick it up, the nurse comes out, giving me an odd look. I smile, like I'm totally supposed to be doing this. "I'll lock up for you," I offer.

"Okay. Just tiptoe. She needs to sleep. Low blood pressure today. Did she have Thanksgiving dinner with you?"

"Yes. Sorry I didn't get her back sooner." I hold my stomach, and she seems to notice my pregnancy.

"Don't you worry about that. She needs to get out every now and then. And not just with that Paul character, either." She shakes her head.

Interesting way to refer to Miranda's fiancé. "Does he come over all the time?"

"Not really, but I don't know what she sees in him. He seems a hanger-on, you know. Lawsie knows she doesn't need anybody hanging on to her in this condition."

My thoughts exactly.

Once the nurse bustles away, I tug at the overstuffed album until the books on top of it finally release their grip. It's getting dark in the suite, but I don't want to turn on a light and wake the Grande Dame. I tuck my bulky plunder beneath my arm, pulling out my keychain. Miranda had a suite key made for me last year.

On the way out, I smile at the elderly people in the TV room. My heart goes out to them, all but abandoned on Thanksgiving. Perhaps I should contemplate having a brood of children, purely for the mercenary motive of having someone to look after me for life. I cover my baby with my hand, pleased to feel more of a bump. Nikki Jo will probably want to take me maternity clothes shopping as soon as it's vaguely necessary.

I speed-walk across the quickly darkening parking lot. After my hunch about Anthony's spying proved to be correct, it's anyone's guess who's watching my every move.

Safe in my seat, I turn on the heat and flip the overhead light so I can peep into the album. Here's hoping I snagged the right one.

A yellowed news clipping lies on the first page. It's Russell's obituary. The corners are worn. Miranda practically worshiped her first husband—why does she need another?

I flip through photos of a young Miranda and Russell, probably on their honeymoon to Niagara Falls. More pics of them draped around each other...then some baby pictures. Must be Miranda's only child, Charlotte. Baby Charlotte is positively cute as a Gerber baby, but I have mixed feelings about grown-up Charlotte. I don't even think she called her mother today.

The pictures of Rose are toward the very end. She poses in front of her flowerbeds, one of which is tightly planted with stalks of bell-shaped purple and white flowers. Exactly like the flowers in my vivid dream.

The look on Rose's magazine-beautiful face strikes me as

disingenuous. Sure, she's offering a warm, full smile. But while her eyes are focused on the photographer, she's not *there*. It's as if she's seeing something else entirely.

The last picture is taken on Rose's front porch, leafless trees in the background. Rose leans over the railing, shielding her eyes from the sun. She wears slim pants and a fitted sweater. And her hand covers her stomach, mirroring the unmistakable protective gesture I make all the time.

Rose was pregnant. Did Miranda—

A movement catches my eye. I roll down the window and turn off the car, peering into the stark, bluish light of the parking lot. I feel someone staring at me, probably from the parked truck a couple cars to my left. Switching my knife from my pocket to my hand, I open the door and walk around my Escape to get a closer look.

Immediately, the black truck revs a couple of times and screeches out, but not before the streetlight illuminates a head-full of long blonde hair. I guess that spying volunteer was putting in some overtime.

25

Three nights in one week, Paul came home drunk. Not just drunk on his normal beer or whiskey. Drunk on moonshine.

I knew he'd hidden quite a few of his father's moonshine jugs somewhere, but I'd never stumbled across them in the house. Since he was already half-delirious by the time he got through the door, I realized he'd stored them outside.

I didn't dare go near him in such a condition. Instead, I hovered at the top of the stairs until he passed out on the couch. Then I went down and stripped off his coal-stained, often vomit-covered clothing and left him wearing nothing but his T-shirt and boxers. He was ruining the couch cushions.

It was painfully obvious to me that he'd started in on the moonshine the day after he'd heard me talking to my mother. I refused to feel guilty about it—after all, who can control appearances from the otherworld? For some reason, I'd received the privilege of seeing my mother again, of having her comfort and encourage me.

It wouldn't take much—just a nudge, really—to get rid of my overbearing, interfering husband forever. Then I could live the way I wanted.

We spend most of Friday and Saturday at the big house, relaxing and noshing on leftovers. I positively crave Nikki Jo's turkey noodle soup, helping myself to it about four times a day. Roger pronounces that it's not *me* craving it, but the *baby*. With the combination of Nikki Jo's soup, the cozy fireplace, and the velour couch, I'm feeling like a big baby myself.

The bear trap story is a huge hit with Andrew and his girlfriend. I've probably heard various incarnations of it every single day. Though it still freaks me out to know there are bears in our woods, I'm finally able to laugh about it.

On Saturday, Andrew and Kelsey bop off to hike, then to zipline in a state park. Thomas and I sit on the couch, pondering if we were ever that enthusiastic about life.

"We're a couple fuddy-duds." Thomas absently pulls on a longer piece of his blond bangs.

I elbow him. "Stop your moping around, old man."

"I'm serious! We never do anything fun anymore. Andrew's right, seems like I'm always working. I even have paperwork to do on the weekends now. And here you are, my gorgeous wife, in the prime of life..." He touches my face with the back of his hand, fingers slowly trailing down to my shoulder.

I snuggle my head onto his chest, waiting for that delicious moment when his heartbeat drowns out all other sounds in the world. After a couple minutes, I sigh. "I know…I *am* gorgeous, in the prime of my life."

He laughs and puts his chin on my head. "Where'd you get that wicked sense of humor?"

I groan, shifting into a sitting position. He knows I don't like questions about my family. Who knows what my genetics look like? Unlike Thomas, my family tree hasn't been traced back to my mother country.

"Sorry." Thomas leans in for a long, tender kiss.

"You're forgiven." I grin, running my hand along the light stubble on his chin. "Maybe we should go back to the cottage for the rest of our fuddy-dud Saturday?"

On our way out, we check in with Mom and Dad, who are attempting to string Christmas lights up the front porch pillars. As Dad starts taping them to the top with black electrical tape, Mom launches into a diatribe about how tacky it looks. Thomas pulls me down the steps and out of the fray.

Nikki Jo shouts, "You two are coming to church tomorrow, aren't you? They'll be doing the Thanksgiving meal after, and I know everyone will want to see you."

Thomas cocks his eyebrow at me. I nod. Nikki Jo loves having her entire brood fill the pew for holidays at church.

Sunday morning, after I try on and discard no less than four separate outfits, Thomas reaches into my closet and pulls out my red dress.

"Just wear this and stop worrying about it."

"People haven't seen me for so long and my skirts don't fit right and I look pale. Besides, I don't have any black heels that aren't all scuffed up."

"Just wear boots or something. That dress looks astonishing on you—no one will be looking at your shoes."

It occurs to me that he just wants to see me in the dress, so I oblige and put it on, along with my high-heeled black boots that seem a bit racy for church-wear.

"We're late!" Thomas rocks in his corduroy sport-coat, checked shirt, and striped tie. It's kind of a multi-pattern cool, like Doctor Who with his trailing scarves.

We manage to get to church just as they're singing the end of *Happy Birthday to You*, for anyone who had birthdays this week. Nikki Jo pats the pew next to her and we slide in beside Andrew and Kelsey.

Andrew's looking downright French in a black shirt and scarf combo. He's also sporting a beret, probably in an attempt to distract from his ponytailed hair. I don't think hats are allowed on men in church, but I guess no one's asked him to remove it yet. Kelsey looks displaced in her leggings and fitted leather jacket. Sitting next to the two of them, I realize it didn't matter what I wore.

Once the children's Sunday school classes are dismissed, the adult class teacher takes the podium. He's so young—probably in his early thirties. Yet he dives into the heavy topic of grief.

The group is eager to respond when he interjects questions, and it's astounding what some of these honest people have to say. Many of them, from the oldest to the youngest, have experienced real grief, in its various forms. I think about my own griefs, such as they are. Namely, my parents. Who knows where my dad is? And my mom, who started selling pills the moment she got out of jail, only to land herself in prison. Where was she getting her prescriptions, anyway? It's not like she had chronic pain.

"...surely He has borne our griefs and carried our sorrows." Thomas sounds very erudite as he responds to something the Sunday school teacher asked.

Guilt washes over me. I learned so many verses in my childhood. Why can't I run to the Bible, like Nikki Jo or even Thomas, to find comfort? Thomas reads it every night before bed. I'm reminded of those cryptic words on Rose's hidden garden stones. Pulling a church pen from the pew ahead of me, I write "Rose rocks" on my hand so I'll remember to pull out my Bible at home.

By the end of our class, I have a newfound respect for young Sunday School teachers. Parents leave to retrieve their children from Sunday school. Petey whirls into the pew, plopping down next to me.

The choir trickles up to the choir loft, Nikki Jo among them. They launch into a kicky Southern Gospel song. Nikki Jo's lilting soprano mesmerizes and is impossible to ignore, even as the other voices meld around it. Andrew and Kelsey whisper together, oblivious to the beauty of the song lyrics.

Petey leans over, cupping his hand by my ear. "Don't look now, but that big guy back there is staring at you."

I wait a little, then twist slightly toward the back. Sure enough, there's Axel, large as life, looking right at me. I'm stalked on every side, from elderly care homes to church.

I nudge Petey. "Does he normally go here?"

"Don't know; maybe?"

Helpful. As the choir switches to their next song, I focus on each and every singer's outfit. Pink tie, white oxford shirt, rumpled chinos. Red sweater, navy polyester skirt, brooch from the 1700s or thereabouts. Hopefully, if I act like Axel's not there, Thomas won't think to turn around.

We make it all the way to the sermon. As the elderly pastor instructs us to open our Bibles, Andrew punches Thomas' arm, jerking his head toward the back row. The look on Andrew's face says something like "Dude, what is *up* with that?"

I sit stock-still, willing myself not to breathe. Axel, get out of here and quit staring at me, you Germanic brute.

Thomas turns.

Then he turns back, looking at the pastor as if nothing's wrong. It takes about two seconds for him to dramatically raise his arm, extend it fully, then position it on the pew behind my back.

Staking the territory. Andrew recognizes this and winks at his brother.

By the conclusion of the sermon and invitation, Thomas has rubbed my head, my neck, and my shoulders, causing no end of coughing and throat-clearing behind us. I finally draw the line when he starts massaging my chin with his fingertips.

Thankfully, Axel's out the door before we get out of our pew. The Sunday school teacher comes over, introducing his wife, who bears more than a passing resemblance to a tan, towering Swedish model. I have no idea what to say to her.

Nikki Jo invites us to stay for the church dinner, but I politely shoot down that idea. On Thomas' last day off, I only want to hang out with him.

I'm quiet in the car, which makes Thomas restless. He peppers me with random questions. "What was that crazy guy doing watching you again?" "Don't you think the choir needed more bass today?" Finally, he hits it. "Wasn't that a good Sunday school class?"

Yes...yes it was. Good enough to make me come back, in fact. I've wanted to ask my burning questions about God for so long, and that Sunday school class seems as likely a place as any to do it.

I rub lotion into my dry hands, noticing the words I wrote. "Thomas, do you recognize the words Mene, Tekel, and Upharsin?"

"Sure. Those were in Daniel, I think. Remember the writing on the wall? Let me think." He gets his intense lawyer look, the one that always makes me want to kiss him. "Weighed in the balances and found wanting; something like that. Yeah, I'm pretty sure that's it."

So Rose felt someone was weighed and found wanting— probably her husband. But I think Miss Rose left a little something to be desired herself. The obvious question is *whose child had she been pregnant with?*

26

One Sunday, I asked Claire to take me to Cliff's church. I told her I wanted closure, but really, I wanted to stay in her good graces. Paul had been ignoring me since the moonshine binges started, so it wasn't a problem to leave the house.

Church was much like I'd remembered, full of starched-looking people who didn't care to talk with me. How did Cliff manage to stay so real when he was surrounded with so many fakes?

Even when one of Paul's poker friends came over, he shifted around, not looking me in the eyes. Was he embarrassed to know me?

Once we sang hymns, I relaxed, recognizing the old words from childhood. Still, what did they mean to me? So many happily married couples here. Who could understand the depths I'd been forced to endure, much less my method for achieving freedom?

For half the sermon, the temporary pastor told jokes. For

the other half, he had us flipping around in the Bible like it was on fire. My disappointment surprised me, since I hadn't been expecting much. I guess I was keenly aware Cliff would've been saddened by the farcical sermon.

On the way home, I told Claire I couldn't go to church again, feigning sadness over Cliff. She said she understood. I wanted to laugh hysterically. No one understood, not even Bartholomew. Not my ghostly mother. And probably not even God.

My alarm bleeps and bleeps. I finally drag myself up, stumble across to the dresser, and contemplate bashing the blue LED into a thousand pieces with my hairbrush.

Realization dawns. I'm meeting with the Good Doctor today at the bistro for lunch. It's already ten o'clock—I must have hit snooze six times. Why am I still tired? Maybe the pregnancy?

Downstairs, I whip up a breakfast of champions: toast and Nutella. I hope the chocolate fortifies me for the day, since I don't have time to brew coffee in our old-school French press.

Finally, I feel relatively presentable in my baby bell-bottom jeans and purple shirt. I throw on some silver ball earrings and matching mesh bracelet, for a touch of class.

The house phone rings. I don't recognize the number, but I pick up.

"Aw, good, honey—it's you. Listen, I been down here in this cell just a'thinkin about you all Christmas—I mean Thanksgiving. I wanted to be there, you know I did."

The smoky voice pulls at me through the phone line. My mom. Calling from prison. I back onto the couch and sit, trying to harness my emotions.

"How are you doing, Mom?"

"Now, don't you go gettin' all sly on me. Is it true you're pregnant?"

Oh, good land. Who told her that?

"Yes, Mom, I am. Found out not too long ago." Well, maybe a couple months…

Mom coughs directly into the phone—a nasty phlegm-filled cough. What if she has bronchitis in that comfortless cell? I need to find out which prison she's in and go see her. I shouldn't have distanced myself so far from her problems.

"Now listen, I just need to get outta here, then we can go get you some baby stuff." Mom doesn't even know where I live, much less that I don't need anything bought with her drug money. *If* there's any left.

"What did the judge say about when you're getting out?"

"Now don't you worry your pretty little head about that judge. Momma's gonna find a way out of here; wait and see. I'm tired of sitting around, all do-less."

Oh mercy.

She coughs again. I hope the guard's standing by with some Clorox wipes for the phone.

She finally breaks the silence. "Okay, well, better go, sweet girl. See you later."

Click. That's it. No time for a rebuttal, question, or reply. My mom makes up her mind and there's no stopping her. Unfortunately, she nearly always gets set on doing the wrong things.

I rush to the SUV, running late. Any cohesive thoughts are lost, like someone pushed the *reset* button on my game system. I can't even remember one topic I wanted to broach with the Good Doctor.

I flip on the Christian radio station, hoping for something to fill my soul. Instead, I get nothing but lovey-dovey songs. I feel anything but that.

Turning it off, I focus on the serpentine pavement ahead. I might be the worst child ever. I don't even want my mom to know this grandchild. Hiding the baby and myself away seems a legitimate plan right now.

Point Pleasant comes into view way too soon. I almost turn the wrong way down a familiar one-way street. Finally, I pull into a parking spot near the restaurant.

When I get out, the nippy air braces me. By the time I push open the bistro's heavy wooden door, there's a fifty-fifty chance I might be lucid enough to interrogate Doctor Cole.

I scan the room. He smiles at me from a darkened booth and waves me over. There is *no way* on earth he could be from the same decade as Miranda. The first question I should ask is "How do you stay so well-preserved?" Between the strong chin, the shock of white hair, and the impeccable wardrobe, he's a regular elderly Don Juan. Today, I fixate on his shoes— soft gray suede lace-ups.

He stands as I walk to the booth—an old-fashioned gesture that doesn't fail to impress. He grabs my hand and covers it with his own. "Tess, so good to see you. How's the pregnancy?"

I try to inject some edge into my voice. "Doing okay, but that whole episode with Miranda was pretty traumatizing. She still seems weak—is that normal?"

The Doc's gaze sharpens and he goes into doctor mode. "Perfectly normal with that kind of overdose, I'm afraid. I've been racking my brain, trying to determine how that could've happened."

"I have some ideas, one of which is a specific volunteer over at The Haven. Have you noticed a pretty blonde working there?"

"Actually, the volunteers are there on weekends, during the mornings. I usually round in the afternoons."

Our waiter sidles over and reels off the list of specials, his eyes never leaving my face. I order a peach sweet tea and Caesar salad, and the Doc orders a crab salad sandwich and sweet potato fries. When the waiter finally turns back to the kitchen, I breathe a sigh of relief.

The Doctor gives me a knowing look. "Must happen all the time, huh?"

"What?" I feign oblivion.

He smiles. "Rose had that problem, too. When you're beautiful, you attract attention. When you're beautiful *and* approachable, you attract even more."

It takes me aback, this comparison to Rose. Lately, I've been hating on her for her indiscretions. Which puts me in mind of a question I need to ask the Good Doctor. I lean across the table.

"I know you and Rose were close. I also know you pronounced her death. Please be honest with me. Was she pregnant when she died?"

The Doctor inhales some of his coffee down the wrong pipe. After coughing and sipping water for a minute, he tries to answer, his face still red.

"I wonder"—cough—"how you got that idea?"

"You've said it yourself, Doctor. I'm pretty intuitive. I've been putting some pieces together with pictures, stories, and the like. I also know you could have fathered that baby." I calmly take a sip of sweet tea. Sometimes it feels pretty daggone good to be "top banana in the shock department," as Holly Golightly says in *Breakfast at Tiffany's*.

The Doctor takes one last cough, then recovers his composure. "Bravo, Tess. Good sleuthing. Yes, Rose and I were involved. And you're right, it *would have been* my child."

I didn't expect this quick admission. "Would have been? But wasn't she pregnant when you pronounced her?"

His habitual smile dissolves. "I know she wasn't pregnant then. She'd had an abortion."

My face freezes. "But why would she do that? I thought she wanted a child more than anything—at least, that's what Miranda told me."

The waiter brings our food, derailing my train of thought with his unwelcome stares. He carefully places the plate between my hands, saying, "Careful, now, that's hot." He leans closer and whispers, "*Just like you.*"

I catch my breath. Did he really just say that? He stands by my chair, not even asking if we need anything.

The Doctor doesn't fail to miss these intrusive overtures. He gives the waiter a look that could melt glass. "Excuse me, but we'd like a little privacy."

The punk gives me a long smile, then moseys back toward the kitchen. I try to process the horror of what the Good Doctor told me.

"You said Rose got an abortion? How do you know?"

The Doctor dips his fry in ranch dip, then slowly chews it, gazing out the window. "I know because I asked her to."

What? What about the physician's creed: *Do no harm?*

He continues. "I know what you're thinking. How could I do that? Well, I'll explain. Paul would have killed Rose if he knew. And I'm not exaggerating. Rose always had bruises, and those bruises came from her husband. She never told Miranda."

Fire works its way into my chest, until I'm ready to shout at all the injustices. "Don't you think you should've *told* someone? Even now, Miranda's getting ready to marry Paul! If he lays a hand on her I'll kill him! And why didn't you get Rose out of there, if you loved her so stinking much? You could've saved the baby and her!"

"What are you insinuating? That Rose could have been saved? She committed suicide."

"Of course that's what I'm insinuating. What if Paul found out and *he* killed her?"

"Ridiculous. Impossible."

The Doctor's tone is borderline condescending. "Why's it so impossible, Doctor? You said yourself that Paul was violent. What if she pushed him too far?"

He leans toward me, templing his fingers. "I think it's more a case of Rose's psyche. You like to study people. What do you make of Rose, from what you've uncovered?"

"There's no way I can understand someone who died forty years ago. Here's what I do understand: if she killed herself, she was probably in the depths of despair because you forced her to have an abortion. If Paul killed her, it's probably because you were having an affair with her. Either way, you're the most direct link to her death."

The Doctor rubs his forehead with long tan fingers, giving me an exhausted look. "Of course I know all this. I've suffered with insomnia since the night she died, all those years ago. Was it my fault somehow? I've had to live with the guilt."

Guilt. The very word is heavy, like a rock dropped into a clear blue pool. And it's something I'm acquainted with, every time I pull out my mental *what if* list. I should give the Good Doctor a break.

"You never married?" I try to sound casual.

He's barely touched his sandwich. Wasted money...like the handsome Doctor's wasted life. He focuses on me with those intense eyes. "I couldn't. I know it sounds horribly old-fashioned, but she really was my one true love."

It does sound quaint, but the Doctor seems honest. Then again, some of the best liars come across as incredibly honest.

As the Doctor pays the bill and I gather my things, I catch a glimpse of the wayward waiter through the kitchen door window. He winks. Jerk.

27

Snow started dumping halfway through the month, blocking us in again. I wished God had never invented December. I was going stir-crazy as it was. The wood stove was the only good reason I had to go out into the mess. I didn't like being cooped up with Paul, or, if I was honest, my mother's ghost.

The ghost had taken to appearing at the drop of the hat. I'd open my closet; she'd be shimmering between my clothes. I'd wake from a nightmare; she was hovering over my bed.

Still, I didn't feel afraid, just uncomfortable. Mother didn't really talk to me anymore, just gave me the feeling she was listening and supporting me.

Then, in the middle of the snowstorm, everything changed.

I didn't want to fix supper, since I was feeling sick to my stomach. Paul brought leftover chicken and rice to me in bed. He walked into my room, then stopped short. He hadn't come in since that day I was talking with my mother.

"Did you rearrange in here, Rosey? Something's different."

"Nothing's different."

He skulked over to the bed with the tray, sniffing at the air. "Feels like there's a draft or something." He set the tray on my lap, then walked toward the window. "This locked down?"

"Yes, Paul. Stop fretting."

He came over and sat on my Wedding Ring quilt. His dark eyes were impenetrable as he examined my face slowly, from eyes to mouth. Finally, he spoke, his drawl exaggerated.

"You doin' drugs?"

"What?!"

He grabbed my arms. The pain no longer affected me.

"You don't let me in your bed now. What am I supposed to do, Rosey?" He leaned in closer, eyes nearly wild with passion. "I married you because I need you!"

I sat calm, unmoving—an ice queen. "Unhand me."

"What?" He dropped his hands, shrugging helplessly. "I don't know what to do," he said. Then, like a baby, he laid his head on my lap and started sobbing.

I steeled myself against him, even as I rubbed his head. "There's no more time, Paul. It's too late."

Back at our cottage, a strange urge to cook overwhelms me. Though the freezer is scantily stocked, I manage to find a couple steaks I'd bought on sale. I feel disconnected from Thomas, even though we just spent all weekend together. Whether it turns out to be a snow-bloated winter or not, December seems to stretch endlessly. Christmas is a light at the end of the very long tunnel.

I whisk around between my two countertops and the table, making salad and homemade breadsticks. The Doctor's words echo in my head. He was sure Rose had an abortion *because he asked her to.* My stomach twists. The Doc is a murderer, whether he killed Rose or not. Chill bumps creep up my neck, to my very scalp hairs. I sit on the couch, gripping my stomach with both hands as it cramps again. He had Rose kill her baby. I ate lunch with a *killer.*

I run to the bathroom, just in time to lose my lunch. A dull headache replaces the stomach cramps. *What if the Doctor poisoned me at lunch?*

I crawl from the bathroom to the doorway, yanking my purse down from the table near the door. Kleenexes, cough drops, and lip balms scatter around me. I dig until I find my cell phone and call Nikki Jo.

"Hello?" She always acts like she doesn't know who's calling, even though she has Caller I.D.

"I'm sick." I barely manage the words before I lay my head on the floor and drift off.

When I wake up, it's dark and the curtains are drawn. For a second, I'm completely disoriented, until I realize I'm lying under my own blankets.

"Nikki Jo?"

Her blonde head pops in the doorframe, a halo of light behind it. She must have been sitting on the hard step right outside our bedroom door.

"Yes! You okay, honey?"

"What's going on? Was I poisoned?"

"Poisoned? Law, no! You're running a fever to beat the band. And from the looks of that bathroom, you have a stomach bug."

Good grief, I forgot to flush the toilet?

"Now I'm going to get you some ice-cold Coke and a couple Motrin to take down that fever."

"Tylenol, Mom. I can't have Motrin."

"Good gracious, what was I thinking? Tylenol it is. Now you try and rest, and I'll be right back. Thomas is on his way home now—his court case ran late."

I'm probably a bad wife because I don't know which court case that is, nor do I care. I hope the Doctor gets this bug, too—serves that killer right...

I wake with a start, ice cubes clinking next to me. Nikki Jo holds the cold glass to my lips and presses a couple of pills in my hand. "Just sip at it," she says.

The next time I open my eyes, the bathroom light is on. Thomas is curled up next to me, his arm draped over my head. He snores lightly, still wearing his suit and tie.

"Thomas?" I scoot out from under his arm.

"Mm." He rolls toward me, then rouses and half-sits. "You okay?"

"I think so. My stomach seems calmer. Did you know your mom's an angel?"

He laughs, smoothing my hair. "I *think* most angels don't share her tendency to gossip, but whatever you say, lovely. Now why did Mom say you thought you'd been poisoned?"

I grin, my dry lips cracking. "I ate lunch today with the Good—with Doctor Cole. I don't know what to think of him."

Thomas sits up straighter. "Tell me you're not still looking into Rose Campbell's death? I thought you'd given that up."

Given up? My husband doesn't know me as well as I thought.

Thomas is on a roll. "*Why* on earth does Miranda mean more to you than your own safety? Seems like weird things happen the more you get involved with that old lady."

That old lady? Time to lay it on the line for my clueless one.

"Miranda Michaels is more than some old lady, Thomas. She's my best friend. And I'll tell you why. She took care of me when I didn't care if I lived or died. A couple years before you met me, I was ready to do myself in, just like Rose did. Well, maybe not that way. I was going to torch the trailer and jump off a bridge."

Heat flames into my face. "Anyway, Miranda stopped me. Back when she could walk, she would go on these do-gooder expeditions with her church. One day, she came to my mom's jail, where I was bawling my eyes out in the white plastic chair."

Thomas positions himself behind my back, rubbing my head. I've never told him much about my mom, much less Miranda.

"I'll never forget it—Miranda asked me, 'Now, what would make a young girl like you cry like she's got the whole world on her shoulders?' She hugged me, and something in me broke. I told her everything—even how I wanted to kill myself. From that day on, she let me camp in her spare room every time Mom went to jail."

I turn. Thomas' brown eyes glisten, but he says, "Go on."

"So you see why I have to help her? She's marrying Rose's husband on New Year's Day. If he's a killer, I have to stop the marriage. It's *my turn* to repay the debt I owe her."

I tug at his tie, hoping he'll get into PJs or something more comfy. I probably look like a wreck, with my sweaty hair plastered to my head and my feverish face. Yet he's looking at me like I'm a goddess.

"Thanks for opening up, Tess. I never—I just didn't know. I mean, I knew about your mom, but not about you..."

I lean in, ready to stop his unusually awkward speech with a kiss, but stop short as I remember I'm contagious. Instead, I put my finger on his lips.

"I'd better get a shower. Thanks for listening, honey." As I pull clean clothes from the dresser, a strange new happiness electrifies the dark corners of my heart. I told Thomas the gritty truth, and he still loves me. Holding my pajama pants tightly against my little baby bump, I know I'll never be suicidal again.

28

When I sent my Christmas cards out, I wrote something extra on Miranda's envelope: "Come see me."

And she did. She brought Charlotte, all dolled up in a red elf outfit. This time, she didn't have to ask me to hold the baby—I volunteered. I breathed in her clean baby smell, willing myself to say what I had to say.

I had shared so much with Bartholomew. But Miranda needed to know the truth about Cliff. I took a deep breath and plunged ahead. "You've always been my best friend. I know you thought I was having an affair with Cliff. I want to tell you that I wasn't. He was counseling me."

Miranda's dark bangs fringed her wide blue eyes. "Okay."

Nothing more. No, "Why were you getting counseling?"

She took the squirming Charlotte and started bouncing her on her knee. Was this real friendship? Leaving things unsaid? Hiding things? I wanted a true friend more than anything, and Miranda was my last shot at one.

"I'm pregnant," I said.

Miranda nodded calmly. "I know."

"It's Bartholomew Cole's baby."

A half-smile played about Miranda's Clara Bow lips. "I'm not surprised, after the way you two flirted at your dinner parties."

Anger washes over me. "You knew all this time? Why didn't you tell me? Why weren't you there for me?"

"You didn't want me to be, honey. You shut me out long before Cliff came along. I never understood why."

I felt ashamed. Miranda's sharp eye caught my flirting with Bartholomew, but had completely missed the fire in Paul's eyes every time she came to visit. She was oblivious to her own pull on my husband.

Not only was she a true friend, she was the most humble person I'd ever met.

I knew she would guard my secret.

Weak morning sunlight and the overpowering smell of nail polish wake me around eight. I pull out my bathroom drawers to see if Thomas knocked over a bottle before he left.

Light boot-steps sound on the stairs, leaving me little doubt as to the source of the smell.

Nikki Jo opens the door. Her fuchsia blouse and broad smile seem to radiate sunshine. "How are you? I've brought you a pot of peppermint tea. Hardly drink it myself, but I've heard it does wonders for upset stomachs."

"Thanks so much, Mom. I'm feeling better today."

"That's what Thomas said on his way out. Good to see more color in your cheeks. I'll make you some toast."

"Actually, I'm just going to lounge around today. Feel free to go on up to the house—I'll be okay on my own. I need to call Miranda."

"Oh, okay, honey." She blows on her burgundy fingertips. "I'll send Petey down when he gets in from school, just to check on you."

This translates into: "I'll send a meal down with Petey."

I wave at her, trying not to spread my germs around. "Thank you...and thanks for being there last night."

Nikki Jo walks gingerly down the steps, holding her wet nails out at arm's length. I go back and scrounge around until I find an outfit that makes me feel somewhat French and classy—a navy sailor-striped tunic and straight-leg white jeans. I comb my hair out, then fluff and spray it. Finally, I add a dash of lipstick and a couple swipes of blush. I might feel like I got hit by a truck, but that doesn't mean I have to look like it.

Downstairs, I dump liberal teaspoons of sugar into the peppermint tea and take a swig. Wow, this stuff might wake me up more than coffee. I've just finished buttering a toast when there's a knock on the door.

Who would *knock* on my door?

I grab one of my biggest kitchen knives and hold it behind my back. When I open the door, it slips from my hand and nearly stabs my ankle.

Nothing says *Get Well Soon* like an oversized German florist standing on your porch, gripping a large bouquet of black roses.

Axel shifts on his feet, looking sheepish. "Another delivery. Do not worry. I checked the card—Arizona."

I don't know if I want to take the flowers. Axel seems undecided about whether he wants to hand them over.

"Black roses," I say.

"Not so *gut*," he replies.

I don't have to look it up in *The True Meaning of Flowers*. The message is all too clear. Someone wants me dead. I touch an open petal—silk. "They look so real."

"I am good at this work." Axel smiles, his long, nearly white bangs falling over one eye. His lips are surprisingly full. I think Axel could've had any number of girlfriends in college, if he'd just been more personable.

I take a great, sucking breath of fresh air. Smells like rained-on gravel...and some sort of powerful pheromone.

"What do I do?" The words slip out before I think about how vulnerable they make me look. Well, who cares? I am vulnerable! For the love of goodness, I'm a pregnant woman, and some maniac just sent me death flowers.

Axel pulls the bouquet back. "*Nein*, you do not keep them." He steps closer, his eyes wandering down my body as if he can imagine his hands on it. "You want for me to locate this person?"

What Axel's *tone* says is this: "I will cut this person into little pieces if I find them. What do you think?"

I have to stop him, sweetly protective though he may be. "It's okay. I'll be okay. Thanks for bringing these—uh, for taking them away. It'll work out."

His cheekbones look like they're made of steel. If I punched his face, I'll bet he wouldn't even feel it.

176

"You call me for help," he says. It only takes about three of his giant strides to propel him from the porch to his van.

Nikki Jo calls the minute I step into the house, which means she's been watching out her window. I pray she doesn't breathe a word of this to Thomas.

I wouldn't deliberately lie to Nikki Jo, but if I tell her I'm getting black roses from an anonymous weirdo, she wouldn't want me staying alone in the cottage. In fact, she'd probably move me up to the big house, better known as the *armory* when anything dangerous comes along.

I tell Mom the flowers were a mistaken delivery—not far from the truth, since she probably noticed Axel took them back to the van.

Besides, the mystery person *did* just make a mistake. When you push me one direction, I'm quite likely to go the other. I'm going to dig deeper and push harder until I figure out what really happened to Rose. No scaredy-cat stalker, hiding behind a black silk bouquet, is going to stop me now.

29

Revenge was the best slave-driver. It promised everything and required next to nothing on my part—just hatred. And I hated my husband.

Who else did I hate? Possibly I hated Bartholomew, for asking me to do the unthinkable. But I loved him, too, for his willingness to protect me at all cost. If I was truthful, I hated my father for never being there to hug or encourage me.

Still, I was alone in my hatred. There were days I wanted to call Bartholomew so I could lie in his arms and wrap myself in his comforting presence. But my comforter was something of a threat, so I couldn't call him. I wanted to share more with Miranda, but she knew all she needed to know. My mother stayed around, but I knew better than to speak to her aloud anymore. She seemed to almost read my thoughts.

So I poured all my venom into my journal, knowing it would tell the tales I could not.

I wait a couple of days before I go visit Miranda—I don't want her to catch my stomach bug on top of her heart problems. In the meantime, she's called me twice—once to ask about flowers for her wedding, and once to ask if I'd like to be her wedding coordinator.

Um, that would be a resounding *No.*

Unfortunately, I can't extricate myself from my debt to the Grande Dame. The woman is a saint, and I'm not going to begrudge her the happiness of remarrying in her later years. So I didn't say no to her directly. I just fell back on my typical run-myself-down routine: I'm not crafty; I'm not good at decorating; I haven't attended a wedding since my own. Thankfully, Miranda bought it. She's supposed to be asking around at The Haven for any leads on reputable wedding planners. Charming juxtaposition—asking around an assisted living home for marriage tips.

The day I finally get over to visit, the beautician is hard at work on Miranda's still-thick hair. Miranda waves me to the couch, and we chitchat while the frizzy-haired woman rolls each section on hot rollers. I wonder if I'll get my hair fixed when I'm nearly seventy, or if I'll just let it go *au naturel.*

"I'd play you a game of chess, but I'm afraid it'd be discouraging for you." Miranda's in fine form today. "You keeping your food down now?"

"Yes, sure am. I'm able to eat more every day. And how are *you* feeling? Having any weak spells?"

"A couple here and there. Last time I had one, Paul was over. He gave me the nitro pill right away, and it seemed to work."

She says it like I'm supposed to stand up and clap. Hopefully it's not obvious I still don't approve of Mr. Paul Campbell. In the lull that follows, I finally speak. "Fast thinking on his part."

She smiles. "I thought so. He's already ordered his tuxedo. Can you imagine—a tux at his age! It seems very romantic."

Romantic was not the word that sprang to mind.

"Oh, and Tess, I got the invitations in the mail today! Go over and look in that box on my bed."

Feigning enthusiasm, I walk into her bedroom. Sure enough, they're very proper wedding invites—all white, with scrolling dark green cursive letters. Green ivy forms a border around each card.

I read over them, feeling a bit nauseated. *Welcoming the New Year as Husband and Wife—Paul Campbell and Miranda Michaels.* Isn't the wife's name supposed to be first? I know she's waiting to hear my reaction.

"Classy-looking!" I shout.

Miranda shouts back. "Could you address a few of those cards for me? The guest list's sitting right next to the box. My handwriting's so shaky now."

"I might could." I pick up her rough-scrawled list of names and addresses—probably twenty, tops. "I'll just address all of them, Miranda."

"Oh, honey, I hate to have you do all that." She rolls herself into the room, hair perfectly coiffed—a true Southern Belle. She pats at her hair. "That NonaBeth never sprays my hair enough. This thing'll go flat by afternoon."

I peek out the door. "We alone?"

She nods. "What's on your mind?"

I've spent two long nights wondering if I should be straightforward with Miranda about her second anonymous note, not to mention my cryptic bouquet. I still don't know. I won't be responsible for giving her more heart palpitations.

"Can we talk about Rose? I met with the Doctor—you know, Doctor Cole."

I wait, hoping the Grande Dame will delicately fill in the blanks. She doesn't. I try a different tack.

"I took your photo album when you were sick—trying to figure out who would hurt you. I saw the pictures of Rose and I noticed something. Turns out, she was pregnant. Did you know?"

Miranda sighs. "I swore I'd never tell anyone. But she's been dead all these years now. Yes, she was pregnant. I couldn't believe she wasn't more excited about it, but it was like something was hanging over her head."

I don't want to be the one to tell Miranda about the abortion. Smoothing her luxurious, dark red velour bedspread, I wait and hope she'll continue.

"She had me over one day and told me it was Bartholomew's baby—wanted to clear Cliff's name. That was only about a month before she died. So I always figured the baby died right along with her."

I can't hide the truth from Miranda. "That's what I was asking the Doctor about: if she was pregnant when she died. He said she wasn't."

It only takes a second for Miranda to read between the lines.

Wheeling herself to her night-table, she takes a tissue to dab at the corners of her eyes. Then she discretely blows her nose. "Was it a miscarriage, or did she get rid of the baby?"

Not the most politically correct way of phrasing things, but sadly true. "Yes, she got rid of it." I sit in a nearby wing chair and start addressing and stuffing envelopes. I can't handle Miranda's tears.

My mind whirs. Maybe Rose made that will before she got the abortion? Or is the Doctor lying, and she was pregnant when she died? That points to murder, since I doubt a pregnant woman would kill herself.

Miranda absently twists at her tissue. "Such an ugly end for that poor child. There's so much I don't understand...I can't explain." Her voice trails off, then gathers strength. "Tess, you think someone deliberately changed my pills?"

"Honestly, I do. I don't know why yet, but I don't think it was an accident."

"But I only got the one note. I thought that was it, just a warning."

She leaves the door wide open for me to fill in the blanks. "There was another note, that same day you had the overdose. I found it on your counter."

She wheels closer, the spicy, vanilla scent of her perfume wrapping her much like the Black Cashmere it's supposed to represent. She leans toward me and takes my hand. "Look here, I don't want you worrying over me, Tess Spencer. Whatever that note said, don't let's think about it." It's just like her to be comforting *me* over her own threatening letter.

I focus on her hands. Alabaster white, veins slightly pronounced, and covered with age spots. Tears fill my eyes.

Whether there's a killer after us, or whether it's just that ever-crouching Death, I want to hold it back for my valiant friend. I wish she could go back to that vivacious, mobile woman she used to be.

Miranda sighs. "I need to think on this. Something's not right here."

I look at my pensive friend's face. Miranda knew Rose, Paul, Cliff, and the Doctor better than anyone else. Miranda's at the crux of everything: the notes, the overdose, and indirectly, my flowers. Someone's figured out I'm helping *her*. Someone is gunning for *her*.

So the question is not *Was Rose murdered*, but *What does Miranda know?*

30

My mother's ghost whispered to me in my dreams. "Poison."

Every day that long December, I read my book and hid it under my mattress. I set about to prepare just the right dosage for Paul. There could be no mistakes. I wanted to ask Bartholomew for help, but he couldn't be suspected of anything. That's why I wanted to use my own flowers.

Then one morning, Paul brought me coffee in bed. There was strange taste to it, like the half and half had gone bad.

I sipped at the drink, then yelled for him. It took him scarcely a minute to get in my room, like he was waiting outside my door.

"Didn't we just buy this cream?" I set the mug on the bedside table.

"Yes, just bought it yesterday."

"It must be rancid; tastes so bitter."

"What?" He grabbed the mug and took a tiny sip. "Tastes fine to me, Rosey." He stalked back to the door, glancing at *me. "You getting up today? I was thinking about taking a walk down by the creek."*

"Not today."

The same minute he pulled the door to with a slight slam, a voice drifted over to me. "Poison." And then other voices joined it, first singing, then shouting the word, "Poison."

A chorus of angels? A rabble of demons? Or just my own mind?

Didn't matter. I pulled out my red book.

I finish addressing Miranda's cards, then play chess and hang out with her until five-thirty. Suppertime at The Haven is at five forty-five sharp.

It's already getting dark as I swing by McDonald's for a coffee with cream and sugar on the way home. Might not be a grande cinnamon-vanilla swirl from Kelly's, but I have no desire to go all the way into Point Pleasant for a fancy cup o'joe. Our poor baby is going to come out of the womb fully caffeinated, but I just can't give up coffee yet.

Christmas music plays on practically every station, and I'm glad for it. I need to get in a Christmassy mood. Nikki Jo will probably have her house decorated this week. Every year, she chooses an ornament theme for her fake white Christmas tree. So far, I've witnessed two: the dove theme, in which an unnatural number of red-eyed, pigeon-type birds were jammed into every possible cranny, and the Little Drummer Boy theme, in which the song played on an endless loop while tippy glass drums threatened to break each time you walked past.

At home, I putter around the house, looking for the few Christmas decorations we own. Generic red stockings, check. White lights and garland for the tree, check. Ornaments? No idea where those are.

I venture into the stationary bike closet-room, hot on the chase for my missing ornaments. In truth, we might have a total of about twenty ornaments, five of which say *Our First Christmas*.

The dark room smells musty, and we don't even have a basement. Who knows how long this umber-colored paneling has been on the walls. I should paint it white, or better yet, have Thomas take it down. Not that he has any time to play handyman.

I flip the light then peer out the window, just to be certain. No one out there.

Rummaging through the boxes piled in the corner, I hear footsteps in the living room.

"In here, Thomas!"

No reply. In a split-second, my heart leaps to my throat. I hit the light and crouch in the darkness, feeling for sharp objects I can use as weapons. I try to replay self-defense strategies from college. There's dead silence in the house now.

Then I hear it—loud and clear, coming from my purse—my *Doctor Who* ringtone. Oh my word. Oh my word.

Will the trespasser pick it up? Would they even dare?

Once the phone gets quiet, I peek into kitchen—the only room that's lit. I'll wait three more minutes, then I'll run into the kitchen, grab a huge knife, and scream like a maniac.

The front door opens. Once I get out in the open, I wonder if that crane move from *Karate Kid I* could actually save me. The element of surprise...

"Tess!? You in here?" Thomas' rich voice fills the empty spaces in the house.

I nearly fall over. "Yes! Here! Oh my lands, where *were* you?"

He rushes into the closet-room. "I was at work, of course. Why are you hiding in the dark?"

"Someone was in the house! I—"

He stops me, whispering. "In the house?"

I nod.

He pulls his ever-present Sig Sauer from his belt holster and starts combing the rooms. I have to snicker, since he looks all serious, like a cop on *Law and Order.*

Doctor Who calls, again. This time I sneak out into the kitchen and grab my purse.

I pick up without checking the caller. My voice comes out as a half-whisper. "Hello?"

"Tess? Bartholomew. Are you sitting down?"

Not Miranda, please, not Miranda. I sit on the kitchen chair. "Yes."

"A masked person broke into my house tonight and took a shot at me. If the intruder hadn't had atrocious aim, I might have been killed. The police are here now." He whispers into the phone, "I wondered if it had to do with what we talked about at the bistro."

Why would he assume that? I grip the phone, trying to still my shaking hand. "Someone was in our house, too! It doesn't make sense—we don't have anything vaguely valuable, except maybe guns."

"I don't own any guns—just a minute." The Doctor covers the phone and talks with a police officer. His deep voice cracks when he speaks again. "The officers are wondering if it's possible the intruder *knew* I had no guns. Maybe it's someone we both know. Shall I send the police to your house?"

Thomas comes down the stairs, gun sheathed. He shrugs. "Nothing's missing."

"No, don't worry about it, Doctor. Everything looks okay here. Just call me tomorrow and we'll compare notes. Try to stay calm and decompress."

Yes, Tess Spencer, housewife, is giving medical instructions to a physician of forty-plus years. Beautiful turn of events.

When I put the phone down, Thomas asks, "Who was that?"

I explain the Doctor's close call with a masked gunman.

"You mean someone broke into both houses tonight? And someone *shot at* Doctor Cole?"

"Well, technically, they just *walked* into our house, Thomas. Not really a break-in."

"*Be serious,* Tess."

His tone shocks me into silence.

He continues. "Look. You know Doc Cole. Doc Cole knows the Grande Dame. It's a circle of danger."

I want to say, "As opposed to a circle of life?" but I manage to restrain myself.

Thomas' strong shoulder muscles bunch up, and he pulls me into him. I look up into his dark eyes, clouded with anger. He has a little stubble beard, like he forgot to shave this morning. "I used to think you could take care of yourself. But now...now that you're carrying our child, I'm not so sure."

I'm not so sure, either. Yes, I've had judo and self-defense and I know how to use a knife. But this perp has a gun.

Uninvited, a memory washes over me: the first night we were alone after my dad walked out. Me, huddled on my bed, wishing for a nightlight we couldn't afford. Mom, crying and gasping so hard I thought she'd choke and die.

Thomas tightens his hug. "I want to take care of you now," he murmurs into my hair.

31

I wasn't sleeping and Paul knew it. I abandoned my room when it grew dark, unwilling to share it with the ghosts. My mother seemed to have friends now.

Curled up on the couch, I'd watch the gold chair, wishing Cliff could comfort me. Why couldn't I see his ghost? Maybe he didn't approve of my idea to poison Paul? But he had encouraged me to stand up for myself.

I hated myself, because I'd started doubting whether Paul had actually killed Cliff. Yet nothing else made sense—Cliff was a good driver, and I doubted his heavy truck could've slid off the road without some kind of push.

Some nights, Paul sat in the living room, stoking the fire and smoking cigars. Just like a magnet to metal, he wouldn't leave me alone. He'd be possessive to the bitter end.

The way he watched me, so intently, I wondered if my malevolence was leaking out into my face. But my mother had always said I looked like an angel, with my cloud of light hair and fair skin. I practiced my innocent, helpless look in the bedroom mirror, so I could turn it on Paul at any time. I hoped it made him feel like the predator he was.

I wait until Thomas is snoring to check the house for missing items. I find only one—Miranda's photo album.

I don't know which of my fears was greater: that the footsteps were all in my head, or that the intruder was somehow connected with Miranda and the Doctor.

When I finally climb back into bed, chilled outside and in, Thomas shifts in his sleep and lays his hand on my leg. I love these little expressions of love, even when he's half-conscious. I still remember Roger's quiet words right before I walked up the aisle: "There's not a man alive that will love you more than Thomas."

I sleep late and wake to a cup of now-cold coffee Thomas left for me on the night-table. He also left the Glock in the chair next to our bed. I have no doubt it's loaded. He's always telling me not to pick up the gun unless I'm prepared to kill someone with it. I might have reached that point.

My cozy, broken-in slippers beckon, a respite from the cold wood floors. I could use a new pair, but who can afford it? I already feel bad that my in-laws have to pay my obstetrician bills. Every necessary purchase just makes the law school debt loom bigger.

I take the Glock and my coffee cup and pad downstairs. While the coffee heats in the microwave, I check my cell phone. I turned it off before bed, so the ringer wouldn't freak me out like it did last night when the intruder was creeping around, stealing the album.

I missed an 8:30 call from the Doctor this morning. He sounds unnerved in his message: "Hi, Tess. Sorry for calling so early. I wonder if you were able to sleep at all—I know I couldn't. I couldn't find anything missing, but we need to talk. Call me."

I hesitate. Wouldn't he be working today? I'll just leave a message.

I call, and after one ring, the Good Doctor answers.

We're very familiar with each other, calling on cell phones. I'm not sure how I feel about that. I can visualize him all too clearly in his nerdy glasses and gray arm-patch sweater.

His deep voice is soothing. "Did you sleep?"

"A little." I focus on my scuffed slippers.

"You got my message?"

"Sure did. I *did* find something missing, Doctor—uh, Bartholomew. Miranda's photo album."

"That confirms it. We need to talk, somewhere private."

My face flames. "Okay."

"Could you come over today? I don't know your schedule, but I took today off work."

I agree, and he gives me directions to one of the tonier sections of Putnam County.

While I'm showering, I wonder if I should tell Thomas where I'm going. I decide against it. Miranda might understand, but then I'd have to tell her about the break-in. Not an option until I'm sure her heart's back to normal.

I step on my porch to figure out the weather. Nikki Jo waves from her back yard, where she appears to be stringing lights from her red maple tree. I wave back, determined not to get into a discussion in which I would undoubtedly spill all my secrets.

Bucking against my need to look hoity-toity for the Doctor, I don my bomber jacket instead of my dressier peacoat. I slip the Glock into the pocket where it fits so neatly. Since I don't have a concealed-carry permit, things could get complicated if I get pulled over. I determine to drive carefully. Only a fool would go meet the Good Doctor unarmed, since it's still unclear if he's actually trustworthy.

Sure, he *says* he got shot at by some masked gunman. But I've read enough mysteries and watched enough police dramas to know that could be totally faked. In fact, he could have been the one sneaking around my house the same time he was allegedly attacked.

I ease the SUV out of the driveway, trying to make as little a spectacle of myself as possible. I wave again at Nikki Jo, who seems preoccupied with her project. Still, I know she sees all, which is comforting on some level. How did someone sneak into our house, anyway? They couldn't have pulled down the drive without Thor barking like a fiend and Dad, Mom, and Petey all peering out the windows. Maybe the intruder parked somewhere off the main road and walked down through the woods?

On my way to the Doctor's, I only get lost twice. As I pass a Dunkin' Donuts, I plot a victory stop for coffee when I retrace my steps out of this small town. At the Doctor's gated drive, I pull in slowly, marveling at his Italianate stone house with terracotta roof tiles. He couldn't have chosen a more atypical house to plop in the middle of West Virginia, land of Depression-era homes and trailer parks.

And how did an intruder get in here? He'd have to throw a rope over a tree branch and scale the metal fence. Curiouser and curiouser.

The Doctor stands on his white gravel drive, waving me forward. When I park, he walks over, opening my door.

He looks slightly rumpled. A couple pieces of his white hair stand out at odd angles—probably cowlicks like my own. His black turtleneck wasn't ironed. Other than that, he's handsomely intimidating as ever.

Walking past stone walls and marble urns, I feel like I've stepped into the Old Country. Impulsively, I ask the Good Doctor if he's Italian.

"Mostly boring English. But it's rumored my mother was partly Sicilian. That might explain why I'm drawn to opera and pasta. What nationality are you? Your coloring is so rare—the pale skin, blue eyes, and dark hair. Much like Miranda used to be, except her hair was a dark red."

I slow to a near crawl, hoping I'll lose him in the driveway.

He stops right alongside me. "If it's not too forward, I've noticed you never mention your parents. Yet you're from around here, if I'm not mistaken?"

"Boone County." That's all I want to say on that.

"Coal country." He smiles. I don't smile back. Yet he continues probing.

"I can't help but think you have so many similarities with my Rose. She was like a Botticelli, only so fully *alive*."

This strikes me as indecent, coming from an abortion-pushing murderer. I don't want to know just how lively Rose was. I push open the wide, carved front door. The dark wood flooring immediately captures my attention.

He motions to the rough-edged planks. "Reclaimed from a barn that used to sit here. Amazing what they can do with wood these days. Please, come into my den."

An all-too-clear flashback of our trapped bear flies into my mind. I shiver.

"Here, I'll turn on the fire." I absorb the room's details as the Doctor starts the gas fireplace. Leather chairs flank the fireside. Medical books are neatly stacked on dark bookshelves, and Murano glass vases add color to the space. I recognize some very convincing Modigliani prints on the textured walls. I've always loved his paintings of elongated women with their classically irregular features.

I feel the Doctor's eyes on me. "A stark change from Botticelli," I remark. "You value imperfections, then?"

The worn leather creaks as he sinks into his chair. Taking a pipe from a black lacquer box, he fills it, lights it slowly, and takes a long puff. "I do."

He gazes into the fire. Maybe that's all he wants to say about that. We're dancing around the key issue here, but the earthy smell of pipe smoke and the warmth of the fire lull me into a relaxed state I haven't felt in weeks. The Good Doctor puts people at ease—a handy talent for a doctor. For a moment, I even feel an urge to open up and tell him about my childhood.

Something holds me back. He can't sort out all my emotions. I have to do that myself. I wish I could talk with Thomas about the things that move me most, but I don't want to look like a blubbering fool.

I wonder if Rose was similar to me in this way, too?

32

Bulb catalogues arrived in the mail, cleverly scheduled to make housewives start salivating mid-winter. This year I pitched them into the trash. My future in West Virginia died with Cliff. It died when Bartholomew asked me to kill our child. It died the day I opened my mind to my mother's ghost.

Pregnancy was hard; harder than I'd ever guessed. Miranda came over often, sharing her prenatal advice and books with me. Many days, her words seemed to flow right past me. Miranda had always been strong—probably why Paul had found her attractive when they used to come for dinner. That indomitable strength he knew he couldn't crush—couldn't even get close to.

One time at dinner, we'd been discussing a local man who'd beaten his wife to death. Miranda had declared, "If any man laid one fist on me, he'd be a dead man next morning." No one doubted she meant it. How did she luck into a good man like Russell, when I had to cringe and bow to Paul?

Not much longer. The ghosts told me so. I wanted to tell Miranda about the ghosts. About Paul. About everything. But she would never understand.

My red plant book had gone missing for three days. Why would Paul take it? Now, when I went to my room and the ghosts were cackling "Poison," I felt they were trying to warn me. What if Paul knew of my plan? What if he tried to poison me first?

I had no backup plan, save the journal I would leave behind. I wrote in it furiously every day.

The Doctor and I sit in silence, content for the moment to watch the fire. My booming ringtone shatters our peace, bringing an amused smile to his face.

"Just a minute." I pull the phone from my purse, its eerie tones getting louder. "Hello?"

"Hey. Mom said you went out this morning? I thought you'd visited the Grande Dame yesterday. You in town?"

I can't lie to Thomas—can't even stretch the truth. "I'm at Doctor Cole's house, comparing notes on our break-ins."

Thomas seems surprisingly cool with this. "Hm. Where does he live? Over in Putnam county? Hurricane, is it?"

"No, he lives past Hurricane. Ask your mom if you want to know so bad. I'm sure she knows where he lives. I'm leaving soon, anyway. I want to make stuffed shells for dinner." Hopefully that mouth-watering tidbit of info will divert him from my sleuthing mission.

"Okay, talk to you tonight."

I hang up. The Doctor has started pacing in front of the fire. I clear my throat and he looks over.

"Sorry. I had a reason for asking you over, Tess."

"I know. We needed to talk about the creep who shot at you."

"Indirectly, yes. But I have something in my possession that at least a couple of people might want to get their hands on. I think it might help you. However, if I give it to you and the wrong person knows it, you'll be even more of a target. I don't think I can do that—you're pregnant. I already have one baby's blood on my hands—yes, I know that's how you think of me. It's how *I* think of me." He clenches his jaw. In a low mutter, he says, "The life of the child for the life of the mother."

Directly above the Doctor's angst-ridden head hangs a Modigliani painting of a sad, reddish-blonde haired woman. She represents Rose to him, no doubt. Her eyes are black, but instead of looking empty, they're filled with sorrow and a strange vulnerability. Yes, the Good Doctor appreciates imperfections. What was Rose's?

He walks to his bookshelf and pulls on a mildewed book on the top shelf. In an empty space in the shelf below, a drawer slides out.

No *way*. A secret drawer!

The Doctor takes out a yellow legal pad. As he hands it to me, I recognize the writing at once—same as Miranda's anonymous notes. Presumably this was Rose's.

He nods. "I see you know who this belonged to."

"How did you get it?"

"It was sitting right next to Rose's bed the night she died. I took it, hoping to find some clues as to why she committed suicide. I didn't want Paul getting it. I'm glad I followed my instincts that night. At this point, I think I've read it over a hundred times. I can guarantee Paul would have burned it."

I flip through the dry, crinkled pages. "You know I have to take this with me."

He adjusts his handsome-nerdy glasses. "I understand. You're putting everything together, trying to protect Miranda. I don't want her marrying Paul any more than the next person. This was Rose's journal, so you have to be careful, and you have to be covert. Don't let anyone know you have this—not even Miranda."

I don't make any hasty promises as I put on my bomber jacket and hide the notebook under it. I think the Good Doctor's just ready to get this thing off his hands, and he's astute enough to realize I won't stop until I get it into mine.

He walks me out to the car. I have the urge to hug him goodbye, maybe because he had such a close call. Instead, I remember a question I forgot to ask.

"What did the person look like? Your intruder? You got a look at him, didn't you?"

The Doctor nods. "One thing I know—it wasn't a *him*. It was a woman. She may have been dressed in black, wearing a mask, but I'm a doctor, for goodness' sakes. I'm not oblivious to anatomy." He smiles.

I keep reading innuendo into everything the Good Doctor says. Doubtless, I'm seeing something that isn't there. He's an older man, wrapped in the memory of his dead lover, and probably oblivious to his effect on females.

Still, he's so alone. We're both in some freakish stalker's

sights. I give him a quick hug. The spicy smell lingers in the fibers of his turtleneck. I'm surprised to feel muscles tighten in his arms as he wraps them around me.

What passes between us is indescribable. Comfort. Understanding. Some kind of shared, mutual hurt.

And yet he's still hiding something. It's there, beneath his unruffled exterior. It's behind the words of every sentence he utters. This journal was his cry for help.

Maybe I'm fighting for freedom here—freedom from the ghosts surrounding Rose's death.

33

I missed my last chance to get right with God. I didn't recognize it when I saw it. When was it? Maybe when I was walking in the woods, wrestling with the perfect, chaotic beauty of this state. Maybe when Cliff earnestly implored me to get back to church. Maybe when I realized I'd made the mistake of getting pregnant with the wrong man's baby.

Instead, I turned away from the living, hoping the empty dead would fill my heart. They rewarded me with nothing but shame. They laughed at my weakness, shouting unspeakable things about my illegitimate child.

I'd cast my lot with the devil. Yet somehow, I was certain he'd help me carry through with my plans.

As I pull away from the Good Doctor's house, a parked blue

car swerves onto the road behind me. Crazy driver.

I can't get home to read Rose's notebook soon enough. But first I have to make good on my plan to get Dunkin' Donuts. As I pull through, picking up a regular coffee with lots of cream and sugar, the blue car zips into a nearby parking spot. Odd—must be having a donut emergency. Still, no one gets out. The windows are tinted, so I can't tell who's in there. I thought that dark tint had been outlawed.

I sip at the hot coffee and slowly pull out. Sure enough, the blue car reverses and follows me.

My first instinct is to drive right back to the safety of the Doctor's gated home. But another part of me tells me I can lose this loser.

I drive below the speed limit, sipping along and watching. Sure enough, the blue car slows right behind me. Obviously, this person has had no training in basic stealth techniques; otherwise, they would have let at least one car get between us.

I continue at my leisurely pace, contemplating speeding up to 60 in the 45 mile-an-hour zone. That's the quickest way to get police attention. Then it hits me—police attention is the last thing I need, with a Glock sitting in my pocket and no concealed carry permit. Still, the thought of my forgotten gun comforts me no end. If the stalker drives up close enough, I have the option of pulling out my loaded metal friend.

I toy with my devoted, unidentified follower by turning into random locations: the library, the bank, and finally the gas station. Sure enough, I can't shake him or her. Probably *her*, given what the Doctor said.

What if my plan fails? What if she stays on my trail all the way into Buckneck? It's possible she already knows where I live—she could've been our house invader. But I can't bring some wacko back to Roger and Nikki Jo's safe haven. *Unless* I call Roger first and have him load up half the arsenal for our unsuspecting guest.

All this for a journal? It's the only thing I have worth anything, unless the stalker feels I'm a personal threat. Regardless of the reason, all my poking around into Rose's death has stirred up a hornet's nest. When I ran into a hidden hornet nest hanging in the tree this summer, I learned how mean hornets can be. One stung my head, then fell on my hand and stung that twice, for good measure. I felt vindicated when I found it buzzing in the grass and ground it into a pulp.

Once I get to Buckneck's Main Street, I pass the law office and think about calling Thomas. I can't really predict what he'd do, though, and I don't want to put him in harm's way. As the blue car edges closer, I decide to bite the bullet. I pull up right in front of the police station and lay on the horn.

It doesn't take long for a cop to emerge—a tall guy who looks vaguely familiar. Thomas hangs out with cops a lot, and it's entirely possible this guy knows him. I'm not above hiding behind my hubby's good name.

I lean out my window, hoping he won't ask me to get out. "Hi, I'm Tess Spencer. My husband Thomas works at the law office—do you know him?"

The burly, red-faced guy nods. "What can I do ya for, Mrs. S? You got a problem out here?"

"Yes, actually, I do. See that blue car parked there?" I point out my side window, then suck in my breath. Two seconds ago, the car was parked at the curb. Now it's gone.

The officer shields his eyes and squints. "I don't see a blue car, Mrs. S. Someone bugging you?"

"Someone trailed me all the way here from Putnam County! It was a little blue car with tinted windows—maybe a Kia?"

"D'you get the license number?"

I sigh. "Sorry, I didn't."

"Any reason somebody'd be following you?"

Uh-oh. Now we've gone to meddlin'. "None that I could say."

"Okay, Mrs. S. I can't do much. You wanna call your husband?"

"No, I won't bother him at work. I must've made a mistake."

He nods and walks back to the station. I stay parked for about five minutes, waiting to see if the car reappears. It doesn't. Guess I'll have to take my chances and go home. I'm getting hungry and I need to make good on my stuffed shell promise to Thomas.

Winding along the familiar one-lane road, I wonder if I should call Dad, just in case. There's no other car in sight, but that's no guarantee she's not behind me somewhere.

How long until I'll feel safe again? I kick myself for going to the Good Doctor's house. Hornet's nest. The minute I tell Dad about a stalker, he'll move Thomas and me into the big house quicker than we can say "Scat."

I want to celebrate our second Christmas in our own little cottage. I want to stop fearing for the safety of everyone who means anything to me.

There's one other option, and I take it. I call Thomas' cell.

His phone rings and rings. Right before it goes to voicemail, he picks up.

"Yes, what?"

"Sorry to bother you. Are you in the middle of something?" I tap the brake as I steer into one of our 180 degree-curves.

"As a matter of fact, yes, I am."

Woah. Rude. Suddenly, I feel so tired. "Okay. I'm just on my way home. Thought I'd let you know." Forget about telling him anything else.

"Okay, thanks for calling." He hangs up. On *me*.

I slow, swerving into the Spencer driveway. How dare he? Yes, I married a real gentlemanly prince. *Not.*

The familiar sight of Petey's red head at the big house does little to allay my fears. I don't want Thomas' kid brother anywhere near some gun-toting trespasser. I feel guilty for letting him dig those traps in the first place.

He runs off the porch to greet me. I roll down my window, letting in a gush of fresh air. "You've gotta see the lights in the back, Tess! Mom stuck up lots of the sparkly white ones. They look like stars."

"Okay, I'll check them out tonight. I need to get some lights up myself."

"Aw, don't worry about it. I think Mom's got enough up for all of us. You should see our tree this year! Mom said I can't tell you the theme." He snickers, like he got caught with his hand in the cookie jar.

Petey knows how to pique my interest. I shift the car back into drive. "Tell you what, I'm going to get something to eat, then I'll come up and look at it, okay?"

He grins. Thor tears around the side of the big house, barking at my car. A little slow on the draw, you teeny, completely pointless guard dog.

As I coast around the back of the house, I slow. There's already a car in my driveway. It's Thomas'.

34

One drab, rainy day, I'd tried and tried to light a fire in the outdoor wood-burner, but to no avail. Gusts of wind and spraying rain consistently snuffed out each match I lit. I was cursing at the devilish device when Claire Hogan rounded the side of my house, wearing sturdy brogans and a plastic rain cap. Immediately, I smiled in the most approachable, angelic way possible.

"Rose Campbell, ye don't have to try and fool me. I know the sound of a desperate woman when I hear one. Here, give me a try."

She took the matches from my wet hands. She proceeded to rearrange the pine cones and newspaper shreds, then finagled her body to block part of the wind blasts. In just a matter of seconds, she'd gotten the blaze roaring and clamped the metal door shut.

She dusted her hands on her corduroy pants. "There we go. Sometimes it just takes a little more experience, 'tis all."

I knew what she was saying in her own disguised way. She wanted to care for my child. And she was right—she did have more experience. Claire Hogan's kids had turned out better than any other kids in town. We both knew Paul would never allow me to have a baby that wasn't his.

A fire started in my head and tingled its way down to my toes. I had to fight the impulse to throw myself on Claire and choke her. How dare she be so bold? Surely I should keep my own child. Yet the ghosts' whispers echoed in my mind, tainting my love for the unborn baby.

I searched her face for reminders of Cliff. The resemblance was muted, but still there. A stronger, non-ghostly voice spoke into my fevered mind. "She's the one."

At that moment, I let go of the bond I felt with the child. The only way to save the baby was to save myself, and I had to focus on that. Claire Hogan would have to provide all the love I lacked.

I coast to a stop behind Thomas' car and run into the cottage. "Thomas?"

"Up here."

My stomach cramps as I walk up the stairs. I need some kind of snack—probably something light after all that coffee.

The scene in our room would make a pacifist weep. Thomas' twelve-gauge lies propped in the chair. He's wearing his wife-beater T-shirt, loading magazines for his dad's new

Socom 16 semi-automatic rifle. That magnificent, intimidating gun is currently deposited in the middle of our bed. Not once does he look up at me.

It's not hard to pinpoint the cause of his palpable anger. I lean against the dresser, hoping to quell the latest stomach clench. "You're worried because I went to the Doctor's house."

"You think so, Tess?" He jams the magazine into the magazine well.

"Hey, take it easy. Arming us to the teeth isn't the answer."

"You think not? I think it might do a world of good, when my dear wife won't stop meddling into something that's none of her problem in the first place."

When Thomas is really mad, he can't articulate properly. Quite often, I've used his cute quirk to defuse him. Not this time.

I turn around and walk out. I'm getting food before I discuss this.

The clicks and shucks continue in our room. I grab a granola bar and a yogurt and set water boiling in my teapot.

Sitting on the couch, I shout up to him. "You're going to get in trouble for taking off early all the time."

He doesn't answer. I switch on the TV. Then he shouts back.

"How can you watch TV? I had a call from my cop friend, Jimmy. Guess what he told me? My pretty wife laid on the horn today because *some lunatic followed her all the way from Putnam County*." He stomps down the stairs, his Sig Sauer exposed in its belt holster. "Please explain to me how you've been awarded all this undue interest?"

I retrieve the legal pad from the hall table where I dropped it, holding it like the Olympic torch. "This. Someone's looking for this. A dead woman's journal. Now tell me *why* someone would want a dead woman's journal bad enough to break into houses and follow a pregnant woman around. *Riddle me that.*"

He walks over to inspect it. "I take it you're still talking about Rose Campbell? Why can't you just let water flow under the bridge?"

I repress a grin, putting my hands on his shoulders and looking right into his stormy eyes. "I swear I would if I could. But Miranda's marrying Rose's husband. I can't let her ride off into the sunset with a murderer."

"*If* there was a murder. Anyway, this sounds like a job for Miranda's own daughter—does she live around here?"

Good thought. Maybe I should contact Charlotte. Thinking back over Miranda's wedding announcements, I don't remember addressing a single envelope to her daughter. Charlotte could give me some backup. "I think she lives in the panhandle somewhere."

"I want you to unhand yourself of this burden, Tess. You're extricating yourself from this. I want you to return that notebook to Doc Cole—promise me—or *I* will."

I sigh. He's dead-set on this, and maybe he's right. We're coming up on Christmas. I couldn't even shop in a public place if someone's following me.

He looks around. "By the way, where's the Glock?"

Blast. How can I distract him? If he finds out...

He peers into my face. His voice roughens. "*Tess.* I said, 'Where's the Glock?'"

Dip me in butter, I'm about to get toasted. If my lawyer honey finds out I've been packing heat with no permit, it could be grounds for divorce.

My bomber jacket lies on the arm of the couch. I sidle over that way, sitting down and patting the cushion next to me. He gives me a doubtful look, but joins me.

"Close your eyes." I use my most seductive voice.

He obliges. I slide the gun out of the pocket and into his hand. "Live and Let Die, my dear."

As his hand closes around it, the kettle whistles. "I have to make my tea. You want some?"

He follows me into the kitchen. "No, I don't. I want you to promise you'll get that journal back to the Doctor. Let him figure out what to do with it."

"Okay, tomorrow then. I'll have to figure out a place to meet him." That means I need more coffee so I can stay up all night reading it.

Mollified, Thomas smoothes my hair and kisses my head. "Thanks, beautiful. I enjoyed waiting for a surprise on the couch—too bad it was just the gun."

I smile as he goes upstairs, taking the steps two at a time. Poor boy, so easily distracted. I suspect men don't make the best detectives.

I pour the hot water and yell up to Thomas. "I'm going to run over and see your mom's tree."

He laughs. "It's the craziest one yet!"

As I crunch along the gravel, the rain starts—first a light mist, then heavier drops hit me square on the face. Serves me right. I've been running around like a chicken with my head cut off for weeks now. It's about time I *extricate* myself, as Thomas said, and start celebrating Christmas. Yes, that journal is out of here.

On Nikki Jo's front porch, Thor rushes over to greet me, barking every bit as furiously as his tail's wagging.

Petey cracks the door. "We can't let Thor in here. He knocked off two glass balls jumping around. Mom said he has to stay outside, then go straight to his crate at night."

"Where is your mom?"

"She's upstairs—just got back from the gym. She's starting her resolutions early. Hey, come on into the sitting room!"

The sitting room reminds me of the Conservatory in the Clue game—full of windows, plants, and linoleum flooring. But every year, Nikki Jo clears a spot for the tree right in the middle.

Petey pushes the French doors open and I stop short. Bowling-ball sized hot pink, turquoise, and green balls hang on the white limbs. Pink candy canes and *sock monkeys* festoon every level of the tree. Green monkeys dangle sideways. Yellow monkeys climb the branches. And on the tippy top—a fluorescent orange monkey with a green tie flexes his arms.

Petey watches me, waiting for a reaction.

I clasp my hands behind my back. "I...there just aren't words."

He makes a face, scrunching up the freckles on his nose. "I know, right? What was Mom thinking? She said it was some kinda deal at Belk. You should've seen Dad when he saw it!" In a more subdued tone, he adds, "I can't even bring my friends over till after Christmas."

Sock monkeys at Christmas. *Fluorescent* sock monkeys as tree-toppers. I chuckle, then chortle, then fall into a full-on, snorting fit of laughter. Petey starts laughing at me.

I wipe my eyes and straighten up, clamping my hand on

Petey's shoulder. "Petey, my boy, you cannot *ever* tell your momma I just did that. Because honestly, on some level, I think she's brilliant. Why shouldn't we get a kick out of Christmas?"

35

Paul was getting up early, making his own breakfast and bringing me food in bed. He probably thought I stayed in bed all day, since the laundry had piled up this last month of marriage. It was a mercy on my part—I was preparing Paul for life alone.

I still hadn't found my red poison book, which heightened my fears. Every time Paul set a food tray in front of me, I hesitated to eat it. I just gave him a smile and a peck and shooed him out. Then I dumped the food in the toilet, or waited until he was gone to throw it out in the woods. Who knows how many forest animals died from his poisoning attempts. I was fairly certain the poisoning motivated all his feigned kindness and concern. He wanted me dead as much as I wanted him dead. I wondered if he still thought I'd left him everything in my will.

The ghosts became a part of me. It seemed my mother had gone somewhere else, leaving me with ghosts of murdered wives. They shared stories of chokings and stabbings and even one particularly gruesome one about a beheading. I lost more and more sleep, as the ghosts were only too happy to supply me with images to back up their tales. They hadn't come to me for justice or for comfort. They came to torture me.

Some nights, I'd lie in a fetal position, clinging to my tiny stomach. I wanted to pray for my child, but I couldn't even pray for myself. I tried to remember the Bible verses I'd learned in Sunday school, but they'd been erased from my mind. When I opened the family Bible, the words were a jumble of symbols on the page. If only Cliff were still around, he'd steer me to the right verses and make sense of my life.

But Cliff would never come back. And I knew I could never join him.

Once I hug the freshly-showered Nikki Jo and rave a bit about her humorous tree, she invites me to a new women's Bible study starting up in January. It's called *The Weeping Prophet: The Life of Jeremiah.* Doesn't sound too cheery, but I promise to think about it.

I follow her into the kitchen, where she pulls out a red Fiestaware plate and starts cutting into some delicacy on her counter. "Now listen, sugar. I just whipped up this tiramisu Yule log last night and I want to know what you think. Take that on down to your cottage. By the way, is Thomas home early? I thought he wasn't off this week."

Love the casual lead-in to her real question.

"Yes, he came home early." How to explain this? Maybe it's time to let Nikki Jo and Roger in on some of the insanity. Especially since they already know about the traps, although they thought Petey was doing some kind of science project.

"Mom, we've been having a little problem. It has to do with Miranda." I take a deep breath. "Well, anyway, somebody's been stalking me. I've been checking into Rose Campbell's death, and someone doesn't like that too much."

Nikki Jo's hand flies to her chest. "Good *lands*, honey. Why didn't you tell us? You know your dad will do anything to protect you and the baby."

I take a moment, savoring the sound of "your dad." Roger *is* my dad now, and he wants to protect me, not run away from me. I send up a silent *thank-you* to God.

But some deep part of me doesn't want anyone else fighting my battles. Of course, Thomas would say this isn't even my battle; it's Miranda's, or even Charlotte's.

I finger the cedar boughs on the counter. "We'll let you know if we need help. I'm going to stop nosing around during Christmas break."

"Good, that's smart. Did I tell you Andrew's coming in for Christmas? It was last-minute. His fraternity was supposed to do a ski trip, but they canceled for some reason."

"Is he bringing Kelsey?"

She chuckles. "Oh, he's bringing his girlfriend, but it's not Kelsey."

"What? What was wrong with Kelsey? I thought she seemed sweet."

Nikki Jo gives me a long look. Apparently she wasn't as endeared to Kelsey as I was.

She pinches a bite off her half of the Yule log. The creamy swirled center makes my mouth water. "It's some Norwegian girl—Helga, I think. Can you imagine someone named *Helga?* Goodness only knows if she even speaks English."

I smile. "Mom, I'd better get this Yule log over to Thomas before he heads back to work."

"Okay, honey. You call us if you need *anything.*"

Once I take one step out the front door, Thor jumps all over my legs, leaving tiny pawprints on my dark jeans. Someday, I will get a real dog that will put you in your place, crazy squirt.

I walk slowly down the brick path, soaking in the trim beauty of Nikki Jo's back yard. Boxwoods have been pruned to perfection, despite Roger's crazy clipping at Thanksgiving. Dead butterfly bushes have been lopped off for next year's purple display. Next summer, I will make our yard look gorgeous. I'll plant some things our baby can enjoy.

When I was in fifth grade, I got a free packet of wildflower seeds at school. I remember running home, so excited to take my old metal shovel and dig up the dirt in front of our trailer. I scattered the seeds and watered them, just like the instructions said. But the trailer was tucked so tightly in the valley, the sun didn't even hit the front of it. Black mildew was the only thing that flourished in our yard. Every one of those seeds died. I'd promised myself to have flowers galore someday, and a house positioned so it could drink in the sunlight.

As the brick path trickles away, I stop at our driveway. I look over our little white house with its green metal roof. Our cottage faces north, so we get only the purest sunlight—the sunlight artists love to paint by. Yes, there's much to be thankful for today and every day. Our little one will come into the cozy Spencer world, wrapped in closeness and love and wonderful food.

Thomas' car is gone. I carry the Yule log in to our kitchen counter, cutting off a generous piece before I look around for the note. Thomas always leaves a note.

Sure enough, it's on the coffee table.

Hi Gorgeous,

Had to go back in—will work late tonight. Guns loaded on the bed upstairs. Don't forget the 12 gauge kicks, so lean into it if you use it. Stay up at my parents' if you want. Don't forget to call the Doctor and get that journal out of here tomorrow.

Love, Thomas

So. He didn't forget about Rose's journal.

I grab my cell phone and scroll down for the Good Doctor's number. I love the picture I loaded next to his name: the fifth Doctor Who.

The phone rings several times then turns me over to voice mail. I hadn't really planned a speech.

"Doctor, it's Tess. I have to get this uh…thing…out of my house. Like tomorrow. So let me know where I can drop it off. Thanks."

Pretty inept, but I've done my duty. Time to make coffee, curl up in our upstairs arsenal, and read over the journal. I wish Thomas would finally install a real lock on our front door. I might be armed to the teeth, but anyone could sneak up those stairs before I got a grip on a gun.

36

Miranda was getting nosier and nosier. Every time she came over, she wandered around the house, a perpetually-smiling Charlotte on her hip. She was searching for something, but what?

Finally, I broke down and asked her. "What are you looking for?"

She was nothing, if not completely transparent. "Well, I checked out a book from the library for you, and they want it back. Apparently it's been gone for months. It's a book on poisonous plants. I remember it had a red cover with a skull and crossbones on it. Have you seen it?"

I was able to be completely honest for a change. "I remember that one. I haven't seen it anywhere."

Miranda sat on the couch and bounced Charlotte on her knees like a personal trampoline. I had no idea where she found the energy. I'd been tired for months.

She looked closely at me, her eyes taking in everything, from *the circles under my eyes to my stomach, which seemed to be shrinking instead of growing. Her next question was abrupt. "You seen a doctor yet?"*

"Of course. Bartholomew's been over."

She continued prying. "When? When's the last time he checked you?"

I hadn't said he'd checked me. Just that he'd been over.

I shrugged.

Miranda hit the roof. "You're going to get yourself checked out. Are you embarrassed to have him do it? I'll find another doctor for you. But something isn't right. You need vitamins, or...I don't know what. You're looking as peaked as a dead possum."

She dragged a chuckle out of me. "Okay, Miranda. I'll let you find me another doctor in January, how's that?"

"Alrighty. But in the meantime, I'll bring you the rest of my vitamins so you can get started." She turned back to Charlotte, squinching up her eyes at her plump, healthy girl. "Can you believe you'll be a mother before Christmas next year?"

I swallowed to stave off tears. Yes, I was going to give birth before then, but I'd be no mother to this unfortunate child.

Creamer always makes my coffee cool too quickly. I take a sip of my lukewarm Amaretto-flavored brew before cautiously moving the guns to the floor. Before I get under my fake-down comforter, I arrange all the gun barrels so they're pointing at the bedroom door. Then I lay my Glock on the table next to me. Retrieving Rose's journal, I prop up on my pillows to read.

The first page, covered with quips written at random slanting angles, looks almost biblical. Each sentence talks about judgment on the wicked and oppression of the innocent. It's like Rose created her own handbook of verses. Strange, and not at all what I expected from someone involved in an adulterous relationship.

I skip over a handful of blank pages, then stop short at a roughly scrawled drawing of a skull and crossbones. Four familiar words line the bottom of the drawing: *MENE, MENE, TEKEL, UPHARSIN.* I replay Thomas' words: *"Weighed in the balances and found wanting, something like that. Yeah, I'm pretty sure that's it."*

Vindicated—it seems like Rose felt vindicated, having an affair on Paul. What did he do to deserve it?

I turn the page and squint. She's written in pencil here, and I have to read the first sentence three times to register what it says.

"December 2, 1973. I have a delicious secret. I'm hiding it from Paul, because he doesn't deserve to know it. The first time he hurt me, he ended our relationship. My mother understands this."

She's doodled several flowering plants on the pages before the next entry. From the realistic details on them—stamens and pistils and other plant names I've forgotten—she seems to have been talented at drawing.

"December 5, 1973. Miranda knows about B. She thought it

was C. Doesn't matter. I know what Paul did to C, and I know what he's trying to do to me. I think he must suspect something."

The phone jangles downstairs, making me jump. I should run down and answer it, but it's so comfy sitting on my bed, surrounded by a sea of guns. Straining my ears, I barely make out Nikki Jo's voice when the answering machine beeps. She's probably sending something over for supper again, bless her.

I dive back into the now-familiar handwriting.

"December 6, 1973. Paul has stolen my book. He's trying to poison me."

I re-read that last sentence. What? Paul was trying to poison his wife? For how long? Maybe this explains her affair? I read on.

"Every morning, he brings me breakfast in bed. I pretend to eat it, then dump it out. Mother's given me insight into his underhanded plans."

Why does Rose keep talking about her mother, when she never left her house? Did her mother live with them or nearby? Was she aware of the illegitimate pregnancy? I'll have to ask Miranda.

"December 8, 1973. B came over today. I can't believe I've tricked him—a doctor! I guess it's because I'm eating next to nothing. He'll help me get out of this marriage."

A deep voice carries into the house from the front doorway. I freeze, listening.

"Tess? It is I, Axel."

Nikki Jo must've been calling to tell me the flower truck was outside. I'm such an idiot—I should've picked up the phone. Even if I pretend I'm not home, he might barge right in. He acts like he's concerned about my welfare. But *what if* he knows the one sending me flowers? Or what if he's sending them himself for some warped reason?

"Tess?"

Even though I probably can't trust Axel as far as I can throw him, I go downstairs. Sometimes my inner voice might be muddled, but right now, it's saying, *"He's okay."*

Downstairs, Axel's peering into the fast-darkening living room. His blond hair looks phosphorescent in contrast to the twilight outside. He's holding some kind of wreath.

I step boldly into the room. "Yes? I'm here. What do you need, Axel?"

He smiles in my direction, but I don't think he sees me clearly yet. I hit the light switch and wait for his gasp.

I'm pointing the Glock right at him.

To my bewilderment, he acts like the gun is perfectly natural. He takes another step, holding up the greenery. "I have brought to you this wreath, since you are full with child."

I continue aiming at him. "Please put it next to the door."

He continues smiling—a psychopathic thing to do when a gun is aimed at your chest. Then he says, "Do not fear. All will be well."

With that, he deposits the wreath on the floor and walks out, firmly pulling the door to. He leaves behind him a heavy spruce scent and a growing conviction that my inner voice might just know what it's talking about.

37

Ghosts don't obey rules. They're awake all hours of the night. Between my weight loss and my sleep loss, I was a jittery mess. Sometimes I thought it would be better to eat Paul's poisoned food, taking the child and me out of our haunted house.

But Claire called faithfully, planning for the big day. Just like her son, she gave me hope. She was so excited, buying baby clothes and cleaning up her old wooden crib.

Bartholomew called, too. I peppered him with questions about poisoning, instead of the pregnancy questions I really wanted to ask, like: was it normal to feel nauseous all day? Was dizziness okay? How much weight did I need to gain?

To distract myself from the ever-hovering fiends, I read up on flowers. I wanted to choose a name for my child that would link it to me. The baby should know I would remember it forever, regardless of the fallout from my plans.

Sleeping on the couch proved difficult since it made me more accessible to Paul. I'd refused him for so long, I knew it was only a matter of time before he forced himself on me. Unfortunately, I was still his wife.

Sure enough, one chilly night he snuck downstairs. I felt the heavy quilt lighten as he moved it to the side. He stood in the dim light in nothing but his boxer shorts. "Rosey?" he whispered. His words were too quiet—he didn't expect a response.

I gave him one.

Sitting bolt upright, I dug my long fingernails into the exposed flesh on his thigh and dragged them straight down, like a cat. He yelped, then turned and fled up the stairs, shouting all the way. "Crazy! Woman, you're plumb crazy!"

Pure energy coursed through my veins, and my pulse pounded in my wrists. As the ghosts cackled at the sight of blood under my nails, I sank to the floor. I didn't deserve to live.

I hang the wreath on our front door as a talisman of Axel's good will. The frosted needles, interspersed with blue and silver twigs and baubles, give it a fairytale effect, like something out of *The Snow Queen*. Axel really is good at his job. I wonder if he trained in the US or Germany.

I chop up an onion and drain the beans I've soaked overnight before filling a pot with water and adding a little oil. Brown beans, wilted greens, and cornbread are my favorite comfort foods, and the only thing I feel like eating tonight.

Thomas opens the door, giving the wreath a cursory glance.

Circles shadow his eyes, and I feel horrible for ruining his day. He deposits three brand-new locks on the kitchen table.

"I'm installing these tonight. Where's my drill?"

No kiss. I point to the closet room. "In a plastic bin in there, I think."

The bean water finally starts bubbling, filling the cottage with its familiar heavy scent. The Good Doctor never returned my call. Maybe I'll have to take the journal to his office? Where is that, all the way over in Putnam County? I should probably read a little more tonight.

Thomas lays the drill on the table and winks at me. Has a man ever looked so ripped in a dress shirt? As he walks upstairs to change, I'm tempted to follow him. Instead, I mix up the cornbread and grease the cast iron pan.

When he comes down, looking more delicious than ever with his old *Pac-Man* T-shirt, I wave my spoon at him. "You're a handsome man, Thomas Spencer."

He manages a grin. "Thanks, babe. How was the rest of your day? Anything of note?"

"Nothing." I smile, trying to repress how I welcomed Axel with a gun.

The phone rings, and I hand the spoon off to Thomas. "Could you stir?"

Miranda's on the other end. "Hi, Tess. Just wondering if you could come over tomorrow for the Christmas dinner? It's in the dining room. You can dress up a little if you want."

I hadn't really planned on it, and I'm still reeling from the encounter with the blue car from Putnam County. A million excuses run through my mind as Miranda continues.

"My daughter's driving in tonight, so she'll be here. So will

Paul. I thought it'd be a good chance for you to get to chat with them before the wedding."

Ugh. *Charlotte.* I've heard so much about her, and none of it impresses me. *Charlotte* is a vegetarian. *Charlotte* loves to travel to Europe, since she's footloose and fancy-free with no husband or kids. *Charlotte* likes Jimmy Choos. I wonder if she'll wear them to the party. Still, I owe it to my friend to meet her daughter.

"Okay, what time does it start?"

Thomas has ditched the spoon, and stands poised by the front door, drill in hand. The minute I hang up the phone, he starts up a ferocious racket. I run over to the oven, checking my cornbread and stirring the beans lightly, hoping they aren't stuck to the bottom of the pot.

In between drills, he shouts over to me. "Royston isn't happy that I keep leaving work early. He's afraid when you have the baby I'll turn into some weakling who runs home to change diapers."

"Oh, what*ever*, Thomas. You work harder than he does, and he owns the place. Besides, I'll probably be a stay-at-home-mom, considering the fact I haven't been job-hunting for a couple months. Good grief."

He drills a couple times, then stops. "What's that? You said you're thinking about staying home?"

I hear the hope in his voice. He's always wanted me to stay home with our kids, just like his mom did. I've balked at the idea, until now—now that I'm some kind of target. Besides, it seems nice. Staying home, cooking, snuggling with your baby...I don't even have a proper rocking chair yet. We don't have any baby furniture yet! What kind of parents-to-be *are* we?

"Yes, you heard me right." I flip the cornbread pone onto a plate and slather it with butter.

Thomas runs around the corner, embracing me. "I've been praying about this! I just knew you'd come around!"

Not *exactly* the most romantic thing to say, but I'll take it. He's excited as a little boy opening Christmas presents. I peck his cheek. "What else have you been praying about, my man?"

"That's for me to know and you to find out." He darts back into the living room.

After supper, and after Thomas gets two locks on the door, he goes upstairs to unload some of his guns. I sit on the couch, resting my hands on my miniscule baby bump. Yes, little one, I'm going to stay home with you, even if it means we're poor for a while.

I think I kept one of my old baby blankets somewhere—maybe the closet room? I walk in, rummaging through the boxes. The box of Christmas ornaments still sits on the floor where I dropped it when our house was invaded. We need to find a tree, even if it's just a little Charlie Brown scrapper from the woods out back.

This room has nothing but bad memories. Faces in windows, hiding from intruders...I need to cheer this room up. I wonder if we could extend it out the back and make a play room.

I peer out the window at the oak. Such a big tree—I breathe a quick prayer it'll never fall, because it'd turn our cottage into splinters. The thick limbs sprawl every which direction. But there's something on the lower limb.

That something is a woman, a halo of long blonde hair

floating around her face. It's a face I'll not soon forget. Her slitted eyes focus on me, and her mouth hangs open at a weird angle. I must be seeing things. She can't be real.

I back away from the window. "Thomaaas!"

He rushes downstairs. "What? What is it?" The Sig's still sheathed in his holster.

My hand shakes as I point to the window. "Someone was sitting in our tree, staring at me. How could anyone get up there? Am I seeing things? Am I going crazy?"

38

Christmas is coming, the goose is getting fat…

Dame, get up and bake your pies…

God rest ye, merry gentlemen…

I finally dragged our flocked Christmas tree out of the attic. After straightening some of its oddly-bent branches, I draped multicolored lights and green garland around it. It wasn't an impressive display, but Paul and I would be the only ones to see it.

I decided to get creative with the decorations. I drew foxglove, hellebores, and belladonna, laughing as I used colored pencils to make them realistic. Then I cut them out, glued them to cardboard, and hung them on the tree.

When Paul got home that night, he walked in a slow circle around the tree, fingering the ornaments I'd made. I could tell he wanted to say something.

"Cat got your tongue?" I asked.

"Naw. You've got a real knack for drawin', Rosey. Maybe

you ought to draw pictures for catalogues or magazines or something. You know, advertising."

"And how would I get to work? You take our only car with you."

"I don't know. I reckon we could buy a new vehicle, if that's what you need. I been talking some with Miranda. She thinks you need to get out more."

And what other things has Miranda been telling my husband on me? Tattler.

"I haven't left this house in months. You know that, and you know why."

He walked over to me, his warm breath tickling my face. "That's just it. I don't know why. Used to be we'd go to parties, visit your family. We'd even go to church." He ran his hand through his thinning hair. "Only thing I can figure is that things changed when you—"

"Don't you dare mention it, Paul Owen Campbell."

I stalked over to the tree, ripping off each of my handmade ornaments. I had wanted to hurt him, figuring he'd recognize the flowers from my book he'd hidden. I didn't want to consider getting a job or take a walk down memory lane.

Christmas was coming and the goose was getting fat. Paul had no idea what was coming to him.

After a sleepless night, in which Thomas alternately peered out the window and checked the newly installed locks, I have to pinch him awake. He managed to miss three snoozes on the alarm clock.

I go downstairs while he's in the shower to brew some strong coffee for both of us. I need to get my act together to go to a Christmas dinner at The Haven, which I'm quite certain is an extravagant affair. Guess I'll be pulling out the red dress again.

Thomas looks wasted as he pads to the bottom of the stairs. His eyes are glassy and he gives some short coughs.

"You getting sick? You look like you have a fever."

He feels his forehead. "I don't know. I can't keep up this pace."

I feel reprimanded. "It's not my fault someone's after me, you know. I didn't plan for this to happen when I started helping Miranda."

"I know, I know. Are you getting that journal back to Doc Cole?"

He's lucid enough to remember that niggly detail.

"No, he hasn't called me yet. I could take it with me today—maybe I'll give it to Miranda. Wait, that's stupid. That would make her a target again."

"Maybe you should just burn the thing," Thomas suggests.

"I can't do that without asking the Doctor first."

Thomas grabs his favorite UVA coffee mug and fills it with some of my black brew. "Then give it to me."

All in all, I have to admit this is the best suggestion yet. We decide to make a public display of the journal handoff, in case we have an unseen audience.

As Thomas leaves, I slowly follow him, then hand him the legal pad through the open Volvo window. If he's willing to relieve some of my stalker stress, more power to him. I won't stop him from being my hero.

After my second cup of coffee, I attempt to curl my hair with the curling iron. Since only certain pieces are long enough to wrap around the barrel, it comes out resembling a bad perm. I rewash it before trying to spruce up my red dress with my big fake pearl earrings and bracelet.

The SUV is a great place for mulling things over. Today I ponder that waitress, Rosemary. There's just no logical way she can resemble Rose so perfectly unless she's a blood relation. An *immediate* blood relation. She's around the right age to be Rose's child, and her name is so similar to Rose's, it can't be a coincidence. The Doctor was convinced Rose had an abortion. Miranda was convinced she was pregnant. Is *this* what Miranda knows that's worth killing for?

Maybe Paul doesn't want a daughter getting in the way of his money—all that money he'll be getting when he marries the Grande Dame. Still, it doesn't make sense he'd switch Miranda's pills *before* they get married.

The Haven looms ahead of me too quickly. The front porch is awash in white lights: an exorbitant display reflecting the income level of its residents.

A caregiver greets me at the front door, ushering me into the long, rectangular dining room. Forest green damask tablecloths have replaced the usual paper placemats at the round tables. The lights are dimmed, and short glowing candles adorn each table centerpiece. Not a good idea for the residents with waning eyesight.

Miranda waves me over to her table. Her hair is done up higher than usual, and she's wearing her pearls and an elegant black cashmere sweater. Paul sits on her right, fiddling with the lemon in his water glass and looking uncomfortable in an outdated sport coat.

It takes me a minute to place the woman on Miranda's left as her daughter. Sure, she has the same chocolate-cherry hair color Miranda had when she was younger. But she's quite tan, not pale like Miranda. Instead of wide blue eyes, she has darker eyes that angle slightly upward, like a cat.

As I come closer, she stands to shake my hand. She must be a full four inches taller than me. It's interesting to extrapolate how Russell looked from the variations between mother and daughter.

"Tess! I've heard so much about you. You're a Godsend to my mother."

We both sit. As I tuck my feet under the tablecloth, I catch a glimpse of Charlotte's retro black pumps under her long skirt. They actually look like something I'd buy, and I doubt they're Jimmy Choos.

"Thanks. Thanks so much." I wish I could say the same about her. "Where do you live again?"

"I'm right outside Morgantown, so I'm across the state from you. I teach over at the college."

WVU. Did Miranda ever tell me that Charlotte's a professor?

"What do you teach?"

"Ceramics, actually." She smiles. "Are you from around here?"

That question again. Miranda jumps in. "Tess grew up in Boone. But she moved here after college—you would've been over in China then. Then she married that charming Thomas Spencer. You remember, Roger and Nikki Jo's boy?"

Charlotte smiles. "Oh my land, he was such a cutie as a kid! I remember him in church. Little tow-headed booger who liked to climb under the pews!"

I snort. So my sophisticated Thomas was a bit of a whippersnapper as a kiddo. I'll have to tease him later.

Miranda looks around impatiently. "When on earth are they going to serve us? I didn't have time for breakfast this morning."

Charlotte and I both jump to the rescue, waving down caregivers. Meanwhile, Paul maintains his silence on the other side of the candle.

Turns out, the food is going to be served buffet-style. The head honcho gives some kind of hand signal and the caregivers release the tables one at a time. Charlotte picks up her mother's plate, shooting a quick, disgruntled look at Paul. That look tells me everything I need to know.

We walk up to the buffet together, leaving Paul in the dust. I decide on a blunt approach. "So...what do you think of this marriage?"

Charlotte stops mid-scoop on her mashed potatoes. "He's okay, I guess. Not like my dad, though."

I put a slice of ham on my plate, surprised to see her deposit a piece on each of her plates. So much for the vegetarian lore. "How was your dad different?"

She shrugs and some of her perfume drifts my way. It smells like roses and citrus—probably Parisian. "My dad joked a lot. He was quiet, but fun." She jerks her head toward Paul, who's pulling up the rear about five people behind us. "*He's* just quiet. But I haven't gotten to know him yet."

Obviously she's the kind of woman who gives people the

benefit of the doubt. I prefer to assume bad stuff first; correct it later.

Charlotte takes a couple of yeast rolls and a handful of butter packets. She turns to me with a calculating look. Her unusual eyes remind me of the polished smoky topaz stone in my childhood rock collection. "Did Mom say you're looking into Rose Campbell's death?"

I nod. Why does she care?

Charlotte dips her head toward me, whispering. "Let me tell you something. I've never believed it was a suicide, either. Count me in on your quest."

39

One face repetitively visited me as I went to sleep. Dragging blonde locks, empty eyes, twisted smile—the misshapen ghost shared my own face. When I screamed at her, she'd disappear—just like I was going to.

I made it a point to write in my journal, ridding myself of all the thoughts I wanted to peel off like a discarded snakeskin. Paul was right—the miscarriage early in our marriage had changed me. We'd only been married for three weeks when I lost the baby, but I'd been pregnant for months. Paul had taken advantage of me when we were engaged. It was his fault I'd lost the baby, with his obsessive, hovering ways.

When I'd told Miranda about it later, she'd tried to comfort me with words about how the baby was in heaven. But the loss of the child had twisted something deep inside me. I wouldn't have strapped myself into our loveless marriage if I hadn't been carrying Paul's baby.

Then Bartholomew came along, giving me the one thing I

wanted most—another child that had no connection to Paul. I was determined to give this child the future my first baby had lost.

But I had to keep the ghosts at bay. For the past week, Paul had been asking specific questions. If he knew I was seeing ghosts, he might tell Miranda. And if she told Bartholomew, my whole plan could be thwarted.

I got to where I responded to Paul with nods or shakes of my head. The concerned look in his eyes should have been touching, but it made me hate him more. He should've been more concerned when he pushed me around as a girl. I was a woman now—a woman who would not be stopped.

Miranda, Paul, Charlotte, and I form a surprisingly jolly group. The other residents seem a quiet, stolid bunch compared to us. Miranda and I joke throughout the meal—about the tough ham, the governor's new gun regulations, even her lopsided artificial Christmas tree. Charlotte's laugh is rich, almost musical. Even Paul gives an occasional dry laugh, making a rasping sound like he hasn't done it in ages.

Somehow, we get around to discussing racial relations in West Virginia. Miranda straightens the napkin on her lap and leans closer. "I'm going to tell you something about the Klan. You know what? My momma and daddy were in the Klan way back when. They'd put the pillowcases over their heads and wear sheets. But it wasn't to get rid of colored people. No sir. Daddy had plenty of close colored friends. It was to put the fear of God into men who beat their wives. They'd burn crosses in their yards—a symbol that next time, they'd come and kill them. Once word got out a woman was getting beat, the Klan went to work. Too bad it went the other direction by the time I got bigger, otherwise I would've joined up. As it was, I must have heard of three or four wives who got beat to death, just in Mason County."

We all sit, speechless. The Ku Klux Klan used to be more about wife-beaters than racial prejudice? This was something I'd have to Google for sure. Was Miranda's memory slipping?

Paul clears his throat. "Remember that young gal got killed when we were young, Miranda? Left four children behind. Her husband got a thrashing over at the coal camp where I worked—beat within an inch of his life. Never married again."

A hard glint creeps into Paul's eye. I visualize Rose's slanted writing on the yellow paper: *"Paul's trying to poison me."* Who is this man who looks down on wife-beaters, yet tries to poison his own wife? I stare at him. His half-smile seems honest enough, like he's seen more than his share of sorrow. I can't get sucked into it. I need to get Miranda alone, so I can tell her about Rose's journal.

Miranda covers my hand with hers. "Tess, your daddy worked in the camp down in Boone County, didn't he?" Her memory must be slipping—she knows I don't like talking about Dad.

Paul jumps on this information. "What's his name?"

Great. Just great. My wounds are laid open for the whole table. Charlotte must notice my flaming cheeks. She jumps to my rescue.

"Good grief! My glass has been empty for half an hour! Do

we have to go into the kitchen for refills?" She loudly taps her glass with her fork, but no caregivers appear. Charlotte stands, her towering figure drawing every pair of eyes like a lightning rod.

She takes the handles of Miranda's chair. "Well, Mom, I guess the dinner's over. You ready to get back to your room?"

Miranda looks at me intently. I nod, trying not to be upset with her. "I'm just going to hit the Keurig in the hall, then I'll be down." More coffee is never a bad thing, and I need to be alone.

Charlotte raises her eyebrows. "Coffee? As in, caffeinated? While you're pregnant?"

I nod. "I don't hold much truck with some of that medical advice. It changes every other year, anyway."

Charlotte winks. "I gotcha. Enjoy the coffee."

As I walk out of the dining room, Paul follows me, a little too closely. *What* is his problem? I stop walking and face him, pulling him up short.

"Could I help you?" My hot cheeks continue to betray my muddled thoughts.

He wraps his long fingers around my arm, but I control my recoil and hold still. His dark eyes stay on mine. Is he waiting for me to flinch?

"Tess, I know almost everyone from those camps. What's your father's name?"

I pull away, walking the remaining steps to the Keurig machine. Rifling through K-cups, I act like I have all the time in the world. Finally, I push the button to brew a Raspberry Mocha. I shouldn't answer Paul, but some deep-seated Southern compunction forces me to speak when spoken to.

"His name's Jimmy Lilly. Most people call him Junior."

Paul's angular face softens. "Junior Lilly. I know him well."

I focus on the chipped white mug, waiting for him to continue. He doesn't.

"Well, I need to get back to Miranda," I say.

Paul steps closer. "Could we talk somewhere private?"

The knife in my pocket seems almost radioactive, I'm so aware of it. Yet Paul seems so intense, so driven to say something. I owe it to Miranda to listen to her fiancé.

I give in. "Okay. How about that couch in the hall?"

We walk down the long, dimly lit passageway. You'd think they could afford to replace the bulbs in here. The leather couch barely sinks under Paul, he's such a lightweight.

"Miranda told me you're interested in Rose's death?"

Miranda's been talking a lot lately. Did the overdose mess with her head?

I look deep into his eyes. I'm going to ice his nosy cake. "Yes, I sure am. I've been reading her journal."

His face reflects shock, not anger. "She had a journal?"

My mind races ahead, grasping for explanations. He's going to wonder where I got it, and I can't very well say from Doctor Cole. Maybe one little white lie...

"I found it in your library—recognized the handwriting."

He sighs, like he's Atlas holding the world on his shoulders. "What do you think about what you've read?"

I hedge. He doesn't need to know about Rose's pregnancy. "She was a very passionate person, it seems."

He leans forward, burying his face in his hands. I manage to make out his muffled, "She never loved me."

Well, aren't we candid today. Still crunched over, he talks

to the carpet.

"Our marriage was like a stale brownie—started crumbling apart the minute we got hitched. She had a miscarriage and it threw her, bad. She never let me get near her after that."

I focus on the tremor in his voice and hands. He's brittle—a glass man, ready to break into shards at the slightest bang. Unwanted compassion floods me. Only a woman could make a grown man this fragile; hurt him this deeply. My dislike for Rose grows as he continues.

"She had a book on poisons—I didn't know what she was going to do with it, so I hid it. Then she started seeing things, talking to people when she thought I wasn't around. I think they were haints, but she never came out and said it. She'd wake up screaming on the couch."

I carefully probe into the gaps, feeling like a psychologist. "So she didn't let you near her? How did you deal with that?"

He looks at me full-on, and I could swear there's no artifice in his answer. "I did think about other women—how could I not? I almost acted on it one day...I thought Rose was having an affair with a pastor. I'm ashamed to say I went to a bar, hoping to find someone. If she could enjoy her life, why couldn't I? But I didn't want a loose woman. I just wanted my wife. She was prettier than all those roses she grew." He drops his gaze, wringing his hands.

I sip the cold dregs of my coffee, taking in Paul's worn jacket, his scuffed shoes, and his mismatched socks. Could Miranda's strength heal him?

I stand. "I need to talk with Miranda. Thanks for sharing with me, Paul. You've helped me understand some things."

He stands alongside me. "Miss Tess, I know what your

daddy's like. You ain't nothing like him. God bless you." As he walks toward the front doors, my stomach flutters. I cover my baby with my hand, and I'm met with another flutter, like butterfly wings. The first kicks.

40

For the first time in a couple weeks, I pulled on my boots and gloves and walked into my woods. I soaked in every detail—the icicles blanketing the sides of rocks, the frozen ferns poking through the melting snow, the deer droppings near the iced-over creek.

I wanted to shout loud enough to fill the woods and sweep the ghosts away. Where was my angel now? I had none. God had abandoned me.

My feet seemed to move of their own accord, right along the creek bed, to where Cliff's truck hit the ground. I stared at the drag-marks where they'd pulled it out with a tow-rope. Paul had done this and more. He'd stolen my life from me.

I put my hand on my stomach, hoping for movement. I thought I'd felt something in the night, but it could have been hunger pangs. I wasn't eating enough, but I could never be sure if Paul had put poison on my favorite foods in the refrigerator. I'd forced myself to subsist on foods I knew Paul ate—things I hated, like olives and tuna. I felt nauseous almost all the time.

I closed my eyes, imagining the snow swirling up into solid walls around me, like when Moses parted the Red Sea. I wished it would swallow me and take me to another world, one where I had a healthy baby and no regrets.

Miranda's tastefully decorated suite brings back memories of her classy home in Buckneck. As I finger an antique Mrs. Claus on her tree, I remember the two Christmases I spent in her huge home in town. That next year, I got married, and Miranda had a stroke that landed her in a wheelchair.

I glance at Charlotte, who's stirring something in a wooden bowl in the kitchen. Why didn't she come home from China to sit with her mother that year, instead of shuttling her off to The Haven?

Miranda sits on her blue couch, looking at pictures of flowers in a wedding magazine. She holds up a picture of a bouquet of red and white roses. "Do you like this one?"

Roses? Not so much. I remember the ivy on her invitations. "Maybe more greenery? And a different type of flower?"

She groans. "I don't know what I'm doing."

Does she mean planning her wedding or getting married in the first place?

Charlotte comes in, dusting flour off her apron. "I told you, I like those white mums, Mom. They're more like you somehow." She motions to me. "Would you mind helping me roll out my dough? This counter is miserably small."

I nod, pecking Miranda's head first. "It'll be beautiful, whatever you decide."

Charlotte stands by the sink, pounding at the dough with all her strength. This could qualify as a gym workout for her. "Honestly, I'm not at the rolling stage yet, but I wanted to talk with you. What are your theories? Mom showed me her note. Who would do that?"

Should I take her into my confidence? My face must give away my conflicting thoughts, as she rushes in to fill the silence.

"Oh, I don't blame you for keeping things to yourself. It's just…she's my mother. I worry about her."

"You do? I wouldn't know it." My bluntness startles me. Where did my manners go?

Charlotte stops mid-punch, setting the bowl on the counter. "I'm so sorry you think that."

She doesn't explain herself, like I would. She just stands her ground, sticky dough on her knuckles, waiting for me to say something.

I put my hands on my hips and oblige her. "You were in China when Miranda had her stroke, right? How hard would it have been to come home and take care of her, do you think?"

"Well, as a matter of fact, it would've been pretty hard. The colleague I was traveling with had a miscarriage over there. I had to stay with her in the hospital and make sure she was okay. I knew Mom needed someone to take care of her immediately, so I looked up all the assisted living homes in the area, and this one had the best reviews." She pushes a strand of dark hair behind her ears. "Besides, I knew you didn't live far away. She loves you like another daughter."

I'm speechless. Charlotte dusts more flour into the dough, punching it into a fluffy round lump. She's so self-contained, it's intimidating. Was Miranda like her as a young woman?

Pulling out drawers, I find a green rick-rack trimmed apron and tie it around my waist. I wash and dry the counter, then lightly flour it. "What are you making?"

"Cinnamon rolls—Mom's favorite," she answers, smiling.

"Count me in."

As we work on rolls together, I tell her everything. By the time we've put two pans into the oven, Charlotte's come to the same conclusions I have.

"Can you get the journal to me?" she says. "No one would think I'd have it."

I untie my apron. "I don't see why not. Are you staying here?"

"No, I'm in Mom's old house. She never sold it. I'm trying to clean it up—had some mice."

Back in the living room, Miranda's fallen asleep on the couch. "She's so tired now," Charlotte whispers. We prop up her feet and cover them with a blanket.

I make my vanilla butter cream frosting for the cooled cinnamon rolls. Charlotte covers a pan with tin-foil for me to take home. As I put on my jacket, I promise to drop off the journal tomorrow.

Outside, the fast-melting snow soaks the thin, fake leather of my boots. Most of the dinner guests have already gone. Realization hits me—God's answered a prayer I hadn't even voiced. I needed someone who understands my urge to protect Miranda, to get to the bottom of Rose's death before the New

Year's Day marriage. God answered it with the most unlikely of people—the citified girl I'd despised for no real reason. Turns out, Charlotte isn't a vegetarian and she doesn't wear Jimmy Choos to Christmas dinners. But she's *tres formidable*, just like her mother. And she's an ally I can trust, unlike the Good Doctor or Paul.

The SUV skids a little in the slush as I head out the drive. When I adjust my rearview mirror, something catches my eye—a dark-windowed black truck parked flush against a storage building. It's conveniently tucked behind a bigger red truck. I shift into reverse, rolling backward until I come up next to it. Peering at the windshield, I can't see anything. In a complete stroke of déjà-vu, the truck's engine revs. I pull the SUV directly in front of its large chrome grill and open my door, determined to thwart a repeated escape attempt.

The driver gets out, too. "Lady, you're crazy! Can't you see I'm trying to pull out?"

I walk toward the familiar strawberry blonde. "I can see just fine, Rosemary Hogan. But I can't let you go anywhere until you answer my questions."

41

I called Miranda in the middle of the night. Russell, ever the gentleman, answered the phone before handing it to her.

I only managed to say, "I need you to come over right now." She hung up. I prayed God would bring her to me quickly. Paul wasn't even home yet from work—or drinking, I wasn't ever sure which.

The bleeding had started early in the evening. I couldn't figure out what to do to stop it. Finally, I lay on the couch, stretching the phone cord taut so I could reach it without moving around.

I should have called Claire, but couldn't risk arousing Paul's suspicions. If he came home, I could easily explain Miranda's presence.

Around one-thirty, Miranda rushed in the door, which I'd neglected to lock. She must've been freezing in her thin gown and housecoat.

"Is it the baby?" She ran over to me, kneeling by the couch.

I nodded.

She touched my stomach lightly and I yelped. "Rose, we have to call Bartholomew. Something isn't right."

"He can't know...he can't know." Lights flashed on the edges of my vision.

"Is there blood?"

I nodded again.

"Lots of it?"

I shook my head.

She sighed. "Good. That's good, I think. Has it slowed down?"

"I don't know."

By the time Paul clomped in the front door at three, Miranda had me cleaned up and tucked snug in my bed. The bleeding had stopped, but I saw the haggard ghost's face peering at me from my closet.

"Will you stay?" I grabbed her hand, holding on for dear life. When she was nearby, the ghosts hid.

"Of course." She snuggled on the bed next to me, wrapping my extra quilt around herself. "Let's pray."

Her words flowed over me, touching the God I'd felt isolated from for years. My heart joined her as she pled for the health of the baby. For one night, I fell asleep with no hateful faces and words tormenting me. For one night, I forgot my hate and my fear. Surely heaven was hemmed tight with friendship.

Rosemary leans against her truck, one pale hand on her curvy hip. It's possible her navy caregiver shirt is a full size too small. No wonder Anthony was impressed with her hotness.

I point at her. "You're following me around."

She sighs. "Mind if I smoke?"

"Yes, I do, actually. Keep your hands where I can see them."

She salutes me. "Yes, ma'am. What's the bee in your bonnet?"

"For starters, I'm very interested to know why a waitress from Point Pleasant would suddenly start lurking around an assisted living home in Buckneck."

She purses her lips. "Okay. I'm going to lay the cards on the table—I have nothing to hide. I was adopted, okay? I've always wondered who my parents were. Then I had these customers from Buckneck who were always saying I'm the spitting image of a dead woman over here. I decided to look into things."

My wet toes are frozen. "By 'look into things,' what do you mean exactly?"

"I knew her best friend lived in The Haven, so I volunteered here, hoping to find out more."

"And that's it."

She smiles. "I didn't say that."

Don't smile yet, girlie. "You were outside in my woods, weren't you? You came into my cottage that night!"

The Haven's heavy front doors close and someone moves toward us. I glance over to see Charlotte plowing through the slush in her heels.

"Tess, what's going on? I saw you out the window!"

Rosemary turns to face her. As she gets closer, Charlotte gasps.

"Why do I always have that effect?" Rosemary laughs.

"Has my mother seen you?" Charlotte grabs my arm to stop her own forward motion, eyes fixed on our intrepid waitress.

"Who, Miranda? Of course not—I'm not a total idiot. I don't want to give her a heart attack. I stay out of the way, washing sheets and mostly working in the basement."

"What about Doctor Cole?" I ask.

"I don't think I've met him. But why does it matter?" Rosemary kicks at the slush. Cold muddy water splats my good red dress.

"Hey, knock it off!" Charlotte steps in front of me.

"Try and stop me." In one surprisingly fluid movement, Rosemary jumps in her truck, starts it, and backs up. Charlotte pushes me out of the way as Rosemary tears out to the side, scraping the red truck as she goes by.

We lean against my SUV for a few minutes. Charlotte brings an abrupt end to our breathless silence. "She can't get anywhere near Mom."

"Agreed."

"She's stinking crazy." Charlotte examines her mud-splattered skirt, then my dress. "Hope our outfits aren't wrecked. You were right; she's a dead ringer for Rose. Her daughter, you think?"

"Has to be. There's no other explanation. She must be in her late thirties, maybe forties?"

Charlotte grins. "Do I look that good? I'm forty."

"You look better. She only *thinks* she looks that good."

She laughs. "You go home, pregnant momma, and get some sleep. I'll take that journal off your hands tomorrow."

I sigh. I'd forgotten the journal. Hopefully Rosemary will

keep her curious self in Point Pleasant tonight. I'd hate for her to get shot creeping around the Spencer property, but she must realize that trespassing around people's homes isn't a formula for safety.

On the way home, in the cocoon of my SUV, I feel some measure of closure. Rosemary's my stalker. She was the one in my woods and in my house. Did she follow me from the Good Doctor's house in the blue car, too? There's no telling what she's done. I guess she's figured out that she's Rose's daughter, and if she's figured that out, the next part is self-evident.

Rose didn't die on New Year's Eve, 1973.

42

Like Thanksgiving, Christmas meant nothing to me. Bartholomew stopped in, bringing me a bright Hopi scarf from Sedona. I smiled, and he gave me a hug, assuming he'd pleased me. In reality, I was thinking I'd wrap our baby in it.

Still, his gray eyes were shadowed as I answered his questions. I felt I was saying something wrong, but I had no idea what. Why couldn't people stop interrogating me—Paul, Bartholomew, even Miranda?

I decided to ask my own questions.

"Is everything lined up?"

Bartholomew nodded, stroking my cheek with his hand. "You know how much I love you, right?" He pulled me into his chest. I felt his silent sobs.

"Of course I know. What's wrong?"

He held me, still shaking. "I'm worried."

"About what? Paul? He won't be a problem, once they get their hands on my journal."

"No, Rose. I'm worried about you. You'll be on your own for a while."

That was the whole point. The only way to still the ghosts was to leave West Virginia—to leave myself.

I draped the scarf around my shoulders, whirling. "I'm more resilient than you think, Bartholomew. Trust me."

Roger is burning brush behind his house when I drive up to our cottage. He walks over and opens the car door for me, wrapping me in a big hug.

"How've you been doing? Haven't seen much of you lately."

"I was visiting Miranda today. Her daughter's in from Morgantown."

"Isn't that nice? Good when family comes in. Speaking of family, Nikki Jo's flurrying around again for Andrew's visit. But I know she was looking for a Christmas shopping buddy…"

He gives me a mischievous grin. I read between the lines.

"I'll give her a call," I say.

Roger beams at me, which makes my day. "Thanks, Tess. I can't handle malls anymore. Sudden moves just put me back in Iraq."

Roger, a retired National Guardsman, had been called into the War on Terror way back in 2002.

"No problem. Thanks for burning our brush."

He pats my back and returns to his work. I can't believe he

didn't ask about my mud-splattered dress. I think men really do have one-track minds.

I muck through the slush, griping all the way. "Stupid mud. Not a drop of sunlight. It'll probably snow tomorrow."

Petey emerges from the woods behind our cottage, the ever-faithful Thor right behind him.

"What are you up to?" I ask.

He adjusts his lopsided wool cap. "I heard some weird woman was in your tree out back."

Where does he hear this stuff? Thomas?

"Don't worry about it, Petey. I think it was just my imagination."

He spits in the snow. "Not like *you* to imagine stuff. Anyways, just checking it out."

Thor careens into me, jumping up for a pat on the head. I oblige. Why not add his muddy paw prints to the mud on my dress? If we're going for utter ruination of the thing, let's just dive in headfirst.

"Get down, Thor!" Petey bops the little dog out of the way. "Sorry. I see you're all dressed up. I'll get him outta here." He picks up the wiggling dog, holding him tight. "How you feeling, Tess?"

I won't dump all my woes on my young brother-in-law. "Doing okay."

He grins. "Come over sometime to play Xbox, okay? You need some practice."

I tweak his ear. "Keep dreaming, bud. I'll still thump you soundly."

I wave and head into the cottage, suddenly ready to sink into the couch. No one told me pregnancy could make you this tired. But then again, I haven't had time to read many pregnancy books.

I have a baby growing inside me. That's the strangest thing, when you come to think of it. A little person, relying on me for nutrients and care. And the reliance only gets stronger once the baby is born.

Did Rose have a good pregnancy? Apparently it came to fruition, since Rosemary's walking around. Rose must have faked her suicide. How do you *do* that? Bartholomew has to be lying. Did Paul also know she wasn't dead? Or Miranda? Surely Miranda hasn't been lying to me.

Their whole era seems tainted now. It's an odd world where the younger generations seem more trustworthy than the older ones.

Rosemary *Hogan*. I've heard that last name somewhere. I flip through conversations stored up in my head and finally latch onto Nikki Jo's voice saying, *"I hear the Methodist church is doing a joint service with that little independent church—you know, Miranda, the one Cliff Hogan pastored way back when?"*

Pastor Cliff—Cliff *Hogan*. But Rose wasn't having an affair with him. And he must've been dead before Rose, since Miranda took her to his funeral. Rosemary said she was adopted.

A string of words tumbles into my mind. *"Oh what a tangled web we weave..."*

Someone has laid an elaborate plan, one I'm only beginning to unweave. Each strand of the web leads back to something—something that's been covered up for forty years.

I have less than two weeks to figure this out and stop

Miranda's marriage, if need be. But the web is tightening around me.

This summer, I watched a particularly voracious spider killing bugs on our porch. Once, it caught a bee. Though the bee buzzed its wings for all it was worth, it couldn't get out. It tried desperately to sting the spider. The next day, I checked to see who won. The bee was dead in the web.

Only one way to get out of a web like that, with a spider that dangerous. You have to cut the web.

I call Axel's shop and leave a message with the girl. Snip one.

Next, I call Nikki Jo. All this time, I've had a wealth of reliable information sitting right next door. Snip two.

By the time Thomas comes home, pizza and wings in hand, I'm ready to give him my undivided attention. I'm no longer merely a well-armed victim. I'm going to hunt down the spider.

43

New Year's Eve, 1973. What better day to leave my oppressive life behind? I'd beat Paul to the punch. He was waiting for me to keel over from his poison—now I'd give him the pleasure of watching me die.

All day, I worked to get everything in place. I touched my kitchen towel for the last time, cleaned the bathroom for the last time. Only when I walked into my garden did I hesitate. As I took off my ring and arranged my special stones to hide it, I hoped someone would discover it someday and understand the message. I'd weighed Paul and found him wanting. So I was leaving him forever.

And I was happy to frame him with my death. Sure, there would be the evidence of poisoned food in the fridge. But I needed to leave more behind: thus the rock message, wedding ring, and my journal. Still, I had just one more bit of information that I needed to drop first.

Miranda came over halfway through the day. I gave her

some gingerbread—the last batch I'd ever make. Charlotte climbed over my chairs and couches with abandon, and Miranda barely noticed. "Girl's a regular monkey," she said.

I wanted to feel that kind of enthusiasm again. I wanted freedom from the vows that had wrecked my life.

I sat in the gold chair, wishing for Cliff's presence. I felt fake, even to myself. And I knew the truth.

Miranda's wide blue eyes fixed on me. "How's the baby? Any more spotting?"

"None." I shifted in the chair, uncomfortable broaching the topic. "I know how you feel about men who beat their wives. I don't know how to say this, Miranda. Since we met, I've been hiding something from you. Paul hits me."

Her face went crimson. "He what?!!"

I nodded.

"While you're pregnant, too?"

"No, not lately. I...I just thought you should know."

She rubbed her forehead. "Why are you telling me now?"

"It's just...if anything happens to me, you know."

"No, I don't know. What's going to happen to you? Do we need to get you out of here?"

I slouched in the chair, trying to hide from the ghost that hovered on the stairs, a look of riotous glee in its black eyes.

"No, I'm okay. Bartholomew knows too. Even Cliff knew."

"But you didn't tell me? Your best friend?"

"I couldn't. I knew you'd have Russell kill him or something. I know how you hate wife-beaters."

She sighed. "Yes, I do. My great-granny, God rest her, got beat to death by her no-good drunk of a second husband." Her gaze sharpened. "So what does he do to you?"

I knew this question would come, and I was ready for it.

"Just little things that bruise me. He's never punched me, but I always worry about it. Especially when he drinks his moonshine."

Her eyes widened. "He has moonshine? You have to get rid of that."

"Then he'd hit me."

"Oh, right." She bit her fingernails. I knew she'd look for a solution—it was her nature. She didn't talk through problems; she looked for ways to solve them. "Okay. I'll talk with Russell and get back to you next week. We'll figure something out."

I gave a half-smile, more to the ghosts than to her. "Thanks, Miranda."

Thomas finally consented to leave the journal at home so I could pass it off to Charlotte today. The minute he walks out the door, I start skimming it, hopeful for a clue I've missed.

Instead of reading each entry, I focus on the flower doodles. If I look closely enough, each flower resembles a face—a face with warped features. In fact, they look downright evil. Why was the lovely Rose scrawling demented flowers?

My phone rings and the Fabled Flowers number pops up. I grab it.

"Hello?"

"Ja, Tess. You asked something of me. I traced the Arizona card back to Marilyn Davis. Do you know this woman?"

"No, I don't, but I'll look her up. Thank you, Axel."

He doesn't speak.

"Axel?"

"Ja, I was just thinking that perhaps you need my help?"

I smile. "No, I'm okay, thanks."

Another pause. I ask, "You still there?"

"Ja. I must return to Deutschland soon. More training for the flowers."

"You're going all the way to Germany for that? I mean, you're so good at it, why do you need more training?"

"It is hard for me. Your West Virginia mountains and forests are like a small Schwarzwald—Black Forest. But also I have family, and there is sickness at home."

"Oh, I'm so sorry. You've truly helped me so much. Thank you. *Vielen Dank.*"

"We will meet again, Tess Spencer. Come to the flower shop to find me someday."

After our bittersweet goodbyes, I sit and ponder why Axel came back into my life at the exact time I needed his help. I never got to ask him why he moved to West Virginia. And yet...I feel oddly certain I will see him again at some point.

Finally, I pull out a notebook and write *Marilyn Davis* in large letters at the top.

Nikki Jo gave me a name, too. I write it at the top of the next page: *Claire Hogan.* Cliff's mother. She moved out of Buckneck, but one of Nikki Jo's church friends knew her unlisted number. If Cliff faked his death, surely his own mother would know. And she must know something about Rosemary.

I dig my favorite trouser jeans out of the bottom of my drawer. The top button doesn't close anymore. "Getting big, are you?" I pat my stomach and receive a small flutter in reply.

I can't wait to see this baby on the ultrasound. Thomas doesn't want to find out if it's a boy or girl, but I do. I want to know everything about our child.

I drive into Buckneck, parking next to the curb in front of Miranda's three-story, light green house. Charlotte comes out onto the porch barefoot, waving at me.

"Get in that house! You're going to freeze out here!" I climb the steps and rush her inside.

She laughs. "Thanks for your concern, Momma Hen, but it's probably forty degrees outside. I dated an Iditarod racer—lived in Alaska one summer. This doesn't *begin* to be cold."

"Oh, excuse me. Whatever, girl." I look around the familiar living room. It's dusty and most of the knick-knacks are gone, but it's retained its homey feel.

Charlotte follows my gaze, misinterpreting it. "I know—it's a wreck. I'm cleaning everything with Pine-Sol. You can imagine how long that takes in a house this size." She walks me into the kitchen, where the smell of freshly brewed coffee and cinnamon rolls greets me. She pours the coffee and heats a roll for each of us.

We sit at the round table where I had so many heart-to-heart conversations with Miranda. "So, what are we up against?" she asks.

I toy with my silver hoop earring. "I think we need to talk with your mom first."

"You think she knows something important?" Charlotte takes an oversized bite, then a big gulp of coffee. For a city girl, she's astonishingly uninhibited.

"I know she does. She just doesn't know what's important. I have to figure out the right question to stumble onto the right answer."

Charlotte giggles. "I feel like George—you know, Nancy Drew's tall friend? And you're Nancy. We need to find a Bess."

I wish I shared Charlotte's excitement. But I'm married, almost in my second trimester, and sick of getting stalked. She just signed up for this gig.

"I can read your face," she says. "I know this is dangerous. Listen, it means so much to me that you care about Mom like I do. We'll wrap this up before she marries Paul—or doesn't marry him."

I pull Rose's journal out of my quilted bag. "Read over this and see if you can make more sense of it than I did. My takeaway was that Paul hit Rose and that Rose was obsessed with poisonous flowers."

"Paul beat Rose? But he talked like he was part of the coal camp chain gang that took out wife-beaters."

"I know. Nothing fits."

"Let's ask Mom."

44

After Miranda left, I called Paul's supervisor at the coal camp and left a message that I felt lightheaded. I hoped it'd be enough to bring him home earlier. He didn't leave then, but he did get home around six that night—definitely earlier than usual.

A strange nostalgia swept over me as Paul pulled off his dirty boots, walking across my floor in his work-blackened pants. He knelt by the gold chair where I sat in my favorite rosebud-cotton gown.

I offered him my hand. "I'm feeling some better, but I'm still a little lightheaded. Could you bring me something hot to drink?"

Paul stared. He wasn't used to my touch, much less a direct request from me. And I knew this request left the door wide open to poison me.

"Sure—sure thing, Rosey."

As he walked into the kitchen, I hoped he felt the full weight of his murderous thoughts. He'd be alone for life, but he'd chosen that. He didn't deserve happiness any more than I did.

Bartholomew was on his way over. I'd called him the moment I saw Paul's car. He had a trumped-up excuse ready. In reality, he had to arrive before Paul started examining me.

Smiling like a cat staring at an open fish tank, Paul came back, holding the full mug in front of him. I wished I could stand and punch his face. Instead, I smiled back as he handed me the swirling, bubbly cocoa. I touched the liquid, dropping the pills in as I blew on it. What goes around comes back around, Paul Campbell. You reap what you sow. I took one gulp, then another.

The effect wasn't immediate, but quick enough for Paul to see it. My hips and legs lost their strength. The room was too hot, so I let go of the mug, its spilled contents warming my lap. When the stringy-haired blonde ghost shot toward me from the stairway, yawning black eyes ready to swallow me whole, I knew I'd succeeded.

The temperature's dropped by the time we get to The Haven. I pull my bomber jacket tighter, then fixate on Charlotte's light hoodie. "What is it with you and underdressing, Iditarod Groupie?"

I really hope Rosemary's not here today. I wouldn't mind talking with her again, asking more questions, but today we need to focus on Miranda. Maybe if we let her see the journal, it'll float some important detail to the surface.

We knock on her door, and the Good Doctor opens it. My thoughts scatter, then realign with proper Southern manners.

"Doctor Cole. Nice to see you. This is Charlotte, Miranda's daughter."

Charlotte reaches out to shake his hand. As her warm, flashing eyes meet his calm, sea-gray gaze, the words *Fire and Water* spring to mind. I hadn't thought of it before, but the Good Doctor is very much like water, fitting in wherever he needs to. Ever-present, but never obtrusive. Calming, comforting, yet inescapable. My arms get goose-bumps. No matter how earnest and open he seems, Bartholomew is far from transparent.

He leans over to me, spicy scent once again disarming my negative thoughts. That stuff is like Kryptonite. "How's it going?" he whispers.

I lean into the doorframe for support. "I'm hanging in there."

"Good. I'll be home today if you need anything."

He walks down the hall, his long, tailored black coat swirling around him like a cape. Charlotte stands motionless in the doorway. When he turns the corner, she says, "*If* you need anything? What's that all about?"

"Nothing...*seriously*, nothing."

She huffs. "Okay. He's fair game, right? I like older men."

"I think he's taken—by a dead woman. Or at least she used to be dead. And he's in his sixties, just like your Mom."

Charlotte flips her glossy hair over her shoulder and winks. "Like I said, I like *older* men."

We open the door to find Miranda sitting near her dining table, looking out the window. Charlotte rushes to her side.

"Mom?"

Miranda turns, extending her arms to us. "Girls! So good to see you two are friends." We hug her.

I pull out the journal, feeling a little guilty, since Bartholomew told me not to let anyone see it, especially Miranda. But the greater good is to show it to her so she's warned about Paul. "We have something for you to look at. If it's too hard, you don't have to read it."

She nods, sliding her oversized bifocals down her nose and reaching for the notebook. "Another note?"

"No. Same writing, though. It's Rose's journal."

Miranda drops her hands and gets quiet. "I don't know if I should read it. I never quite knew how she felt about me. It was a tricky friendship."

Charlotte shoots me a desperate look that clearly says, "You have to smooth this over."

I try. "I've skimmed over most of it. Really, she's mostly upset with Paul, as far as I can tell."

Miranda sighs. Maybe that wasn't a comforting thought. I pull out a chair. "Don't worry. You don't have to do it."

She stretches out a pale hand, steel in her eyes. "Yes, I do have to. Time to figure out what really happened. This isn't your burden to bear, Tess."

Charlotte wipes a tear and sits behind her mother. As Miranda turns the yellow pages, Charlotte reads over her shoulder.

Apparently Miranda is a fast reader. She gasps a few times, especially at the flower pictures, but for the most part maintains her Grande Dame composure. She's wearing her chess-master face.

When she reaches the end, she pulls out a handkerchief that's tucked into her sleeve, dabbing her eyes under her glasses.

Charlotte looks at me, and I know we both want to say, "So, what do you think?"

Instead, we sit in funeral-home silence.

Finally, Miranda breaks it. "I'll have to think on this a spell."

Charlotte and I get up, leaving Miranda with the journal. Once we're in the kitchen, I pour water into the kettle.

Charlotte smiles. "Mom's Earl Grey? I remember that tradition."

I pull out a tea bag. "I hope we didn't upset her too much. Maybe that was a bad idea."

"No, Mom can handle it. She always dealt with the big stuff, more than my dad. When we had to put our dog to sleep, Mom broke the news. When my grandpa had a stroke, Mom told me. When the *Challenger* exploded, she answered all my questions about death. Wait...you wouldn't remember the *Challenger*."

I make a face. "No, but I am literate and I've seen the replays."

Miranda's voice drifts in. "Girls? Come here a second."

We race out of the kitchen. Miranda is sitting with her ankles demurely crossed and her hands folded on the journal. "One thing that jumps out at me is the way she talks about her mother. Her mother was long dead when Rose wrote these journal entries."

I'd wondered about that. Charlotte shoots me a horrified glance.

Miranda continues. "And the whole thing about Paul doing

something to C. She must mean Cliff. Maybe she thought he killed him?"

That makes sense, in a warped way. If Rose was beaten, maybe she'd assume her abusive husband would kill someone else—someone who'd been visiting her. Still, I'd thought of both of these things already. There is a deeper truth here, something that fits all these things together.

"She also said that Paul was trying to poison her. Now, she never told me that. But she did tell me he hit her. She told me that right before she died."

Charlotte breaks in. "Mom! How can you marry him? You were just talking about the Klan and wife-beaters and—"

Miranda interrupts her. "Because I didn't believe Rose."

What? Now we're getting somewhere.

"It didn't make sense that in the years we were friends, she never once told me. I never saw a black eye or a broken arm. And her story seemed flimsy. Something about him bruising her, as I recall. Well, shoot, Russell bruised me when he tickled me too hard—didn't mean he was beating on me."

So Miranda doubted Rose's story. Had the Doctor really believed it?

I turn to Charlotte. "Feel like a drive to Putnam County?"

45

She's expecting, this girl who won't heed my warnings. She may be even prettier than I was at her age. Has Bartholomew grown captivated with her beauty, like he was with mine? He whistles when he leaves The Haven now.

Tess Spencer is very good at tracking. It won't be long until she puts the pieces together. I wouldn't be in this mess if Bartholomew had turned the journal over to the police when I died. Instead, he kept it, so he protected Paul.

I shouldn't be surprised. He double-crossed me. And yet I won in the end. Claire flew out and took Rosemary the moment she was born. Bartholomew didn't know about that. Silence was expensive, but I covered my tracks.

Tess still has the journal, as far as I can tell. If I can get close to her house when she's out, maybe I can search for it. If she's like Bartholomew, she keeps it hidden somewhere.

I'm finally free, able to enjoy my second life as Marilyn Davis—the life Cliff wanted me to have. It's time Paul met with justice, and it's time I met my daughter.

After reading the journal and drinking her tea, the Grande Dame seems exhausted. We move her to her bed. As Charlotte walks out to clean up the kitchen, Miranda grabs my arm.

"Listen, honey, God's pressed something on my heart to tell you, and if I don't say it soon, I'm going to pop."

I step closer, fighting the urge to pat my friend's head and tuck the covers around her, like a child. "Do tell."

"Rose was an only child. Her daddy wasn't around much, but her momma took her to church. Rose was the loveliest woman in Buckneck—men threw themselves at her, married or not. Sound familiar?"

I think about it, finally nodding slowly.

"But she made a mistake. She wouldn't go to church or read her Bible. So her views of God got warped, like wet floorboards."

I adjust the flickering light bulb in her lamp.

"I wouldn't be a friend to you if I let you go the same way." She clasps my hand. "We all get in over our heads at some point or another. God never lets you down, even if it feels like it."

I hold my tears in, looking at Miranda's spotty, thin hand.

"Well, think on it. I felt like I needed to warn you. Only the Good Lord knows how much time I have left—no, don't start crying. I'm ready to go. That scare with the heart pills only reassured me of that."

Charlotte comes in behind me, pressing a tissue into my hand. I wipe at my eyes and blow my nose. "Thank you. I will think on it, I promise."

Miranda smiles and clicks off her lamp. Charlotte and I walk into the living room, grabbing our outerwear before heading to the parking lot.

I appreciate that Charlotte doesn't chatter or ask questions. Once we're settled in the SUV and I've regained some of my composure, I turn to her. "We're going over to Doctor Cole's house to ask him some things. He's been lying to me this whole time. He had to know Rose didn't die that New Year's Eve in 1973."

She nods. "Let's do it."

We're both starving by the time we reach Putnam County. When we go through the Wendy's drive-through, Charlotte orders a Junior bacon burger and fries.

Curiosity gets the better of me. "I thought your mom said you were a vegetarian?"

She laughs. "I was when I was in China—safer that way. I could recognize most of the vegetables, but not all the meats. I'd rather eat tofu than pig's feet, you know?"

"They sell pig's feet here in the USA, too," I say.

"I know, and I'm not going to eat 'em here, either! Did your mom ever make kidneys?"

I fight the coldness that creeps into me every time someone asks about my parents. "No, she didn't. But I ate plenty of pickled eggs, let me tell you."

We swap stories until I pull up to the Doctor's drive. I call his number, hoping he'll honor his promise to help out any way he can. Sure enough, he buzzes us in the gate.

When Charlotte gets a look at his house, she whistles. "He must be pretty well-off to build a place like this. Think of all Rose could've had if she'd just divorced Paul and married the Doctor."

Good point. *Why* didn't Rose just divorce Paul? Was she afraid he'd come after her? Another question for Bartholomew, perhaps.

The Good Doctor is nowhere in sight, so we park and walk up to the front doors. I tell Charlotte the questions I plan to ask, in case the Doctor's spicy cologne derails my logic again.

I knock, and when there's no answer, I try the door. Images of black-clad shooters race through my mind. What if Rosemary came back to get what she was looking for?

In the hall, I catch a glimpse of movement toward the left. When I see the Good Doctor waving us into the kitchen, I'm relieved as a hooked fish thrown back into the pond. He's wearing a red plaid shirt and jeans dusted with flour.

"Looks like a cowboy," Charlotte whispers.

"Sorry, ladies, but I'd agreed to make this pasta for the church dinner—my specialty. Come on in."

Charlotte catches her breath as we walk into the kitchen. High wooden cabinets give way to cathedral-height windows. The fridge is cleverly disguised with a matching wooden panel. Natural light floods the marble countertop where he's working.

"This is gorgeous," Charlotte says. "Reminds me of a cathedral in Assisi. Only minus the kitchen appliances."

The Good Doctor looks flattered. "Thank you. Now what brings you two all this way? Must be something important."

Don't look at him. Just talk and focus on his hands. "Doctor—I mean, Bartholomew—I think you didn't tell me the whole truth."

I feel his eyes on my face. "In what way?"

You know very well *in what way.* I am a bullet, speeding toward my target. I am an iceberg, unstoppable in strength. I clear my throat. "In this way: you knew Rose didn't commit suicide, yet you continued to perpetrate that idea to everyone."

He walks around the counter to look in my eyes. The clove-like smell trails right along with him. "Tess, you're right. I confess I lied on that count. I'd made a promise to Rose that I'd never tell anyone. I'm only admitting it now because you figured it out. A true gentleman keeps his word."

And a true gentleman doesn't have an affair with a married woman. I buck up against the cologne's softening effects. "What happened to her after she faked the suicide? And how did she do that, by the way? And why did she go to all that trouble? Why didn't she just divorce Paul and marry you?"

He pats my hand, fingers lingering for a second. "Questions, questions. Where to begin?"

Charlotte interrupts, her musical voice filling the room. "Begin at the beginning, Doc."

He offers Charlotte a forced smile. "I believe I shall. I loved Rose, and I wanted to take her away from Paul. He was abusive."

I interrupt. "You believed that? Did you ever see signs?"

"Quite often, her wrists or arms were bruised. Not necessarily her entire body. But of course I believed her. In my experience, you never question the wife's side of an abuse story. Anyway, I've told you about the pregnancy; how I asked her to get an abortion. I hated to do that, but we couldn't risk Paul discovering it before I could get her out of there."

Should I tell him Rose lied to him? Does he need to know Rosemary is probably his child? I silence Charlotte with a look. For now, we'll keep that information under our hats. It's just a wonder he hasn't run into Rosemary at the bistro or The Haven yet.

"You've read over the journal, Bartholomew. What did she think Paul had done to Cliff?"

His tone flattens. "I've wondered about that many times. I could only conclude she thought Paul had something to do with Cliff's running off the road. She didn't discuss Cliff with me."

I do believe the Good Doctor was jealous of Cliff Hogan. Jealous enough to hurt him? This web just gets more tangled. And who's the spider in the center?

Doctor Who whirs in my purse. I pull out my phone, checking the number. Nikki Jo.

"Excuse me a second." I step toward the dining room, putting a hand over one ear while I press the other to the phone. "Nikki Jo?"

"Oh, Tess! Where are you?"

My heart stops. "Over at Putnam County—what's wrong?"

"It's Petey. He's here at the Pleasant Valley Hospital. A rock dropped on his head."

"A rock? On his *head?*"

"Roger said it dropped from a net in your tree out back." She covers the phone and talks to someone. When she gets back on, she's sniffling. "C-could you come over? I can't handle this without you. Roger's here and Thomas is coming."

"On my way."

The Doctor and Charlotte are deep in conversation about Italian pasta. Both stop talking when they see my face.

277

"What is it?" Charlotte rushes to my side.

"I have to go to the hospital. Thomas' little brother got hurt."

"What kind of injury?" Bartholomew jumps into doctor mode.

"Head. He got hit in the head with a rock."

Bartholomew dusts off his jeans. "I'll come over—is he at Pleasant Valley? Do you want me to drive you?"

"Yes, Pleasant Valley. I'll drive myself, thanks. But could you bring Charlotte? I...need to be alone."

"Of course."

Once I get to the SUV, I bomb out the Doctor's gate. Something deep inside tells me not to overthink things and just drive. So I do.

46

I hide behind a fallen tree, still panting. I'm not as spry as I used to be, but I can still get around in the woods, thank goodness.

I hope they got that poor red-headed boy to the hospital. If it weren't for that obnoxious barking dog, he wouldn't have come around and spotted me in the tree. I had to climb higher, knocking a few stones out of some kind of net they had up there. Maybe it was a trap—for me.

The journal isn't worth this kind of trouble. I still want the police to find it. But there are other ways to make things right—things I can do myself. I'll go back to my hiding place and talk to Mother. She'll know what to do.

Thomas rushes out the sliding front doors of the hospital. He takes my arm and steers us toward the elevator. His yanked-down tie, sad eyes, and stubbly face make me feel guiltier. He starts talking without asking what I've been up to.

"It's a concussion from a contusion—something like that. No bone shards in there, as far as they can tell. Did you know he'd set up a trap in that big oak? Probably after I told him about that woman in the tree. I shouldn't have mentioned it to him." He turns me around, focusing on me with his dark eyes. "Who would do that to a kid, Tess?"

"I don't know."

"If I find out, I'll sue his pants off—or maybe I'll just strangle him instead. Or her. Anyway, if Petey doesn't wake up…" His voice trails off.

I grip his arm tighter. "Don't think that way. He will. He's a tough kid." I have no idea where these words are coming from.

The elevator dings and we walk into the sterile hallway. Thomas dazedly leads us toward Petey's room. I can hear Nikki Jo crying before we reach the door.

Petey lies on the bed, head wrapped in gauze. A bright spot of red has leaked through on the side. He moans occasionally. Nikki Jo rushes over to me, hugging me until my own tears start.

She sobs. "Who *did* this?"

All my pat answers fly out the window. I want to get this son of a biscuit eater as much as they do.

Roger sits in the corner, eyes fixed on Petey. I'm amazed by his composure. Must be his military training. Thomas pats him on the back and sits next to him.

"He needs to wake up soon," Nikki Jo says. "They said if he doesn't, it's a bad sign."

"Maybe we should pray over him." Again, words materialize out of thin air and form sentences I'm shocked to utter.

"Oh, yes. Why don't you do it?" Nikki Jo bows her head.

Good lands. I haven't prayed seriously for years. I glance at Thomas, hoping he'll rescue me, but his head is also bowed.

I try to compose my thoughts as I pray. "Dear God, You see everything. And You see Petey lying here. Please wake him up soon. Help everything to be okay. We can't lose him..." Tears stream down my cheeks as I think of Petey, asking me to come over and play Xbox. I should've gone right then. I should've stopped this stupid fool's errand of prying into Rose's life. I gasp a few times. "And I'm sorry I haven't listened to you lately, God. And...Amen."

The whole room is in tears when Bartholomew and Charlotte come in. The Good Doctor hugs Nikki Jo, then walks over to Petey. As he shines a flashlight in Petey's eyes, Petey sits straight up. Nikki Jo rushes to his side.

Petey touches his bandages. "Wha—what's going on?"

The Doctor eases him back to the pillow. "It's okay. You've had a concussion, that's all. You need to rest right now."

Petey looks around. "Ma? Hey, what are you guys all doing here?" He grins. Oh, thank you, God, for that grin.

He looks curiously at Bartholomew again. "You're a doctor? Where's your stethoscope?"

Bartholomew nods, then turns to us. "If he can remember the word *stethoscope*, he's going to be okay."

Roger clears his throat. "That was quite the powerful prayer you said there, Miss Tessa Brooke."

My in-laws know my full name, and they're the only ones I

let use it. Thomas wraps me in his arms, resting his head on mine. Charlotte winks at me. I'll bet she's imagining Thomas as a little rapscallion, disturbing the peace in church.

Nikki Jo and Roger talk with Bartholomew. I go to Petey's side and pat his arm.

"You look pretty good, for a boy who got hit in the head with a rock."

His freckles blanch as he wrinkles his nose. "Well, you know how it goes when you're out investigating."

I get serious. "No, I don't want you investigating anything else. And *no more traps*—you hear me? The person in the woods won't bother us anymore."

"How do you know that, Tess? There was somebody up in that tree—Thor was barking his head off at her."

"Her? You sure it was a *her*?"

"Sure I'm sure. I know a woman when I see one. She had long blonde hair. Anyway, she was the last thing I saw before I blacked out."

I should track down Rosemary and put the fear of all that's holy into her.

Thomas grins at his brother. "You going to be healthy by the time Andrew gets here tomorrow?"

"You know it," Petey says.

"Okay, bro. I need to get back to work." Thomas turns me around and kisses me full on the lips. "Thanks for coming so quickly."

He doesn't utter a word about how this is my fault, attracting stalkers to our yard with my investigative techniques. He doesn't ask me why Doctor Cole and Charlotte showed up right after me. He doesn't even ask about the journal.

I love my husband.

47

"Nobody knows the trouble I've seen...nobody knows my sorrow." The song keeps playing in my head. I wish I could stake out the Spencer house and make sure the boy comes home, but it's too risky now.

As usual, I have to look after myself. No one else will. Paul never cared, and neither did Bartholomew. I'm at the age where I want my girl to know who I am, so she can make a fuss over me and care for me when I get older. She'll understand why I had to let Claire take her away from me.

I've called Claire's number so many times, just for a chance to hear Rosemary's voice. Yet just this past month, her number was disconnected. What if they've moved? Has my daughter gotten married? Do I have grandchildren?

I wasn't in West Virginia long before the ghosts found me. Mother's still among them. Of course, she was upset I hit that Spencer boy's head with a rock, but I explained it to her. I think she agrees that closure is what we need.

Charlotte and I part in the hospital hallway. She hugs me, then looks at me with eyes that seem more yellow than gray-brown.

"I'll get the journal from Mom and take it back to the house. Do you think I should burn it?"

I nod. "I'm ready to be done with Rose and everything about her. Your mom's been told about Paul, but she believes he didn't hit his wife. I think we have to take our hands off this."

Charlotte fingers a piece of her hair. "But what if he's only after Mom's money? Didn't Rose leave her some, too?"

"Yes, but I figure that has to go to Rosemary now. I don't know all the legal ins and outs of it, though."

I'm tired of straining my brain, trying to figure out everyone's motivations forty years ago. Petey's only twelve, and today his life could've been cut short.

"I'm out of it, Charlotte."

She knows just what I mean. "You should be. You've got a baby you need to protect. *And* you look like you haven't slept in three weeks. Go home and let me handle the rest."

"You'll call before you go back to Morgantown, won't you? Or stop by?"

"Of course. Now go."

I trudge down the hall and punch the button on the elevator. As I wait, someone's body odor reaches me before he does. An older man shuffles along, focused on his feet. He has a bad comb-over and his pants hang so low, they might fall off.

A nurse runs up behind him. "Mr. Reynolds! Mr. Reynolds, time for your pill. Come back to your room, please."

Instead of looking at the nurse, the man fixates on me as I step into the elevator. "Don't ya hear 'em? Them ol' haints are hangin' all around ya! Ya can't escape 'em!"

The nurse grabs his arm, and a large orderly runs toward him. This dude must be on the wrong floor—I think there's a Psych unit somewhere in this hospital.

Haints. That's the same word Paul used—mountain talk for ghosts. I remember Miranda asking me if I believed in ghosts, way back when she got that first warning letter.

I steer my thoughts back to the present. Only the present for me now; enough of the nebulous past. It wasn't *my* past, anyway—it was Miranda's. And now that she has all the facts, she should be able to make her own decision about marrying Paul.

By the time the elevator reaches the lobby, I'm full of new resolve. This Christmas, I'm going to focus on family. For New Year's, I'll enjoy Miranda's wedding and wish her well. Anyway, some part of me actually likes Paul, because he said I'm nothing like my dad.

I suddenly feel hopeful about the New Year. When I try to put my finger on the reason, it comes back to my prayer. God *did* hear me. Maybe He hasn't done everything I wanted over the years, but He's done some really good things for me, like letting me marry into the Spencer clan.

On the way home, I find a Southern Gospel station and crank it. I don't know most of the songs and I can't understand half the lyrics, but I try to sing along. *"No fear, when Jesus is here..."*

I grab the mail and turn into the driveway, trying not to focus on the oak tree behind our cottage. I'm sure rocks still litter the ground right where they fell on Petey.

Andrew's Karmann Ghia blocks our driveway. I stop the SUV and run up to the porch of the big house. As I raise my hand to knock, Andrew throws open the door and hugs me. "I came home as soon as I heard. Who cares about some dumb Latin final?"

Such an attitude does not a doctor make, but I know Andrew's worried about Petey.

"He's fine. I just came from the hospital. He's awake now and talking. In fact, he's ready to get home and see *you*."

Andrew's no-holds-barred smile could surely make millions in advertising. Even sporting his ripped green cargo pants and bleach-stained polo shirt, he looks like he's trying to start a trend.

Eyes wide and innocent, I ask, "Where's Kelsey?" Let's see him explain this one.

He cracks his knuckles. "Kels? Oh, that didn't work out. I was going to bring this other girl, Helga, but she couldn't get out on such short notice."

An entire lecture springs to mind, about dating for marriage and not just for kicks. Instead, I meet Andrew's jolly blue-green gaze and blink. "Hm."

He grins. "I know what you're thinking. It takes *time* to find a girl half as epic as you are, Tess."

Sweet-talker. "Hey, Don Juan, can you move your car so I can pull into my driveway?"

"Oh, sorry about that. Sure thing." He steps into his beat-up Birkenstocks and jumps over the low edge of the porch.

"When's Thomas getting home?"

I shout over his revving engine. "I have no idea! He had to leave work to see Petey."

"Dude. That was a close call for Petey. I think the Spencer men need to go out and find the freak who did this."

The somewhat-comforting image of Andrew, Thomas, and Roger in jungle gear, toting AK-47s, springs to mind. I sigh as he backs up and parks.

"Afraid not. This is something I have to do."

He slides off his leather seat and looks at my stomach. "You better take care of yourself. I still don't see the baby?"

"Andrew, it doesn't pop out till later. But my stomach's getting a little bigger, for your information. My pants don't button all the way."

He grins. "You've got a lot of spunk in you. Thomas needed that."

I laugh. "As if you don't have enough spunk for the whole family!"

My phone rings, and Andrew makes creepy faces to the *Doctor Who* theme. I shoo him off to his house and walk toward the SUV. "Hello?"

"It's me, hon. Hey listen, I forgot to ask if you could come to the office Christmas party on Thursday night? You'll get to dress up!"

"Is that supposed to be an enticement? 'Cause it's not really working."

Thomas laughs. "What if I buy you a new dress?"

"Do you even know my size?"

"You're not making this easy."

I grin as I park the car and walk to our front door. "I'm just spunky, that's all. Of course I'll come. I like to be at your side for any and all social events."

"Okay, I'll sign us up. Oh, and you'll need to bring a couple of desserts."

My keys drop to the ground. "I gotta go. I can't get into the house."

I fumble with the new keys, opening each lock. So far, we have a grand total of two regular locks, two deadbolts, and a sliding chain lock on the front door. I think Thomas adds one every night.

I walk upstairs, prepping for my next mission. I load the shotgun, since I can't find where Thomas put the Glock. I might be the only pregnant woman who's going out this year with a handsaw and a shotgun to gather her Christmas tree from the woods. I'm a real mountain momma.

48

I still can't figure out if Paul really loves Miranda. Her overdose should have scared him good. Instead, he just puttered around the house like normal and dropped in at The Haven a couple of times. Maybe he's just marrying her for my money. In that case, he'll get a little surprise when it goes to my daughter instead of him. I know he must have been surprised when Royston read the will forty years ago, and all that Darby family money went to Miranda.

I don't think he ever walks in the yard. Pity that my flowerbeds look so neglected. I'd trim them up myself, but someone might notice. It's not my house anymore; I realize that. But I miss loading up the woodstove on icy winter nights. I miss dinner parties where I could dress up and our friends would tell Paul what a lucky man he was. I don't miss Paul— he never did anything but hurt me.

Tess Spencer's husband seems like a good man, not overprotective like Paul was. Still, I don't know why he lets her run all over the countryside. I guess times have changed.

I can only think of one way to locate Rosemary—follow Tess around. Unless I underestimate her, she'll be tracking down Rosemary next. Tess Spencer is a rather formidable child of the mountains. I wish I could talk with her and explain things. Maybe someday I will.

I prop my fresh-cut, thin-branched pine in its makeshift tree stand: a tall travel mug. Then I double-string a strand of white lights around it and add a few mismatched ornaments. I'm not sure any presents can fit under the scrawny thing, but who cares?

Nikki Jo calls to say they'll be home late. In a fit of housewifely industry, I thaw some ground beef and whip up spaghetti and garlic bread to take over to Andrew and the late-night crew. Nikki Jo's white lights have automatically come on in her back yard, and Petey was right. They look like hundreds of stars. That must've taken ten strings of lights, easy.

I knock on the door and Andrew yells from upstairs. "Coming, coming!" Thor barks fiercely until the door opens, then runs to sniff the bushes out front.

I hand over the spaghetti pot and carry the bread into the kitchen. Andrew looks like he just got out of the shower. "Good news—Helga's driving in tomorrow morning."

"Really? Does she need some place to stay?"

"No, she'll just be in the den. She's kind of an outdoor girl, so she doesn't mind sleeping on the couch or wherever. It's a wonder she didn't ask to stay out in a tent." He winks. "Alone, of course."

As I walk out, Thor zooms past me at top speed, little claws skidding as he races into the kitchen. Andrew shrugs. "I don't know how Petey puts up with that animal."

I snicker. Andrew and I are on the same wavelength. Well, sort of. I doubt Helga is going to impress me much. Growing up in a rusted, leaking trailer with frequent invasions of spiders and mice takes some of the glamour out of "roughing it."

When Thomas gets home at seven-thirty, he piles spaghetti on his plate and nearly inhales it without even changing his dress shirt. He sits at the table, looking blankly at *The Buckneck Daily*.

"Notice anything different?" I gesture toward the living room.

He turns, confused. "Did you have time to get your hair cut today?"

"No, but nice try. Didn't you see the Christmas tree?"

He peers into the living room. "Oh...that? It's a Christmas tree?"

Ooh. He did *not* just say that.

He stands to get more bread, looking past the counter at the handful of white lights strung on our miniscule tree.

He chews while he talks in a decidedly un-lairdly fashion. "In my house, my dad always picked the tree—back when we got real trees. Then Mom got that artificial wonder and it's been white ever since."

I put my hand on my hip. "Are you saying I shouldn't have gotten our tree?"

He starts coughing. "Crumb," he whispers, gulping at his

water. When he calms down, he comes back to the topic at hand. "Well, where *did* you get our tree, Tess? Surely not the tree farm down the road?"

"Oh, *certainly* not. And I'm hanged if I'll ever get another tree for your ungrateful self."

He tries to put his arm around me, but I jerk away. I grab the sponge from the sink and start cleaning invisible grease off the stovetop.

"Well, that was awkward," he says, under his breath.

"Awkward! *Awkward?* I'm the pregnant chick who busted my hiney to cut down that tree, with a twelve gauge strapped on my back! I'm the one who took time to decorate it, so it could feel like Christmas around here! Yeah, I'm feeling pretty awkward myself."

Thomas groans. "It's been a long day, with Petey's concussion. You seem tired and hormonal. Am I right?"

I grab the nearest ladle and whap it on the counter. "Tired? Hormonal? I'm a *pregnant woman*, for Pete's sakes! You got me pregnant and now you're *criticizing my Christmas tree?*"

"Are those two connected?" He gives me a confused look.

I throw the ladle in the sink. "I'm going upstairs to take a bath! Don't come in and don't come anywhere near me."

Thomas sighs as I stomp up the stairs. Here I've repeatedly put my life on the line for my friend, and all he can do is criticize. Growing up, I rarely had a Christmas tree, yet he berates my tree-choosing skills?

Jerk. What a dadburn jerk.

My mind flits to Rose's marriage. Did Paul make her crazy like this? Was the pregnancy the only thing that made her fake her own death? Does marriage ever get better, or does it get worse?

I sink into the water, heavy with the smell of lavender bath salts. I'll bet the Good Doctor would never say stuff like Thomas just said. No wonder Rose thought he was great. He had his own house, his own career, his own snappy clothes...no ties to anyone else.

Wait. Didn't he have a sister in Arizona? I wonder if she's still there. Maybe I could look her up.

No. I can't keep searching this stuff out. I'm getting way too OCD with this whole attempt to figure out Rose's life. I'm out, like I told Charlotte. Done.

Only I need to talk with Rosemary. Maybe I should take Charlotte to the bistro and threaten Rosemary to stay off our property. Maybe I should take the Glock instead.

Anyway, what was she doing up in that oak tree? It's not like she needs evidence that she's Rose's daughter—that's plain for all to see. I suppose I could save her some trouble and tell her who her dad is. He'd be a really cool dad.

Thomas bangs on the bedroom door. "Tess, I have to come in and change. Okay?"

"Whatever!"

I listen to Thomas' every move, which gives me a good indication of his continued irritation. Drawers jerk open and slam shut. A faint click and the sound of slamming metal tells me he's dropped his gun's magazine and is racking the slide to empty it.

The bath's worked wonders, and I'm feeling calmer. I suppose I should be magnanimous and tell him I'm sorry. But sorry for what? I feel no remorse for letting him know he acted like a Jerk Royale.

He knocks again, this time on the bathroom door. We both know it doesn't have a lock, like every other door in this cottage.

"May I come in?"

"No!"

"C'mon, Tess. I said some thoughtless things. I admit it. I'm the one who's tired. I just want this crazy person out of our woods and everything back to the way it was before."

"Before what? Before your wife went and poked her nose all up in other people's business?"

Silence. Then he says, "Uh, no. I just mean before some stalker started trailing you around."

"Well, it might comfort you to know that I'm giving it up. I'll quit trying to protect my friend from an ill-advised marriage."

"You know I like Miranda, too. I feel bad that she likes Paul—he has too much baggage, what with Rose's suicide, and the will…"

Obviously I haven't brought Thomas up to date on things, like the fact Rose could be alive somewhere. I should probably do that sometime.

Thomas' voice softens. "You know, I was so happy you came to see Petey today. Thanks for praying for him."

He's wearing me down.

He moves closer to the door. "You do too much, little pregnant momma. Chopping down trees, chasing down truths long buried, endearing yourself to my family and everyone else. Would you like a massage before bed?"

I stand and grab my towel. This must be how you make your marriage work for years: you fix things and move on. "Be right out," I say.

49

I sit in Cliff's little church, trying to see through its stained glass windows. I have no idea who the pastor is now. It's been years since I've darkened a church door.

An awareness of my own mortality has been chasing me around ever since I came back to this state. Sun-washed, wide open Arizona loved and nurtured me for years, only to spit me back over to the mossy green captivity of these tree-cluttered mountains. Memories taunt me around every curve. Cliff's radiant face. Bartholomew's irresistible smile. Flowers I grew in hopes of ridding myself of Paul forever.

In Buckneck or some nearby town, my daughter is now a forty-year-old woman. Maybe my entire plan was a mistake, a failure. Perhaps I listened to the wrong voices.

Funny, the ghosts don't follow me into this church. I've been coming here every day so I can think clearly a little while. The parishioners will probably start locking me out.

As I stand in the tiny church bathroom, I examine myself in the cheap gold mirror. My skin's hardly wrinkled and my red-blonde hair is still long. I could pass for about fifteen years younger. What a cruel joke—I'll die unloved, but beautiful. A metaphor for my life, perhaps.

Unless I find Rosemary in time.

First thing in the morning, I walk over to see Petey. Nikki Jo meets me at the door, wearing her exercise clothes and a big smile.

"Just made some fresh coffee—come and join me. How about a ham biscuit?"

Nikki Jo's ham biscuits need to have their own restaurant. I grin. "Sure."

She looks me over. "I do believe I see a baby bump. When's that next appointment?"

"January fifth, I think. I'll call you with the time."

I pull out a stool and sit at the island. "How's Petey?"

She pours two cups of coffee, adding creamer liberally to both. "I'll be doggoned if he hasn't slept like a log all night. I slept on the floor to keep a check on him, like Doc Cole suggested. He was a real angel to stop in yesterday."

I don't think I'd compare Bartholomew to an angel, but I nod and chew my biscuit.

"How are Miranda's wedding plans coming along? Where's she getting married again?"

"In The Haven. I think they have a chapel in the basement somewhere."

"Law, imagine getting married in her condition. Nearly seventy, had that stroke and heart attack—and she's stuck in that wheelchair. I hope Paul will take good care of her. She's taken care of lots of us over the years. She used to come to our church, you know. Always saw the best in people. I remember she told me I was a good mom—this was when I was taking Andrew out to spank him about twice a service. I clung to her words, let me tell you that."

Nikki Jo's right. Miranda's the kind of friend who sees the best in people. Even Paul. Despite his unkempt, plodding ways, she sees something valuable in him. What did she see in Rose, I wonder?

Nikki Jo takes a dainty bite of her biscuit. "You coming over for supper tonight? We'll have plenty of stew."

"I'll try to. I have to run over to see Claire Hogan first. Just want to clear something up. When's Helga getting here?"

"Andrew said this afternoon. Here I was just warming up to Kelsey, too. Did you know she sent me the nicest thank-you for that Thanksgiving dinner?"

"I didn't know that. I sort of liked her, too."

"Land sakes if that boy doesn't give me fits. How he'll ever stick it out in med school, I don't know."

Andrew saunters into the kitchen, sporting a stubble beard. His V-neck tee is about two sizes too big over his flannel pajama bottoms. The old Birks complete the ensemble.

He goes straight to the coffeemaker, emptying half the pot into a huge mug. "Ma, you know I can *hear* you."

Nikki Jo talks to his back. "I don't care. You ought not to toy with girls' hearts that way."

I put down my mug. "Could I go say hi to Petey?"

Andrew snorts. "You could, but he wouldn't hear you. He's dead to the world right now."

"Okay. Could you please tell Petey I said hi and that I'll play Xbox with him if I get back in time? Also, tell him I plan to beat him royally."

Andrew grins. "Oh, I'll tell him that."

I give Nikki Jo a hug. "Thanks for the biscuit and coffee. I'll be on my cell if you need me, unless I lose coverage."

Charlotte calls as I walk back to the SUV. "What are you up to? I'm already bored without you."

I hate to admit I'm tracking down Claire, but it's the last piece of the puzzle—or the last nail in my coffin. It's a toss-up which. But it's the only way to get Rosemary to stop menacing my family and friends—I'll confront her with the truth, once I figure out her relationship with the Hogans and the Good Doctor.

When I tell Charlotte, she's determined to go with me. "Maybe Claire knows more about Paul, too. If so, I need to know, so Mom has the full picture."

"Okay, okay. I'll pick you up in about twenty minutes. Claire lives outside town a little ways."

I double check the cottage locks and then get into the SUV. I can't imagine the miles I've been putting on this vehicle lately—yet another reason to stop this insanity.

In Buckneck, the law office looks unexpectedly festive with red bows and a lighted wreath. Wonder if my Christmas-décor expert of a husband had any say in the decorating. One could only hope so.

Charlotte has it easy: traveling everywhere, spending all her money on herself, looking at life as an adventure. She doesn't have to worry about putting everyone in danger when she pokes around into this Rose business.

She's waiting on her porch, snazzy in her boot-cut cords and a soft orange sweater. When she gets in the SUV, I scold her for not wearing a jacket, then compliment her eyeliner. "Girl, if I wore that dark liner, I'd look like a vampire. You can pull off that perfect smoky eye."

She smiles. "And if I had your porcelain skin, I wouldn't have to emphasize my eyes."

"I guess grass is always greener, huh?"

"You'd better believe it. You know, I've been thinking about my mom. Do you think Rose was envious of her? I mean, Mom had such a great marriage and Rose's was so lousy, from all appearances."

The thought had run through my mind. "Could be."

Charlotte absently straightens the tissue box, sunglasses case, and atlas. "And what if it *was* Rose that wrote those anonymous notes? It was her handwriting. Maybe she heard Mom's marrying Paul and she was jealous?"

"Why would she be jealous if she never loved Paul?"

She twists her gold bracelet. "Maybe…maybe he was like a possession. You know, she could have him, but nobody else?"

"I suppose that's possible. But why the elaborate suicide hoax to get away? Now she wants to get him back?"

Charlotte feigns a British accent. "Oft-times, the human heart is an enigma, even to itself."

I chuckle. "Did you just make that up?"

"Sure did."

In the valley where Claire lives, there's a sudden clearing in the cloud-scudded sky. A beam of sunlight hits the SUV.

Charlotte says, "It's a sign I'm right."

"Maybe so. Let's hope Claire can give us some insights."

We pull up to 213 Mechanic Lane. Turns out, Claire lives in a trailer. Turns out, I can't go in. When Charlotte swings open her door, I sit frozen to my seat. She walks around the SUV and raps on my window. "You coming?"

How do words capture a phobia—something that slithers into every cell and disrupts the way you see everything? I grew up in a rickety trailer. It still bothers me, and I'm a grown woman. I suppose if I dug deeper and psychoanalyzed myself, there'd be a parallel with how trailers' narrow confines make me feel trapped, the exact way I felt looking out for my reckless mom.

No time for explanations. I roll down the window, then grab my stomach. "Not...feeling too good. Can you take it from here?"

Her eyes widen. "Are you sick? Do you need a bathroom? Maybe you could use hers."

"No, no. I just need to lay back and drink a little water from this bottle. I get dehydrated sometimes."

Charlotte looks at the trailer, then back at me. It's a really souped-up place, with white wood siding, flower boxes, and proper shutters. I just can't go inside.

"What do I ask? You're Nancy Drew and I'm only George, remember?"

"Ask about Rosemary. Ask if she adopted her and how. Oh, and where. And even why. Ask how Rose treated her son, Cliff."

"Got it. Who, what, where, and why. Okay, you lie back and I'll handle this."

I feel bad I can't go in to make a mental reel of the questioning. Hopefully, Charlotte will be adept at remembering the key info.

I crank the seat back and stare at the taupe ceiling. Closing my eyes, I imagine myself walking to my mossy rock in the woods. In that leafy embrace, all sorts of impractical notions make sense. Dead trees point to heaven, praising their Maker. Spiders' webs part for me to pass through. Deer don't shy away, but meet my eyes and keep walking.

I'm deep into my woods scenario when the trailer door slams. Claire Hogan and Charlotte walk slowly toward me, Claire holding onto Charlotte's arm. Claire is heavy-set, with sparse white hair and a strong chin.

She peers into the car. "So you're the one asking questions about our Rose, are you?"

I nod.

"I've talked to your friend here. I'm sure she'll explain it. But she tells me you're expecting? Feeling sick, are ye?" The more she talks, the more brogue kicks in.

"I'm feeling some better now, thank you, Mrs. Hogan."

She reaches in the open window and lays a shaky hand on my stomach, letting it rest there for a moment. A blush jumps to my cheeks.

"P'raps ye have a small fever, do ye?"

"No, I'm fine. I just need to get home, I guess."

"That's sure and certain. Get back to home and take good care of your wee girl."

"Girl?" Is she saying what I think she's saying?

"The babe. Did ye know what 'twas?"

"Not yet. But I guess I do now. I'll take care, and you do the same, Mrs. Hogan."

She smiles, her dentures too big for her mouth. "God will take care of ye. Don't ye worry."

We both wave as I pull out. Charlotte offers to drive, but I need something to focus my excitement. A girl! I wonder if Claire is right.

Charlotte watches me closely. "Feeling better?"

I'm sure my emotions are flitting across my face. "Yes, just kinda surprised at what she said."

"About the baby? Yeah, she seems like some kind of mountain sage with that accent, doesn't she? And she had lots of information for us."

All the way to Buckneck, Charlotte fills me in. Yes, Claire adopted Rosemary, because she recognized Rose was pregnant and assumed it was Cliff's child. As Rosemary grew, Claire realized she didn't resemble Cliff in the least, but at that point she loved her so much she didn't care who her father was.

She'd flown to Arizona to adopt Rosemary.

Arizona.

So the Good Doctor had gotten Rose out of West Virginia. Had she lived with his sister? That explains why he went there soon after Rose faked her death. And that's yet another thing he forgot to tell us.

Charlotte tries to cross her long legs, only to crack her knee into the console. She finds the seat lever and slides it back. "I feel like we're getting close, Tess. Really close."

I groan. "It's been one step forward and two steps back this entire process. I want to be out of this, you know. I thought we'd close the case with Claire Hogan—boom! End of story! But we still don't know everything."

Charlotte's phone rings. "It's Claire! I gave her my number." She picks up. "Yes, this is she...What? When was this? Did you tell her?...Good heavens. Thanks for letting us know."

Charlotte's face looks like she saw a ghost. "Someone followed us to Claire's house and asked her where Rosemary lives—someone in a blue car. Tess, pull over. *Pull off the road now.*"

I oblige, pulling onto the narrow gravel shoulder. Hitting my hazard lights, I try to stay calm.

"What? What is it—are they coming to kill us?"

"No. I mean, I don't think so. Tess. The person looking for Rosemary is *Rose.*"

50

Sure enough, Tess is easy to follow, giving me the direction I need. It's surprising to see Claire, looking so run-down and old, as she walks out to the red SUV. Once Tess and her friend leave, I pull up and knock on Claire's door. She recognizes me immediately.

"Ye're here for the child, after all these years," she says.

I speak loudly, in case she can't hear. "I couldn't come before this."

"This bodes ill, your return to the mountains," she says.

"Are you telling me it's a mistake? Because I've made all my mistakes. Now I'm making things right."

"The child's not Cliff's." The old woman leans on the arm of her couch. "Ye misled me."

"Of course I did. It was the only way to give her a home. I trusted you'd hide her from Paul."

"'Twasn't Paul I was protecting her from."

Ungrateful hag. I get close to her face. "Where is she?"

"I willnae tell ye." She pulls her sweater close.

I pull a pill from my pocket. "Oh yes, ye will. Or you'll take this pill and die right now."

Fear fills her eyes. "Ye wouldn't, after all I did for ye."

"Don't push me, Claire. Just tell me where she is. I don't want to hurt her."

"Just being here will hurt her more than ye know. Ye can't make me take the pill."

I take out Paul's revolver—I found it in our house. Not only has Paul never changed the locks on our door, he still keeps his gun in his closet. I aim it at Claire's chest. "I think I can."

We sit in the car, in our far-from-scenic pull-off spot. Several fast-food cups, a beat-up egg carton, and an empty cat litter container dot the grass nearby. Whatever happened to Adopt-a-Highway?

"Rose?" I repeat. "She's here?"

"Yes, and she's not doing well. She pulled a gun on Claire."

"*A gun?*"

"According to Claire, she was desperate to find Rosemary."

"Did Claire tell her about the bistro? Oh my word, we need to contact Rosemary!"

Charlotte shivers. "Claire already called her. Rosemary left work early and is going to a hotel for now."

I rummage in my purse for the phone. "Rosemary should call the police—*we* should call the police!"

"And tell them what? That we're being stalked by a dead

woman?"

"I don't know what to do…your mom! We have to make sure she's safe."

Charlotte calls The Haven. She instructs a caregiver to stay outside Miranda's door 24-7. "Money's not an issue. Just make sure no one goes into or out of her room until I get there."

I turn the key, and the SUV purrs to life. "You going to stay over there instead of the house?"

"What else can I do? I can't move her in with me when I'll be leaving soon. This is such a huge can of worms. Dangerous worms."

"Okay. We have to stay calm. Rose wants to see her daughter, that's all. Who do we need to tell? Paul? The Doctor? Miranda?"

"We won't tell Mom yet—I'll tell her when I get there. Maybe the Doctor?"

I hand her my phone. "He's the Doctor Who number. Just call him at home and see if he's still there."

As Charlotte talks with Bartholomew, my mind races. *If* Rose was in that blue car, she was the one who followed me from the Doctor's house to Buckneck. Does she know where I live? And why's she so keen on following me? She must've ordered the begonias and the black roses, with that Arizona card.

How can we celebrate Christmas if that gun-wielding woman might show up on the doorstep? I won't put any of the Spencers in danger again. But I have no idea how to stop her. Instead of cutting this sticky, deceitful web, I grabbed hold of it and spun around in it a few times.

Charlotte hangs up as I sigh. She pats my hand, just like her mother would do. "It'll be okay. The Doctor says he'll try to track her down."

Small comfort. I know the Good Doctor is still withholding info. I can feel it.

Charlotte observes me with her cat-eyes. "You don't like him much, do you? But then again, you kinda do."

"He's handsome and wealthy; he cooks; he's been loyal for forty years to Rose—admirable qualities, no doubt. But he's not telling me everything. Maybe we should divulge that he has a daughter and see if that rocks his boat."

Charlotte shakes her head. "I don't think this is the right time, when she's in hiding from her crazed mom."

"Okay, we'll tell him later."

As I pull in front of the big green house, Charlotte grabs her purse. "I'll get over to Mom first thing. What about you? Tomorrow's Christmas Eve."

"Oh, shoot, I have a Christmas party to go to. I can't be worried about running into Rose right now!"

She taps her cell phone. "Call me for any reason!"

"Will do."

As I pass the law office, I'm tempted to stop and talk with Thomas about today's strange turn of events. But the last thing he needs is another reason to leave work early. Driving through town, I check my rearview mirror at least seven times to make sure the blue car isn't following me.

Let's see. Dinner tonight with the fam and Helga. Tomorrow night, office party. Then Christmas. We should go to some kind of Christmas program to get in the spirit. I'm sure Nikki Jo's planned a gift exchange under the monkey tree. And I'm in total denial that Rose is on the loose.

As I round the curve before our hidden driveway, I check behind me, then zip off the road without signaling. I hit the brakes to avoid hitting Andrew's Karmann Ghia, which is heading right toward me. Backing down the driveway, he motions me to stop. He rolls down his window, and a tall blonde woman leans over in the passenger's seat, waving at me.

"Tess, what's up with the maniacal driving? You nearly hit My Precious." He strokes his car door.

"Hi." I wave at Helga, who is obviously *not* his Precious.

"Oh, sorry. Tess, this is Helga Ang. She's totally Nordic." He turns to her. "Where are you from again?"

She smiles, showing a row of small, perfect teeth. "Iceland."

I smile. "How exciting! Are you in America for long?"

"One year," she says, her accent heavier than Axel's.

This relationship doesn't have time to get off the ground—which is probably what Andrew's counting on. Scoundrel. Scamp. Scallywag.

"I'll let you two hit the road for whatever adventure you're off to. Nice to meet you, Helga. See you tonight."

I stop by the big house to check on Petey. Nikki Jo opens the door, jogging in place. "I just started my workout, but you go on up. He wants to see you."

Petey shouts at me as I come up the steps. "Tess! You're here!" His door stands open and the blinds are up, letting in buckets of sunshine. He puts down his Xbox controller. "Woah, what a weird day yesterday!"

"I'll say. You remember any of it?"

"Kind of, in a blurry way. Hey, you have time to play Xbox?"

"You'd better believe it." I grab a controller, relieved at the chance to focus on something else. My stomach flutters. "I think this baby wants to see Mommy win."

51

The young man leaning on the counter at the Bistro Americain
eyes me closely. "You related to Rosemary?" he asks. His
manager comes out, shooing him back to the kitchen. "Could I
help you, Ma'am?"

"Yes. I'm looking for Rosemary Hogan. She does work here,
right? There's a family issue—"

The manager interrupts. "I'm afraid I can't share that
information, Ma'am."

I smile, making so much eye contact I get uncomfortable.
"Would you be able to give me her phone number, then?"

"No, I'm afraid not."

I try a different approach. "I'm her mother."

"No, ma'am. I've met her mother—she looks a lot different
than you, and she has an Irish accent."

"I'm her birth-mother. I don't have long to live, and I need
to discuss my will with her." I lean heavily on the counter.

His gaze softens. "Ma'am, I promised her I wouldn't tell

anyone. Rosemary's my best waitress; everyone loves her."

I smile. "I wouldn't expect anything less from my daughter. But I just have to see her before my time comes."

I'm laying it on pretty thick, but hopefully he'll fall for it. He hesitates.

"Why don't you give me your number, Ma'am, and I'll have her call you."

I don't even have a cell phone. To keep up my façade, I reel off numbers I memorized long ago and he writes them down.

I walk out, knowing all hope is lost. It's anyone's guess when Rosemary will come back to work. She could be anywhere in the country, for all I know.

Another Christmas Eve alone. But this New Year's Eve will be more than a celebration—it'll be a victory.

Christmas Eve, and not a speck of snow on the ground. Seems unnatural. Still, it gives me an excuse to walk in the woods and calm myself down before the soirée at the law office tonight. Red velvet cupcakes need to be whipped up soon, but I'm stalling.

Last party, I casually mentioned Thomas' UVA law degree several times, because I felt the paralegal was disrespecting him. I also rambled on and on about his GPA and his position as editor for the law journal. Thomas took me aside and kindly told me to stop making him look like the King of the Office.

Thomas bought a new dress for me, which is helpful because I haven't had time to dry-clean the red dress Rosemary wrecked with her mud splats. I love the navy satin sheath—its tight layers fit me well, without clinging. It hugs my newly-budding tummy perfectly. Thomas has good taste. Every time I tell him, he says, "Well, I married you, didn't I?"

My bomber jacket's a little heavy for the weather, but the Glock's ready to roll, snug in its familiar pocket. I walk in a wide circle around the oak tree, noting the twisted net and the size of the rocks lying beneath it. Not huge, but not pebbles. I visualize Petey, the rock falling on his red head...Petey, the little brother I've always wanted.

My steps are sure and quiet as I blend into the woods. I hope I don't run into Rose or Rosemary out here. I'm sick of trespassers who don't care who they hurt. I understand that Rosemary was trying to find out more about her mother. Likewise, Rose was trying to find out more about her daughter—maybe. Or maybe she's always been jealous of Miranda, and she's come back to put an end to her happiness. She's certainly succeeded in putting an end to mine.

I want to delve into baby books. I want to pick out a name and decorate a nursery. I want to be one of those crunchy moms, who blend their own baby food and use cloth diapers and sew organic cotton baby clothes. Learning to sew is a minor obstacle, one easily rectified with a few lessons from Nikki Jo.

Red-tailed hawk families dip and soar above me as I sit on my rock pew. God seems so real and close here. Has He been watching over me this whole time? I can almost hear Axel saying, *"Do not fear. All will be well,"* smiling with my gun aimed at his chest. Had God sent him to tell me those words I so desperately needed to hear?

Why doesn't God send Thomas to comfort me more often? He's on the outskirts of my life. We're always butting heads about important things. Maybe we're still growing into our marriage. But we have a baby on the way—a baby girl, if Claire Hogan's right.

Did Paul hit Rose? I still need to know if that's true. If he did, I could better understand Rose's retreat into her home, her tendency to throw herself at men who comforted her, and her suicide hoax to protect her baby from her husband. Maybe it doesn't justify those things, but it explains them.

It still comes back to those three who knew Rose best: the Doctor, Paul, and Miranda. One or all of them knows why she's back in West Virginia.

I push my hands onto the damp, cool stone. Both Bartholomew and Miranda pointed out my similarities to Rose. We both have no siblings. She was pregnant and I'm pregnant now, and supposedly I'm beautiful like she was. What good does that do us? The only thing that matters in the end is the love of family, our husbands, and our children. Rose was denied all three. Her parents died. Her husband might have beaten her. She never saw her child grow up.

I picture her—slim pants, Mona-Lisa smile, protective hand over her stomach. She wanted a child—a family. But when she became pregnant, she knew she'd have to give up the one thing she wanted most. I lay a hand on my stomach, and the baby moves in response. Tears flood my eyes and I cry alone: for Rose, for every child that doesn't know its mother, for children whose mothers don't know how to be mothers.

I dig in my pockets and find a used tissue. Wow, I guess there is such a thing as pregnancy hormones, because mine feel out of control.

Brushing off my cold jeans, I stand and whisper goodbye to the hawks—or maybe to God, I'm not sure which. Time to pull this old gal together and get all duded up for the party.

Two trays of red velvet cupcakes later, Thomas comes to pick me up. He has a platter of Christmas cookies from the grocery store to complete our admission requirements.

I meet him at the door, turning in a slow circle for him. He whistles. "Maybe I shouldn't have bought that dress. You'll undoubtedly get plenty of unwanted attention."

"Thanks, hon. And this year, I'll attempt to malign you, instead of singing your praises."

He laughs, giving me a full kiss and escorting me to his car. Andrew shouts from Nikki Jo's back yard, where he sits under the twinkling lights with Helga. "You'd better open that door for your date, bro! Otherwise she might just go home with someone else!"

"Shut it, Andrew!" To me, Thomas mutters, "If he could keep a girl longer than two weeks, he'd know better than to spout that nonsense."

"Shh! He'll hear you!" I swat his rear before sliding into my seat. "And close my door, Date!"

We travel in companionable silence down the twisting roads. I keep the air vents turned on, though my arms are freezing. I get carsick if I'm not driving, and the last thing I need is to ruin yet another dress.

Thomas asks, a little too casually, "By the way, my cop friend was asking if you've seen that blue car again?"

Oh mercy. *"The time has come, and the time is now,"* as Dr. Seuss says.

I try to keep my voice calm. "Turns out, I found out who was driving that car."

"Mm-hm? And who was it?"

"Well, it's a crazy thing—you'll never believe it. You remember Rose Campbell?"

"The young beauty who committed suicide? Her husband's marrying Miranda at New Year's? Yes."

I grip my cupcakes. "Turns out, she's alive. It's her car."

He turns, light brown lashes framing his snapping brown eyes. "When were you going to tell me? And what else are you keeping from me?"

I decide to come clean. "She has a gun. She pulled it on the woman who adopted her daughter."

"A gun! And her *daughter?* I thought she killed herself because she couldn't have kids? But wait—she didn't kill herself anyway…I'm lost on this."

"Me, too."

"Did she have something to do with Petey getting hit in the head?"

If I say yes, Thomas might tell Andrew and they'll do something stupid, landing themselves in prison at Christmas. Probably right next to my mom.

I try to be honest. "I don't know for sure."

My phone rings in my purse. Charlotte starts talking before I say hello.

"It's me. I told Mom why I've got to stay with her awhile. She's in shock that Rose is alive. They just gave her some medicine for her heart palpitations. Is there any way you could stop in?"

"I have Thomas with me, but there's nothing I'd like better

than to hightail it out of the office party early."

"Just bring Thomas along, if he knows what's going on. Mom would love to see him...and she really wants to talk with you."

"No problem. I'll be there."

And that's the bottom line—I'll always be there for Miranda, because she was there for me.

52

Funny thing, attics. They're too cold in winter and too hot in summer. Regardless, Paul never visits his—mine.

Thankfully, Paul hasn't been up here in years. I found an old mattress and some blankets from my bed that he must not have been able to part with. Ironic—maybe he cares for me more, now that I'm dead to him. Wouldn't he have a heart attack if he saw me again?

The thought has crossed my mind...sneaking down to his room in the middle of the night, dressed in a robe...or a white sheet. The ghosts break into a cacophony, excited by the idea of wreaking havoc on Paul. They seem to be getting stronger here. I'll be okay with them, as long as I don't see the blonde ghost who looks like my soul turned inside out. I saw her once, as I passed out from the pills, and I knew she was my own angel of death.

Bartholomew hadn't been sure how the drug would react with me, but he'd given me a dose guaranteed to do something dramatic that New Year's Eve. If it hadn't knocked me unconscious, I would've faked it. Of course, he hadn't realized I was pregnant—I never told him. It was a risk I had to take. Besides, he'd explained they used the drug to lessen pain in childbirth. "Twilight sleep," he'd called it. I knew it would be perfect for my plan.

He did get me out of the house, loading my body in his car, with Paul's awkward help. I don't know how he did the rest, from declaring me dead to getting some kind of ashes to Paul in an urn. But he let me stay at his house until I was back to normal. Then he flew with me to Arizona.

What happened there broke my heart—what was left of it. Yet when I accepted it, I thought I'd healed.

Turns out, the Arizona sunshine lied to me. Only the shadowy Appalachian mountains tell the truth, and it's as dark and twisted as my own heart.

In the office parking lot, I hand Thomas the tray of cupcakes and get out of the car. He eyes the plate. "You made the red velvet ones? These aren't my favorite. I thought you were making plain chocolate with vanilla frosting."

Flames spread up my neck. "Well, first of all, these aren't for you anyway. And secondly, last time I made these, you said they were delicious, as I recall. And trust me, *I recall.*"

He pushes a wayward cupcake back toward the middle of the tray. "I did not."

How dare he? Tape-recorder recall to the rescue.

I make my voice as deep as I can, imitating him. *"You never made these before. Is this cream cheese frosting? They're delicious!"*

He stares. "You're not remembering that right."

This is *so* the last thing I need right now. He knows I can't back down from a disagreement—or what's more commonly known as a *fight*.

"Are you seriously questioning my memory? The thing you're always depending on, since you have miserable recall?"

Thomas checks his watch. "C'mon. We're already fifteen minutes late. And I've never said anything about liking red velvet cupcakes."

That's it.

Before I can stop myself, I grab the plate, smushing my loathsome cupcakes into his ever-loving face. "There! You like them now?"

Oh shoot. What did I just do? What now?

I rummage in the car for the roll of paper towels I stowed for our last trip. When I turn back to Thomas, he's standing stock-still, eyes huge. I overcome the urge to lick the towels to wet them and start wiping his face with the rough paper.

Only his lips move. "You…didn't."

"Sorry. I'm really sorry. You just pushed the wrong button, that's all."

As his nose and mouth emerges, he doesn't look angry, just shocked out of his gourd.

I keep talking, since he's speechless. "You can't go in like this. It's okay. I'll run the cookies in and say I feel lightheaded or sick or something. Then we'll go see Miranda. You can wear your T-shirt."

A silver car pulls into the drive. I shove Thomas toward our still-open car door, then grab the cookie tray from the back seat. By the time the first passenger emerges, I've wiped off stray red velvet crumbs, wielding the tray in front of me. The vaguely familiar woman turns at the sound of my voice.

"Excuse me, would you mind taking this in to the party? I'm just not feeling good tonight. Please tell them Thomas and his wife won't be able to come."

She looks concerned. "Oh, of course, dear! I'll do that."

I walk slowly to the driver's door, not sure what I'll find when I get in the car. Thomas sits facing me. Oh my lands. He looks composed, with his hand crossed in his lap, but his eyes are still gigantic.

I whip out another apology. "Sorry again. I don't know what came over me."

The small interior car light shines on his blond head, flecks of red velvet and white frosting dotting his bangs. He leans over quickly and I scoot back. He wraps his large hand around the back of my hair, pulling me close for a rough kiss.

When we finally pull apart, my lips are tingling. We haven't kissed like that in *ages*. Thomas' voice catches as he apologizes. "I deserved that and more. I was stressing about the party when I should've been paying attention to you. You've been under all sorts of pressure lately—with the pregnancy, Miranda, Petey's accident, and now Rose."

We kiss once more, then I turn the key. "How about we go see the Grande Dame?"

On our way over, Thomas asks, "Is there any other information you've failed to divulge before we visit Miranda?" The way he asks, I know he's fishing for something specific.

I bristle. "What have you heard?"

"Well, Mom was saying something about that florist fellow. You know—the Conan-the-Barbarian guy? She said he brought something over a couple weeks ago."

So, word did indeed trickle out.

"He brought me something and it was a mistake, that's all."

"Hm. You sure he wasn't dropping by just to see you? I don't like him knowing where we live, Tess. Maybe he's a stalker, too. Maybe he's the one that kicked that rock on Petey's head."

"First off, no. To be honest, someone had sent me a bouquet of black roses. I just didn't want to keep it. And Axel wouldn't be up in our tree—in fact, I doubt that oak limb would hold the likes of him."

Thomas' jaw flexes.

The road's getting foggy. I talk into the blackness at him. "Besides, what do you care? I can't read you half the time. Axel's just looking out for me, trying to help out. But when a creepy drunk dentist hits on me in public, you're completely oblivious. What's up with that?"

"What dentist?"

"At the reunion! Didn't you see that dentist next to me? He was hitting on me the whole time you were chatting it up with your old teacher. He called me *gorgeous*. I had to leave the table!"

"Oh—that guy? He's old as the hills. If he tried anything, you could definitely outrun him. Of course I would've knocked his lights out if he did."

"*Outrun him*? So that's the protocol for what warrants your husbandly protection? Well, I felt vulnerable and exposed and you didn't help. And then you fly off the handle with Axel—"

"Axel!? That guy is definitely into you, and he's a much bigger threat than a drunk elderly dentist. I know you liked Axel in college—don't deny it; you're into blonds. And he keeps showing up, leering at you—even in church. Then I find out he's visiting our cottage while I'm gone. Of course I'm not happy about that."

I sigh. "Well, if it's any comfort, he's gone back to Germany."

"Back to join the Hitler youth?" He smirks.

I punch his arm.

"Okay, okay. Just tell me exactly *which* weird guys you want me to beat up and I will. I'm your loving slave."

I wonder. Maybe before Miranda's marriage, Thomas could give Paul a little beat-down warning. Couldn't hurt, except it's undoubtedly illegal.

I hope Miranda has some serious light to shed on this whole Rose-on-the-loose situation. With her heart being so unpredictable lately, I hate asking her anything. Yet she never couches the truth in self-serving terms, like the Good Doctor.

53

The ghosts encourage me to spend all day in the woods. I ramble around, pointlessly wishing for green signs of life. Brown and gray: the colors of December and my soul.

Hopelessness preys on me. I gave Rosemary her name because it means "Remembrance." Claire was supposed to tell Rosemary that her birth mother would always remember her. Ungrateful hag probably did nothing of the sort. I imagine she took Rosemary to church, giving her the same stilted, proper Sunday school upbringing I had. What good had that done me?

Still, Cliff's calm, golden demeanor convicts me. He was settled, peaceful. He wasn't afraid to die. I feel young, but I don't know how long I have left. I'm terrified the ghosts will rip me to shreds—they constantly threaten to do it.

There's one last chance. I could talk with Tess Spencer. She would know where Rosemary is. And if she read my journal, she'll be on my side. Maybe it's time to come out in the open.

Charlotte opens the suite door on the first knock, looking effortlessly ravishing in her orange hoodie and crinkly long skirt. I don't think she's wearing a speck of makeup, but she still has smoky eyes. I think Thomas notices.

She hugs him. "Little Thomas, you grew up! Sorry we didn't really talk at the hospital. Glad to hear Petey's doing better."

Thomas, now in his T-shirt and dress pants, smiles like a goofball. He only gets tongue-tied around pretty women.

"Well, come right on in," Charlotte says. "Mom's in her room. She can't wait to see you."

Miranda sits in her chair, wearing a silky, embroidered red robe. Her hair looks like it's been recently set. She extends her thin arms to Thomas.

"Aw, how I've missed you, delightful boy!"

Thomas returns her hug, giving her a peck on the cheek. "How's my favorite Sunday school teacher?"

"I have to admit, I've seen better days. I assume Tess has filled you in on Rose Campbell's reappearance?"

He nods. Miranda turns to me. "You look lovely, Tess—what a perfect color for you!" She sighs. "I've been walking down memory lane, trying to understand everything. I guess Bartholomew helped Rose fake her death?"

"He did."

Miranda pushes her glasses up. "But he had no idea she was pregnant?"

"None."

"And Claire Hogan adopted Rose's daughter?"

I lean on her bed, all my weariness catching up with me. "She did."

Thomas excuses himself to get a drink of water, but I know he's leaving us alone so the Grande Dame can be more candid.

Miranda spreads her hands on her lap, examining her light pink nails. "You must think I'm touched in the head, marrying Paul after reading that journal."

"Miranda, I'd never think you were crazy."

"Paul and I haven't talked about this, but something was wrong with Rose. I don't mean temporarily, either. From what I've heard, everyone made a big fuss over her from the time she was little. She expected to be worshiped. Then she hit reality smack-on when she got married. Now, I don't believe Paul hit her, not once. But I'll bet he disagreed with her. I don't know why she became a recluse, but I don't think it had anything to do with her marriage."

"So you think the journal was a lie?"

She twists her wedding band. "I guess I do. Maybe I'm a bigger fool than I want to admit. Maybe I have no business marrying Paul. I don't want to replace Russell—it's impossible. But Paul keeps me company. I know he's quiet around you girls, but he makes me laugh something fierce."

The baby kicks. I walk over and take Miranda's small hand, pressing it to the movement. A smile replaces all the darkness in her eyes. She's restored to the carefree Miranda I've known and loved since the day I met her. "You're carrying a little high. Know what it is yet?"

I shake my head.

"I wouldn't be surprised if you were wearing pink at your shower." She winks.

A shower. Good gracious. I hadn't even thought of having one. Miranda reads my look. "Usually your church gives you one. Better get your foot in the door soon."

I love it when she jokes around. "I'm planning on going to the Spencers' church again, don't you fret."

Charlotte comes in, carrying a mug of coffee for me and a cup of tea for Miranda. "Decaf for the both of you. Have I missed anything?"

"Nothing I haven't told you already," Miranda says. "You girls make a good team. Have you talked to Bartholomew— told him about his daughter?"

I shake my head. "No, not yet."

She purses and blows steam off her tea. "You need to do that. It's for the best. A father should know his daughter."

I stiffen at her dismissive tone. "But he wanted Rose to abort her! Why would he care?"

"People change," Miranda says.

"Sometimes they don't." I feel like I'm the devil's advocate tonight. My dad never changed, nor did my mom.

She shoots me a knowing look. "You're right. But if you can help them change and you don't, it's on you."

Charlotte puts a hand on my shoulder. "We'll talk to the Doctor, Mom."

I nod, noticing the dark, starry sky out the window. It's getting late.

"Love you, Miranda. You're an angel to me, and worth your weight in gold."

She smiles. "I'm afraid that's not too much—they keep

telling me to eat more or I'll wither away."

I motion Thomas back into the room for one last hug. Miranda pats his hand. "You keep that gal in line, you hear? She needs lots of attention to keep out of trouble."

He laughs. "You know I'll try."

"You're a good boy," Miranda says. "You remind me of my Russell."

Charlotte walks us to the door. "Thanks for stopping by. She's just wiped out with this whole Rose thing. So...what's our next step?"

"I guess it's Christmas! I'll think about it tomorrow. Your Mom's right—we should tell the Doctor. Maybe he'd want to meet Rosemary."

"I think he would. Okay, we'll take a break, relax, and try to forget about Rose for now."

Thomas takes my arm, walking me down the hall. As we pass the Rec room, a group of late-night television viewers turn to stare. I'm sure we're quite the sight—Thomas in his T-shirt and me in my fancy dress.

The temperature outside has dropped. Thomas wraps his arm around me tightly. "Another memorable date night, I'd say."

I grin. "Let's just go home, lock the door, and eat some cupcakes."

54

Christmas again. How many Christmases have I missed, in my sterile room at Cactus Ridge? Unlike the other residents, I never had pictures of my husband, baby, or even a pet to display.

How many years have been lost? It's been forty years since I died to Paul, but I can't remember when I last felt like Rose Campbell, the girl whose daddy was a big-shot riverboat captain. Maybe I should start acting my age and stop climbing in trees, hiking through the woods, and trusting all the wrong men with my heart.

I sit on my mattress, dressed in layers and wrapped in a blanket. It finally did get chilly, just in time for Christmas. It wouldn't surprise me if we got a skiff of snow. I'm determined not to go out, though. I can't risk being seen too early, and I want to get rested up for when I talk with Tess.

I've done my research. Tess' husband is a lawyer in Buckneck. Tess obviously doesn't garden, given the sparse look of her front yard. I suppose she spends all her time butting into other people's lives, like mine.

All I need is to get her alone. I'm sure that like any other woman, she'll have compassion on me, a mother who had to give her child up at birth. She'll tell me what I need to know about Rosemary.

She's been to Bartholomew's, but I don't think he's told her everything. There's only one reason a handsome, rich man like him didn't get married in all these forty years. He feels guilty. And so he should.

A smile creeps onto my face. It won't be hard to crush him. It was easy enough to get into his house that night. I could've shot him in the head then, but there was no reason to. It was the journal I wanted.

Still, he can never know he's a father. I won't let him steal Rosemary away from me.

Nikki Jo's front porch urns are stuffed with cinnamon brooms and fresh greenery. Roger answers the doorbell, and we follow the smells of bacon, eggs, and waffles to the dining room table.

Helga, Andrew, and Petey have all taken their seats. Helga sits across from Andrew, wearing an icy look. Trouble is afoot.

Thomas and I hug Nikki Jo before taking our seats. Breakfast is somewhat stilted, as Helga's monosyllabic answers to our polite questions only distance her more.

Finally, we gather around the white monkey tree. I notice some new monkeys have been added, Curious George among them. Not to mention banana ornaments.

Individually, we walk over and hunt for our gifts under the tree. I feel bad for Helga, who only gets a small gift from Petey and one from me. My gift for her is a bath gel—not particularly young and hip, but I buy them on sale in January and save them for unexpected Christmas presents. In a total Southern snub, Nikki Jo doesn't give Helga anything.

On the count of three, we all rip into everything at once. It makes for a beautiful chaos, so different from the silent Christmases Mom and I shared.

When I open Nikki Jo and Roger's gift, I gasp. It's a green maternity gown and matching baby sleeper.

Nikki Jo smiles, her red lipstick a perfect match to her turtleneck. "It's a nursing gown. I didn't know if you're planning on nursing, but I couldn't pass it up."

I hug it to my face. "My first baby gift! I love it so much!"

Thomas pats my back, sensing my joy. "My wife, the little momma-to-be."

Helga opens her gift from Petey, and it's a small handmade wooden box. He must have taken quite a few hours to sand that wood, not to mention carving the swirly designs into it.

She smiles at him. "Many thanks, Petey." He reddens, his blush muting his freckles.

Andrew sits perched in the chair next to Dad, oblivious to the fact that his brother outstripped him in the gift department—which tells me Helga's no longer his girlfriend.

After all the gifts are opened, Dad brings in a couple of trash bags. Thomas abruptly walks out of the sitting room.

"What's up with him?" Andrew says.

I shrug, fighting the urge to say, "What's up with *you*?"

Thomas comes back, holding a newspaper-wrapped box tied with twine. He kisses my head. "It's not fancy wrapping, but sometimes the best gifts come in plain packages."

I tug at the lid, wondering why he saved this one till the end. There's a scratching inside the box, and it shifts in my hands. I nearly drop it.

"Open it—it's okay." Thomas grins.

I pull the lid off slowly. A little white, fluffy kitten with huge jasper eyes looks up at me, trying to climb out.

"Oh, Thomas, a kitten!"

Petey scoots over and we *ooh* and *ah* over the tiny fluff-ball.

"Is it a girl or boy?"

"I honestly don't know," Thomas says. "Got it from Gina at work—she breeds them—and had to hide it over here."

Helga joins us on the floor, picking up the kitten and examining it. "Female."

Even Andrew smiles. "Trust Helga: she grew up on a farm. A girl it is."

As I cuddle the kitten, the family debates names for the next five minutes. Petey's fond of *Athena*, but we have enough god stuff going on with the illustrious *Thor*. Speaking of which, I hope kitty will get along with him. Or maybe not.

Thomas suggests *Snowflake*, and I snicker. "Like the traditional names, do we?"

He scratches behind the kitty's pink ears. "You have something better?"

I think of floaty, light words: *diaphanous, ephemeral, translucent, opulent, cerulean.* All adjectives, not nouns.

Nikki Jo reaches for the kitten, her red nails a stark contrast to the white fur. "She's soft as velvet."

"That's it!" I shout. "Her name is *Velvet!*"

"Calm down there, Tess," Andrew says.

Thomas laughs. "How about *Red* Velvet?"

Nikki Jo heads back to the kitchen to cut cheesecake and brew fresh coffee. Petey talks with Helga about how he made the box. Dad and Thomas head to the den for some man-cave time at the TV.

I sit contentedly batting around with my playful kitten. Andrew abandons his chair and sits next to me.

He whispers. "Guess I picked wrong, huh?"

"Are you talking about Helga? What's going on?"

"We can barely communicate. I can't share my life with someone I can't talk to."

Funny. Helga looks like a model—every girl's ideal—and yet she's missing something. Still, it's good to hear Andrew say *share my life* as if he has some longer-term goals in dating.

"What about Kelsey? I thought she fit in with us."

"Kelsey…she's just more intense than I am."

"You need that, Andrew. Contrary to popular college belief, life isn't one big party."

He gets serious, focusing on me with his almost-turquoise eyes. "So, what's the secret to keeping things together? Mom and Dad have it, but they've never been as…sparky…as you and Thomas."

The red velvet cupcake fiasco jumps to mind. I smile. "I think it takes a good sense of humor. And it doesn't hurt to be different from each other. But some people like more similarities. I don't know, Andrew—you just have to find the right one."

He rolls his eyes. "*The right one?*" You really believe that?

Well, how would I know I've found her?"

"If she gets along with your family, you're ahead of the game," I say. "You need to talk with Thomas about this stuff."

"Thomas is always busy. And he's just so much...*older* than I am. You know what I mean."

I nod. Thomas does tend to take a stern line with his carefree brother. "Even if you don't believe in the right one, you have to admit there are some *wrong ones* out there."

He smiles, pointing toward Helga as he picks up Velvet. The fuzzball snuggles into his chest.

"Well, don't feel too low, Andrew. At least Velvet thinks you're not totally repulsive."

Petey jumps up and runs to the window. "Look everybody! Snow!"

We watch the heavy white flakes splat against the glass. I wonder if Rose missed the snow or these mountains when she lived in Arizona.

I won't let Rose hijack my Christmas. I take the kitten back, snuggling my face into her soft fur as Nikki Jo calls us to the kitchen. I don't know where Rose Campbell is spending her Christmas day, but I'm spending it with my family.

55

In the morning, Paul makes a big ruckus in the kitchen. Pots bang and silverware clashes so loudly, I can hear it in the attic. Maybe he's practicing his cooking for Miranda. I wish I could go see her before the wedding, but I have other things to do first.

"Not long," my mother says. She always comes around when I need her.

I've checked to see if Paul has all the ingredients I need— all but one. I hid that one in an airtight jar, before I left this house forty years ago.

I walk to the window and Paul stops his racket. Did the floor creak? I freeze in place.

Quiet—then steps, coming up the main staircase. I yank the blankets off the mattress, throwing them into a pile out of sight. Tiptoeing behind a dresser, I squat near a rafter. I hate hiding, but I don't want Paul to see me until it's too late. This New Year's Eve, it's his turn to die.

The attic door creaks open. "Hello—someone up there?" He flips the light switch. Thank goodness I remembered to unscrew the bulb here in the back.

He walks all the way up, his steps ungainly as ever. He's always repulsed me, even before we married. I inwardly curse my mother for forcing me into it.

I drop all the way to the floor, watching around the side of the dresser. He wears ratty old leather house-slippers. I think he's had them all these years.

When he gets to the small window on the far wall, I entertain myself with visions of sneaking up and pushing him through it.

As he turns back, I catch a glimpse of his face. Haggard. Tired. Anxious. But not really scared. Perhaps there's a ray of hope in those sad eyes. My emotions flip. I was the cause for his sadness, but Miranda's the reason for that hope.

Too late now. I'm baking today—a special batch of gingerbread men.

Our home phone rings first thing in the morning. Thomas rolls over, slapping at the night-table.

"It's not the alarm. I'll get it…you just sleep." I tiptoe down the cold stairs. Velvet tries to follow, but I scoop her up to avoid squashing her.

I grab the receiver just after the call goes to the answering machine. "Yes?"

Charlotte stops mid-sentence. "Tess, is this the real you?"

"As far as I know, I wasn't body-snatched last night."

"Ha, very funny. Mom's doing lots better today. Getting a second wind after that heart scare, the nurse said."

"Good! Thanks for letting me know."

The phone goes silent for a moment. "Charlotte? You there?"

"Yes. Listen, I stayed up late last night, thinking. I'm going over to the Doctor's house today. It's a closer trip for me, and I know you have family stuff going on, so I'm going alone. Plus, I think Rose doesn't recognize my car. I'm going to dangle the Rosemary carrot in front of his nose...but I won't tell him the truth until he agrees to tell *us* the truth. Sound good?"

"Charlotte, you can't go alone. What if he's wrapped up in weirdness and we just haven't figured it out?"

"Like any self-respecting single girl, I carry a handy-dandy can of pepper spray. Try to control your jealousy, you knife-wielding, Glock-waving woman."

I laugh. "Okay. My instincts tell me the Good Doctor's not going to hurt us."

"Where'd you get these infallible instincts?"

I set the wriggling Velvet on the floor. "I don't know."

"Alright, wish me well. Signing off for now."

"Call on my cell if you need me. You know I'd get over to Putnam County in a heartbeat."

"I know. You've got my back. But who has yours, Tess?"

A question I've asked myself many times.

By the time I give Velvet a little food, I'm ready for coffee. I rinse out the French press, then set the pot boiling on the stove. My eyes wander to our nearly-bare walls. We need more paintings. It feels like we're not completely moved in, but it'll be our baby's first home.

For some reason, I think back to my last conversation with Paul—his brokenness, his obvious concern for Rose, and his kindness to me. I almost liked him.

Thomas comes down an hour later, grabbing the last cup of coffee and frying a couple of eggs before giving me a long look. "You sticking around today?"

I swoop my arms toward the fast-wilting Christmas tree. "Well, you know taking down our tree might take a while."

He laughs. "I must admit your tree was slightly more traditional than my mom's this year."

"I'm flattered."

He nudges Velvet away as she starts climbing his leg. "We're going out shooting at the range today. You want to come?"

The range consists of a bunch of buckets and milk jugs propped against a dirt bunker way out on the family property. "Who's going?"

"You know—Dad, Andrew, and Petey."

"Sounds like a guys' day out. No thanks. I'll chill here. I think your Mom will be resting—Helga left already. I saw her rental car pull out earlier."

"Poor Helga. Poor Icelandic beauty."

"You should talk with your brother. He's full of marriage questions."

"Highly appropriate for him to formulate said questions *after* he's dated nonstop for a couple years."

I walk over and rub his strong shoulders. "Thomas. You need to go easier on him. Some people just take a little longer to settle down."

He kisses me, his breath pleasantly heavy with coffee. Those dark eyes make me want to hold his attention forever.

"I hope our daughter gets your eyes," I say.

"Daughter? Did I miss something?"

"Oh, no...it's just that Miranda and this other old woman told me it's a girl."

"Did they really? I'd like that. An itty-bitty Tessa Brooke." He lays a hand on my stomach. The baby kicks slightly under it.

"She says, 'Hi, Daddy!'"

He takes one last swig of the black brew and gently grips my upper arms. "You know I love you?"

I kiss him. "Of course I do. You be careful shooting."

"Always." He runs upstairs to change and get the guns ready.

Hours later, I walk out on the porch, taking in the clean beauty of the fresh-fallen coat of snow. I break off a piece of greenery from my wreath. It's dying fast. I don't want to make the correlation to Miranda—her recent heart problems, her shriveling hands—but she's aged so quickly, just in these past three months.

Our home phone rings—not the call from Charlotte I've been waiting for. Caller I.D. says it's Paul Campbell.

"Hi, Paul."

"This isn't Paul, Tess."

My heart stops.

She laughs. "From your silence, I assume you know who I am. Do you think you could come talk with me today?"

I find my voice. "Why?"

"Because you have Miranda's best interests at heart. And

because I can clear up a few of your pressing questions."

Is she the spider? Or is she trapped in a bigger web?

Velvet snuggles onto my foot, strangely disconnected with my reality. It's like I'm in a car wreck, trapped in that slow-motion, fast-motion moment of impact. This is really happening, and I have to do something about it. "I'll be over in about an hour."

56

She pulls up slowly, easing her red SUV up our long, snow-covered driveway. Smart girl—she knows how to handle our mountain roads.

When she gets out, I'm struck by the juxtaposition of old and new with her. Dark twenties-era bob, battered bomber jacket, and scuffed motorcycle boots. Yet her young, fair face is unlined and innocent—fresh as one of my double-bloomed white roses.

She strides up to my door, full of confidence—formidable.

I let her knock three times, holding my breath on the other side. I try not to notice the cackles of ghosts that race up and down the stairs. I compose my face and open the door slowly, a poem running through my mind:

"Out flew the web and floated wide;
The mirror cracked from side to side;
'The curse is come upon me,' cried
The Lady of Shalott."

Rose is so well-kept, I could be looking at Rosemary. I don't think she's had Botox or facelifts, either. What stands before me is an über-specimen of femininity—a modern Eve.

She smiles without showing her teeth, though I have a feeling they're still white. She must've sold her soul to the devil to stay preserved in time. She doesn't have one white hair on her head.

"Come in." It's a command. Therefore, I hesitate. But she goes ahead of me and sits in the gold embroidered chair.

I sit on the couch. "I feel like I'm seeing a ghost."

Her laugh sounds strange—almost strangled.

"*I'm* no ghost. I'm Marilyn Davis."

Now it's my turn to laugh. "Of course you are. Thanks for the roses, Marilyn—I mean, Rose."

"Don't call me that. I left Rose Campbell behind forty years ago." She says it with conviction. "I sent those flowers to warn you. I even warned Miranda twice. I don't want her marrying Paul."

I brace myself. "And why's that?"

"You read my journal—don't deny it. I understand why you did. You're looking out for Miranda. But you know why she can't marry him. He tried to poison me."

"So you said. And are you looking out for her? She used to be your best friend."

"Of *course* I am." She leans back, looking past me to the window, as if she's soaking up sunrays through its wavery glass. Or is she soaking up some kind of strength?

"Is that why you brought me over, to have me talk Miranda out of the wedding? You know better than I do how stubborn she is."

"I don't question that, my dear. No, I wanted to know where my Rosemary is living. I've seen you poking around and I figured you'd know."

"Hm. Here's what I know—I know you pulled a gun on Claire Hogan, a helpless old woman. Why should I tell you where Rosemary is?"

Rose looks toward the stairs, smiling sweetly. I turn, feeling someone behind me, but there's no one there. Goosebumps cover my arms and I shiver.

She reaches behind her back, pulling out a snub-nose revolver. She lays it on the side table, pointed at me.

"You must be talking about this gun. I did take it to Claire's, but I just asked her the same question I'm asking you. Unfortunately, her information didn't help me much. I was hoping yours would be more accurate."

She waves in front of her face, as if batting away an invisible bird.

Music sounds in my pocket. "It's my cell phone. I should probably answer it."

"Of course, of course." She swipes again at the air.

I try to steady my voice. "Hello?"

Charlotte says, "You ready for this?"

"Um, sure. I'm busy...gardening."

"Gardening? At this time of year?" She doesn't wait for my response, whispering loudly into the phone. "I'm at the Doctor's now. You were right. He's been withholding something from us—something Miranda and Paul sort of understood, but not completely."

"Okay."

"Just *okay*? Tess, where are you? Home?"

"Not mine."

Rose leans forward.

Charlotte's voice returns to normal. "He's in the kitchen, but he knows I'm talking to you. Listen, Rose wasn't *sane* when the Doctor took her to Arizona—well, maybe long before then. Point is, he put her in a psych ward, Tess. She was certifiable."

"Nothing new," I say.

"What do you mean? How did you—wait, where are you again?"

Rose fingers her gun. I hang up, shrugging. "Mother-in-law."

She smiles. "I've made a special treat for us. It was Cliff's favorite. Wait, no, it was Paul's favorite, but I made it for Cliff…oh, everything gets so muddled when you get older."

She carries the revolver into the kitchen. It's the perfect chance to bolt for it, but I feel frozen to the couch. What if I run and she shoots? I can't risk the baby. I wish I'd taken time to tell Thomas where I was going; to get the Glock from him…instead, I'd decided Rose was just misunderstood, not really dangerous. Famous last thoughts, I guess.

She comes back quickly, bearing a tray of carefully-iced gingerbread men in one hand and her gun in the other. "I put my special ingredient in there—see if you can guess what it is." She holds one out to me.

I make a last-ditch effort. "My stomach is off—I'm

pregnant."

Her eyes widen. "You are?"

"Yes. And I get sick easily."

A sudden knock startles us both. She looks to the stairs, asking someone I can't see, "Should I answer it?"

Apparently, that someone says, "Yes." Rose walks to the front door, gun in her sweater pocket.

The door opens before she reaches for the knob. Paul steps in, looking not the least bit shocked. "Rosey...I had a feelin' you were around."

"No. I'm not Rosey. I'm Marilyn."

He grabs her arms. "You're Rose. Remember me? I'm the husband you left in the lurch forty years ago." He pushes her toward the chair. Her legs give and she sits. "What did you go and do that for, Rosey? I had to watch you die!"

She's so close to me again. All I can think of is that revolver.

"Just like you took Cliff from me?"

"I swear, I never saw he'd run off the road. The only thing I was guilty of was trying to find some love at a bar that night. The coroner ruled the pastor's death an accident—you know how icy our road gets!"

Rose ignores Paul's reasoning. She picks up a cookie, handing it to Paul. "Here...it's your favorite."

As he takes it, she pulls the gun, aiming it at me. She quickly regains her composure. "Paul, you were dead to me the first time you hurt me."

He grips the cookie. "When did I hurt you? When you had that first miscarriage? I didn't touch you after that, Rosey."

"Lies! Lies!" She gestures to the stairs. "*They* know you're lying."

"Rose, I don't know what you're talking about. I loved you. You were the one who stayed away from me. You didn't let me near your bed—"

Her eyes nearly shoot sparks as she looks from me to Paul. "You hit me, Paul. From the time we got married."

Bit by bit, he's moving to the right, beginning to block me. "Now, look here, Rose. You know that ain't true. Never once did I lay a finger on you that way. And what were you doing with that poison book? Weren't you planning to get rid of me?"

I lean to the left, thinking of nothing but my child as Paul distracts Rose. He's moving into place as my human shield. At some point, I need to run.

She stands, gun extended. "I won't say I wasn't." She turns, as if listening to something over her shoulder. Paul chooses this moment to knock her arm straight up. The gun clatters to the floor. "Run!" he shouts.

I jerk my body up through what feels like layers of sand, running into the bathroom. As I slam the door, locking it with trembling fingers, a single gunshot rings through the gingerbread house.

57

He's a stupid fool, isn't he, Mother? A liar. Bartholomew and Cliff knew Paul beat me. Everyone knew I was right. Everyone except Tess Spencer, asking all her nosy questions. She deserves to die, doesn't she? She should join Paul.

Blood seeps from his head onto my rug. Once again, you're dirtying up my rugs, Paul Campbell. The ghosts laugh at my joke. Like sharks in the water, they want to see more blood.

"Tess?" I shout. "Come on out! He was lying, honey!"

I walk toward the bathroom, then stop short. My old stringy-haired nemesis is perched above the door, wielding a sword, back and forth, back and forth.

Her eyes are still hollow and her mouth doesn't move. But her screeching command fills my head. "Too late to be a mother, Rosey. Time to eat the gingerbread."

I turn, dropping the gun. The curse has come upon me, brought by a flower-fresh girl with an old soul. A girl who wouldn't stop asking questions. A girl who summoned my death angel from the pit of hell.

I choose a gingerbread woman from the tray, with yellow hair and bright eyes. I've died before, so this shouldn't hurt one bit.

I claw at the library window, trying to open it. It seems to be glued shut. The bathroom doors that stand between us are too flimsy. Rose is calling to me, so I know she must have shot Paul. Poor Paul. All that time, I should've trusted him. Of course Miranda was right to love him.

She's walking toward the bathroom. *Dear God, I want to know you better on earth. Please don't take me to heaven yet. I want to see my baby. Thank you, Amen.*

She stops, talking to someone. A rescuer? I hold my breath, cracking the inside bathroom door to hear better. She walks back toward the couch. There's some kind of scuffling, then a gagging sound, then silence. Maybe Paul isn't dead?

If only I could sneak out and get my phone, but who knows what's going on out there? I pull my knife from my pocket—leave it to me to bring a knife to a gun fight.

I wait. Should I shout? What if she's waiting for me? As if on cue, the baby kicks me, hard. No way I'm risking your life, little one. I'll stay in here as long as I can.

Shadows play off the walls. It's an ordinary, sunny day outside this gingerbread house. But inside...I don't want to think about who Rose talked to on the steps. Someone I couldn't see...

I sink to the floor, resting my head on a bookshelf. Funny how you never wake up knowing it's your day to die.

In the dark stillness, I try to relax. Instead, my restless legs force me to jump up and pace the room. Something has to happen...

After what seems like an hour, after I've worn a trail in the rug, the front door opens. Someone rushes into the house. "Tess! Where are you, Tess?"

It's Thomas. *Thank you, God.*

"Here," I croak, stumbling through both bathroom doors. I'm not braced for the grisly scene in the living room.

Paul lies near the couch, dark eyes open. A pool of blood, darker than what they show in movies, puddles beneath him.

Rose lies crumpled next to him, a piece of cookie still gripped in her hand. She's left a bloody footprint trail, leading to the bathroom door. What halted her from shooting her way in?

The Good Doctor pauses in the open doorway, stoically surveying the scene. Then he moves quickly, touching the necks of this tragic couple. He shakes his head at Thomas' police officer buddy standing by the stairs.

As the Doctor turns to go back outside, his detachment falters for one instant. Recognizing the raw look of disbelief in his soft eyes, I can't hold back my sobs.

Charlotte seems to materialize out of nowhere and hugs me. "You're in shock. We'll get you back to Nikki Jo's. She'll know what to do."

"You...figured it out? From the call?"

"Yes, the minute you said you weren't home, I knew. I brought the Doctor, called Thomas, and we all came here."

Thomas and Charlotte each hold an arm, walking me outside. The Good Doctor stands on the side of the porch, staring at the flowerbeds.

"Wait!" I pull away and stagger toward the Doctor. I fish deep in my jacket pocket, finally finding what I need. I press Rose's wedding band into his palm. "Give this to your daughter, Rosemary," I say. "We'll make sure she finds you."

The Doctor grips the ring, recognition lighting his weary eyes. "You don't mean..."

"You did have a child, Doc. And she looks just like her mother."

I lean against the wall as a wave of lightheadedness hits me. Charlotte and Thomas again close in on me, ready to walk me to the SUV.

A sad smile plays on the Doctor's lips. "Thank you...for getting to the truth, Tess."

When I collapse into the seat, Charlotte gives me a hug. Her warmth seems to pour fresh light into my heart. "Don't worry, it's all okay now."

I remember Axel's confident words: *"Do not fear. All will be well."*

And so it is.

58

Dear Mom,

Thanks for your letter. It came to Nikki Jo's mailbox. My new address is on the envelope.

I hear you're in the Women's Prison over at Alderson. That looks like a decent place—shoot, if it's good enough for Martha Stewart, it's good enough for my momma!

Been thinking about you a lot. We found out we're having a girl. She's doing great, kicking away something fierce. Still thinking about names.

I just want you to know that I'm starting to realize how hard it was, having to raise me with Dad gone. I don't know how you made ends meet with that hotel housekeeper job. I know you felt like you had to help pay my way through college. I wish you hadn't gone about it the way you did, but I know your heart was in the right place.

Funny all a mom will go through for her kid, no matter how old they are.

I don't know when you're getting released, but give me a call when you find out. I haven't checked on the trailer, but I think Billy Jack is keeping an eye on it for you. I called him and he said the heat's turned down pretty low and the hot water is turned off.

I hope you know I'm praying for you, Momma. I'm in a Bible study now and it's all about suffering and pain in our lives. Sometimes it feels like it'll never end, but it always does. I know you still miss Daddy, but maybe it was a bigger blessing that he left us. I can't remember him good enough to say for sure.

Love you Momma.
Tess

GRANDPA JOHN L'S CORNBREAD

Preheat oven to 425 degrees.

INGREDIENTS:

-2 cups *self-rising* cornmeal

-1 egg

-Buttermilk

Mix cornmeal, egg, and enough buttermilk to moisten to a spoonable consistency in a large bowl.

Grease cast iron skillet with Crisco or oil (not spray oil). Sprinkle cornmeal on bottom to keep from sticking. Spoon cornmeal, egg, and buttermilk batter into skillet.

Place skillet in pre-heated oven for 25 minutes. Take out and flip out on plate. Delicious eaten hot with butter.

ABOUT THE AUTHOR

HEATHER DAY GILBERT enjoys writing stories about authentic, believable marriages. Seventeen years of marriage to her sweet Yankee husband have given her some perspective, as well as ten years spent homeschooling. Heather posts monthly on Novel Rocket (www.novelrocket.com) about self-publishing. Her Viking historical novel, *God's Daughter*, is an Amazon bestseller. You can find it on Amazon and Audible.com.

You can find Heather here:

Website: www.heatherdaygilbert.com
Facebook Author Page: www.facebook.com/heatherdaygilbert
Twitter: @heatherdgilbert
Pinterest: www.pinterest.com/heatherdgilbert/
Goodreads:
www.goodreads.com/author/show/7232683.Heather_Day_Gilbert

For updates on Heather's upcoming releases, please follow
www.heatherdaygilbert.com *and subscribe to the newsletter:*
http://heatherdaygilbert.com/newsletter-signup/

Be watching for the second novel in the Murder in the
Mountains series:
TRIAL BY TWELVE

And if you enjoyed this novel, please leave a review on
Amazon or Goodreads! Encouragement is always appreciated.
Thank you!

Made in the USA
San Bernardino, CA
28 May 2014